THESE WOMEN

ALSO BY IVY POCHODA

The Art of Disappearing
Visitation Street
Wonder Valley

THESE WOMEN

A NOVEL

IVY POCHODA

An Imprint of HarperCollinsPublishers

THESE WOMEN. Copyright © 2020 by Ivy Pochoda. All rights reserved. Printed in the United States of America. No part of this book may be used or reproduced in any manner whatsoever without written permission except in the case of brief quotations embodied in critical articles and reviews. For information, address HarperCollins Publishers, 195 Broadway, New York, NY 10007.

HarperCollins books may be purchased for educational, business, or sales promotional use. For information, please email the Special Markets Department at SPsales@harpercollins.com.

FIRST EDITION

Designed by Michelle Crowe

Library of Congress Cataloging-in-Publication Data has been applied for.

ISBN 978-0-06-265638-4

20 21 22 23 24   LSC   10 9 8 7 6 5 4 3 2 1

In memory of Felicia Stewart, an outspoken feminist
and pioneer in women's reproductive health,
who understood these women. And to Matt Stewart.

. . . how do you survive, how do you make it through?
Always listen to the women.

—SESSHU FOSTER, "TAYLOR'S QUESTION"

THESE WOMEN

FEELIA 1999

HEY. YOU WANNA PULL BACK THE CURTAIN, LEMME SEE YOUR face. All I hear is you breathing in the dark. In out, in out like one of them machines. One of them beep-beep motherfuckers. And we got enough of them in here. Breathing for you. Beating your heart for you. Pumping your goddamned blood. Beep, beep. In, out. In, out. In, out. That's all I hear in this place.

So you're not gonna pull it back. You too sick to pull it back? Me, I'm all beat the fuck up. But I'm not ashamed. I'll let you see my face. You—well, it's not on me to invade your privacy. Leave the fucking curtain closed. Sit there in the dark. In, out. In, out. Beep fucking beep.

I'm gonna open the window. Place smells like death even though they're supposed to be keeping us alive. Isn't that just the fucking, what-do-you-call-it. Ironic. That's it. That's what it is. I'm gonna open the window. And don't mind me if I smoke. Let's just hope you don't have some fucked-up lung disease or something. Let's just hope. Well, one cigarette secondhand won't do you worse. You're in here already.

You're just gonna sit there in silence. You're not gonna say a goddamn word. You're gonna let me ramble. You're gonna let me go on about my business. You're not gonna tell me what's up with you, how come you're laid up in this place. You just want to hear my story. Nosy-ass motherfucker.

It's all about how we do in the dark.

You know about that? You know anything about that? You know the streets? Do you? You're really not going to say anything?

It's a hard game out there. There are rules. There are things you do and don't do. Everyone's got to pay to play. Even me, I got to pay it up the chain. Game of skill and luck.

They say you're lucky if someone slows on your corner. Lucky you get to lean into the car window. Lucky if someone takes you for a ride—up around to one of the dirty alleys off Western or down to one of the smaller streets in Jefferson Park. Luckier still to a hotel. Luckier to be returned in one piece.

I'm lucky. I know the streets. At least that's what I thought. Let me tell you—you have to be diligent. That's a big word. Hard to say. But it pays to know it. Diligent. Get knocked up again, that's what I'll name my kid—diligent. Diligent Jefferies.

But fuck if I knew you have to be diligent off duty. When I'm just up at the Miracle Mart on Sixty-Fifth getting a fifth of Hennessy and some Pall Malls. Not even working. Just standing there on the corner, lighting up, enjoying shit, you know. Because the weather's cool for once. And isn't that a fucking miracle. Cool day, cool night. Wind in the trees, you know what I'm saying? Making the trees dance. That's a pretty thing.

Want to know what's fucked up? South Central—everyone says it's ugly, that it's messed up. You ever take a step back and take a good look at it? A really good look. This is a nice fucking place. We got tidy little houses. Yards. Front and back. We got space. Not that I live in a house. I'm in an apartment but all the houses around the way—they're nice. I get to look at them. Also, we got trees. Have you ever noticed all the trees? The ones with pink flowers and the ones with purple flowers. You probably think they're the same. You've got to pay attention.

So this is what I'm thinking about as I light my cigarette and lean against the wall of the Miracle Mart. You know that place? Man who works there is from Japan. And me, I'm from outside Little Rock and he's selling me stuff and I'm buying and we have a nice conversation each day about this and that. And that's what's just happened before I go outside and light up and have my think about how damn nice South L.A. is if you ignore all the people. Or at least most of them. If you look at the tidy houses, the cars in the driveways, the plants, the gardens, the kids playing outside. Squint and you could be staring direct at the American dream.

How come dudes can tell just by looking? You ever wonder that? How come? 'Cause it's not like I'm the only lady out on Western in heels, short skirt, top cut down to there. There's me and there's them like me and there's all the others who dress just the same because that's how they dress. But dudes know.

You know that corner by Miracle Mart? It's dark. That's why I don't work it. Can't see who's who and what's what. But I'm not working, right? So it doesn't matter. Anyway, this car pulls up and I'm not paying attention because why should I? I'm smoking and staring up at those trees that are dancing like a couple of drunk girls at a party—sway, sway, sway.

Window goes down. *Hey beautiful*, or some shit. I just nod and keep smoking. I'm not on the clock. No one's watching to make sure I make my roll.

But then there's another *hey beautiful*. Man's got an accent, sounds like. I don't give it much thought. Because the trees got me thinking about how everyone's always saying they need to get up and out of this place and I'm thinking—why the hell would you want to do that? You been to Little Rock? You been to Houston? Go enjoy what you have in L.A. Go to the fucking ocean. Or just sit and look at the trees and the flowers when you got a moment. Which is exactly what I was doing when I hear this *hey beautiful* again and I'm snapped out of my thinking.

Yeah, I say.

What are you drinking? I don't look at him because I don't want to make eye contact, don't want him to think I'm interested, that I'm looking to trick. So I take a sip of my Hennessy and stare up at the sky.

But the car's still there, rumbling like it's gonna pull a getaway or some shit. And I can feel this guy staring at me and still I'm not looking. Because. Because. Because.

Come on, you don't want to be drinking that stuff.

Now I'm paying attention. Because he's not saying the same shit most dudes say—the *Hey let me see that ass before I decide to buy. You want to give me a little taste so I know what I'm paying for? You're gonna want to get on my thing for free. You're gonna want to pay me.* He's not saying those things. He's talking at me polite. Like I'm a person.

That type of liquor will just make you drunk. That's what he says. And it makes me laugh, because, isn't that the fucking point?

Yeah, I say. *I'd feel ripped off if it didn't.*

Then he says, *You ever had a South African wine?*

They have wine in Africa? I say. Because that has to be some kind of fucking joke. Like zebras and giraffes and wine. But when I look over he's holding a cup out the car window.

Here's the part where I wasn't fucking diligent. Here's when I don't take my own goddamned advice.

Hold up. I need an ashtray. I also need some water. You got water over there? Or should I press this button. They'll smell the smoke, but fuck it if I care. This whole place smells like death and worse.

SHIT. SHE'S GONE. YOU think she thinks she's better or worse than me because she's foreign? What do you think? And she took my smokes. Stole 'em more like. Why'd she come here if she lived somewhere tropical? How come?

Little Rock I understand. You'd been to Little Rock you'd understand too. You'd understand why I left. Any job in L.A. is better than a life there. And so what if my job isn't exactly, what-do-you-call-it, white collar? It's fucking no collar. No collar, no fucking shirt. Not even pants. And so what? At least it isn't in Little Rock. Hell, you might not like what I do, might not under-stand it. But at least I get to be outside. At least I get to walk, to choose my streets, to take it all in—smell the goddamn flowers, which is more than I can say for most folks around here. They don't stop to smell, just cruise on by in their cars, windows up. Me, I smell.

Which is just what I was doing when this guy starts in on me about fucking South African wine and how the shit I'm drinking will just get me drunk and hungover and do I want to taste his booze and then there's this cup handed out the window. And sud-denly I'm, like, what the fuck, why the hell not. So I step over to the car and take the cup. And it doesn't taste all that good. I mean better than most of the shit I drink, but nothing spectacular. Then things get a little fuzzy.

He's like *do you want to go for a drive?*

And I'm telling him he's got it all wrong. I'm not working. It's my night off. And yeah, I get a night off. No one can tell me I'm on the clock seven days. I'm not a free agent—that shit's too danger-ous. If there's one thing I wasn't born, it's stupid.

Shit. But that's the whole goddamn point of this story. Here I am talking about diligence and street smarts and what did I do? I made a mistake.

I get in the car. But I've downed that wine and he's refilled the cup. And my head is swimming like the time I jumped in the river down in Louisiana and the water was too muddy for me to see and I couldn't get back to the surface and all above me was this murky brown churning. That's what it felt like. Which is why I didn't get a good look at the guy.

White maybe? Latino? Not black. That's for sure. White if I had to bet on it.

Here's the secret. Here's what we tell each other. Pay attention. Look for distinguishing marks. Like does this dude have a tattoo? A beard and what the fuck kind of beard? Does he have an accent? A wandering eye? Does he seem hopped up? Jumpy? All these things to look out for in case shit goes wrong. In case you need to run or identify the guy later for whatever fucked-up reason.

And I should be doing all these things. I mean to. But after a while the guys all run together into one angry, horny, sweaty cheap motherfucker who kicks you the hell out of his car the second he's finished. So what's the point. Anyway, like I keep telling you if you're even listening—are you even awake?—is that I wasn't working. I was taking shit in, drinking it down. I was thinking about the palm trees line dancing up there in the sky. Doing the Texas two-step.

I remember leaning back in my seat. I remember unrolling the window to get a better look. I remember the guy telling me to put the window back up. He doesn't like it down. I remember laughing, because who doesn't want the window down on a cool night? Then he slapped me. And for a moment I'm, like, you got no right because I'm not working. That's the fucked-up thing I was thinking before everything goes black.

Remember how I told you about the river in Louisiana? Here's the story. I was ten. At least I think that's how old I was. I was down in New Iberia visiting my cousins. Real country kids doing their country shit. And stealing some kind of moonshine someone's uncle was making. Never mind it was lunchtime. So we go down to the river, or the bayou, you want to call it that. I must have had a couple of swigs from the jar my cousins were passing because I believed them when they said there was a dog drowning. And they point out across that slow-moving brown sludge and there's something rolling in the current. Rolling. Bobbing. Fucking spinning. Drowning. That's what I thought. My cousins are just standing there on the bank talking about this drowning dog and not doing anything. And they're saying: *Feelia, you so concerned, you jump in.* And that thing's not too far in front of me spinning and spinning. *Yeah you save it*, they're saying.

And next thing, I'm kicking off my sandals and pumping my arms at my sides and I'm jumping off the bank far as I can toward the dog. Then the water's up over my head, thick like melted ice cream. I can see the sun, sort of, so I know which way is up, just not how to get there. Have you ever had one of those dreams where you are running but you can't move a motherfucking inch? That's what being in the water was like. Except worse because there was no air. And that sun overhead was getting farther and farther away like that pinpoint of light at the end of a Looney Tune.

The dog is in the water above me. Spinning. I can't reach it. I can't do anything. That thick-ass water is up my nose, in my mouth. It's crawling down my throat like a warm milkshake. The dog is spinning away from me and I'm sinking way the fuck down. I'm not going to save it. So I close my eyes and I fall.

You know I didn't drown. Of course you fucking know. Which makes this a stupid story. One of my cousins jumped in, grabbed my arm, dragged me to the bank. I lay there panting on my back, staring up at the sun as if it were a long-lost friend. A boat goes chugging past, one of those shrimpers belching diesel smoke, stirring up the water. Making waves. And my cousin has left me and scrambled back to the rest of them. But I'm too exhausted to move. So I lie there, the waves from the passing boat lapping at me and suddenly there's this thing on top of me. Cold and bristly and bloated with river water. And motherfucking dead. The dog, I'm thinking. But it doesn't feel like a dog. It feels like human skin—swollen, clammy skin. Pimply and prickly. My chest hurts too much to scream because this dead thing is all up over me, pressing on me, heavy as fuck, its scratchy hair ripping my skin. And somehow I get out from under that shit, roll to the side. And I'm lying face-to-face with a dead hog. Its glassy eyes and blue snout inches from my own. I kid you not.

Why am I telling you this shit about something that happened to me when I was ten, some prank my cousins pulled? Here's why. Because when I come to in that car after being slapped, it's like I'm back on the bank of the bayou, disoriented and exhausted, that fucking pig on top of me. But this time the pig isn't dead. It's biting and snorting and saying all these things that sound like it's talking to someone who isn't me, some other woman in some other place who's done some other shit to get the pig mad.

I can feel its piggy skin on my own. I can smell its dead pig smell.

And then I go out again. I feel the car moving. And next time I'm awake it's because there's a pain like nothing I've felt before. It's sharp and clean. Like glass. It's almost beautiful. Like mercury sliding in one of those old-time thermometers. I didn't know pain could be so beautiful. So fucking beautiful that it takes my breath away. Literally. Straight across my throat, so I can't scream, because when I try I feel a bubble of blood running from my throat down to my neck.

And then there's something over my face, something that makes it even harder to breathe. Something that makes the world even farther away. Foggy, like I'm looking through a cloud of weed smoke. And I'm rolling, rolling, like that dead hog in the water. Except below me the ground is hard. I can feel dirt, trash, and glass. And I'm lying on my back, staring straight up at the moon, which is blurry behind whatever's over my face that's making it impossible to get air. And even still, I'm looking for the palm trees, trying to remember them. Because if I can find them . . .

PART I

DORIAN

2014

1.

———

THE GIRLS ARRIVE AFTER DISMISSAL. HOW OLD ARE THEY?
Fifteen? Sixteen? Seventeen? Dorian's lost the ability to tell. They
flood the small fish shack, spinning on the stools bolted to the floor,
splaying their bodies over the counter. They've rolled the skirts of
their uniforms high, revealing thigh, even a little cheek. A flash of
underwear trimmed with lace. They've unbuttoned their blouses,
yanked down their polos, showing bra and breast.

I could get—

Gimme—

Lemme get a—

Their voices pile on top of one another as they wait for their
food.

They're loud, performing, making a big deal of their adoles-
cent selves.

Dorian checks the temperature of the oil, making sure it's hot
enough that the food crisps instead of sweats.

The girls are growing impatient because the world isn't moving at their speed. Soon they're trying to outdo one another with
their takedowns, their bold profanities.

Bitch. Whore. Slut.

Dorian slides them iced tea, soda, and double orders of fries.

The girls' voices rise, twisting and tangling.

Let me tell you what this bitch got up to last weekend.

Don't you dare.

This bitch—

Who are you calling a bitch, bitch?

Like I said, this bitch went over to Ramon's place.

Don't you say another word.

Come on, you're proud of it. Don't tell me you're not. Or else how come first thing you did when you got home was text me and Maria all the details.

Dorian shakes the grease from another batch of fries.

My order ready yet?

How come this shit is too slow.

She dumps the fries into a Styrofoam container.

Bitch went down on him.

Dorian drops the fryer basket, missing the grooves. Oil splatters onto her forearms.

The girls are laughing. Pinching each other. Congratulating themselves on leaving childhood behind. Leaving safety and sanity.

Dorian turns, exiting the kitchen, and approaches the counter with the food.

All you do is open your mouth and close your eyes. No big deal. Like nothing at all.

Dorian drops the fries. She reaches across the counter, her hand grasping the speaker's forearm. "Lecia!"

The girls fall silent, their invincibility interrupted.

"Get your hand off me."

Dorian holds firm. "Lecia," she says, her voice brittle with panic.

"I said, get your hand off me."

"Lecia," Dorian says, shaking the girl's wrist to stop her talking the way she's talking.

"Who the fuck is Lecia?"

She feels a hand on her own arm, the present reaching into the past. "Dorian." Willie, her helper at the fish shack, is at her side, his voice soft but firm. "Dorian."

Dorian's holding fast, shaking her kid back to reality.

"Tell this bitch to get her hand off me."

Bitch. Lecia would never call her mother a bitch.

Dorian lets go. Willie pulls her back into the kitchen.

"Easy," he says. "Easy, easy." As if she's a dog that got too riled.

The girls scatter, leaving their half-eaten food. The gate to the fish shack bangs behind them. Dorian can hear their voices mocking her as they hit the streets.

Fifteen years later, nothing is going to change the fact that Lecia's still dead. Yet somehow the past keeps calling. Dorian puts her hands to her temples to settle her mind, sort imagination from reality. Still everything remains tangled.

2.

_____

THE EVENING RUSH IS OVER. DORIAN DROPS SOME SCRAPS
into the fryer and turns up the volume on the radio. It's tuned to
the classical station that plays the obvious hits of Mozart and
Beethoven, and because this is Los Angeles, John Williams and
Hans Zimmer.

The fryer spits. Dorian shakes the basket. After nearly three
decades running the fish shack on Western and Thirty-First,
Dorian should be sick of the fried stuff, but if you can't stomach
your own grub, you can't serve it. She shakes on a little extra salt.
Reaches for the hot sauce.

Long ago her customers stopped caring, noticing, or remem-
bering that it's a white woman running the fried fish place at the
southern edge of Jefferson Park. If they knew she'd never had
collard greens or catfish before she met Ricky on the other coast
and allowed him to bring her cross-country, they'd put it out of
mind. If she'd told them she'd never cooked cornbread or fried
okra in her life before Ricky died, they'd chosen to forget.

"Hold up."

Someone's banging on the grate covering the kitchen window.

"I said, *hold up*. How many times I've told you I don't like hot sauce on my fish?"

It's Kathy. Dorian knows the voice—a gravel singsong that she hears up and down Western.

Didn't want you anyway.

Probably too small to find in the dark.

You buying or wasting my time?

Dorian opens the back door to the fish shack.

Kathy's standing in the alley. She's short, compact, like she did away with anything she didn't need. She's wearing a denim miniskirt, a fake fur bomber jacket, ankle boots with pencil-thin heels. She's pale and her bleached, frizzy bob only washes her out more. *My great-grandmother was raped by a plantation dude,* she told Dorian once, *and all I got was this yellow complexion.* Then came the manic cackle Dorian can recognize from a half block away. Dorian didn't bother with the math to see if Kathy's story was even possible.

The things she's heard from Kathy's mouth. The things she's heard from the rest of the women who work Western.

Half assault, half work, is how I'd tell it.

No worse than choking on a raw sausage.

Couldn't keep an umbrella up in a light wind.

Thirty seconds wet and sloppy, but done is done.

Smell like the reptile house and I know you know what I mean.

There are more. More about the life. More about the men. More about the discomfort, the drugs, the antibiotics. The nightly bump and grind.

After thirteen years of feeding the women on the stroll, there's not much they can say that would shock Dorian. They try though. Make a game out of it. Dorian could run a late-night sex call-in show with the information she's gleaned. She could give a twisted anatomy lesson.

She wedges the door open with her foot. "Are you coming in?"

"Hold up." Kathy squats down, getting close to the sludge running off the dumpster. She reaches out for something. When she stands up, Dorian can see tears in her eyes.

She's holding a dead hummingbird. It's a Costa's—its purple crown slicked by the runoff from the dumpster.

Dorian cups her palms and Kathy drops the bird into them. It feels impossibly light, as if minus its soul it's hardly there.

"Fuck is it with the world?" Kathy says. "Beauty's nothing but a curse. That's what I tell my kids." She wipes her eyes.

Dorian should have told her daughter, Lecia, the same thing. But Lecia learned that lesson before her eighteenth birthday.

And there it is—the black flash of rage. A punch to the gut. A hand closing over her throat.

"You gonna feed me or not?" Kathy says.

Dorian holds the door open and stands aside.

The kitchen barely fits two people. Dorian presses herself against the counter and Kathy slides past, taking the container of fish trim to the far end by the window. She eats with her hands, dipping the fish in tartar sauce and raising it to her lips, then licking the sauce from her fingers.

Dorian gets a Pullman pan from the overhead rack. She places the dead bird inside it, then checks the temperature of the oven. It's two hundred give or take. She slides the loaf pan in and turns up the heat a bit like she's drying jerky.

"That's fucked up," Kathy says.

"It's how I save them."

"Save," Kathy says. "That's a good one. How many you got now?"

On top of the refrigerator are two shoeboxes of dead birds perfectly preserved and nestled in cotton wool.

"Twenty-eight," Dorian says.

"Shit," Kathy says. "I wouldn't want to be a bird around here." She takes a bite of fish. "You gonna do something about this situation?"

"What situation?"

"Somebody's trying to fuck you up. Somebody's sending you a message. It's straight-up cartel. Dead birds. Hell, I've seen girls do shit like that to other girls. Back them off their turf. Seen pimps do worse."

"I'm not on anyone's turf," Dorian says.

"Seems like it," Kathy says, polishing off another piece of fish. She cocks her head toward the radio. "The fuck you listening to?"

"Classical."

"Lemme change that." She swipes at the radio, shifting it to the other NPR affiliate in L.A. that runs *All Things Considered* on a slight delay.

Idira Holloway is talking. It seems that ever since the verdict was handed down about the death of her son—all officers found innocent although they shot the kid at point-blank range in broad daylight—the woman's been talking nonstop, swamping the airwaves with her rage. Dorian could tell her a thing or two about how the rage is senseless. How it accomplishes nothing. How all that screaming and anger only digs you in deeper, alienates you, makes people pity and fear you—as if grief is contagious.

"Bitch is pissed," Kathy says. "Bitch is mad pissed."

"Wouldn't you be?"

"Hell, someone kills one of my kids, I'd kill a whole bunch of motherfuckers in return. No shame in that. Only shame in doing fuck-all."

Sometimes Dorian imagines there's a city full of women like Idira Holloway. Women like her. A city of futile, pointless anger. A country. A whole continent. It's a fantasy she hates, but it comes anyway. It makes her claustrophobic, like she's going to choke on the proximity of all these grieving mothers.

"Only one way to get justice for Jermaine," Kathy says. "Law of the streets. An eye for an eye. It's like how I tell my girl, Jessica— don't look for trouble, keep a low-pro, because when shit goes down, you've got to represent yourself. What's more, I tell her if she gets herself into some real shit, there's a chance I'd have to go to work on her behalf. And neither of us want that." She roots around for any fish she's missed. "What I wouldn't do for her or the others. Protect them to my grave."

Yet here's Kathy, night after night, strolling Western, putting herself out there, right in the way of danger. A strange form of protecting her kids if you ask Dorian. But choices are choices. And some people don't get too many.

Maybe Dorian had doomed Lecia from the start. Maybe choosing Ricky, a black man, to be the father of her child was her first mistake. Growing up in small-town Rhode Island, Dorian didn't understand the curse of skin tone.

On the radio, Idira is still raging, shouting down the cops, the lawyer, the justice system. As if any of it will change a thing.

Kathy finishes and crushes the Styrofoam. She pulls a compact out of her gigantic shiny red purse and touches up her makeup.

"How do I look?" she says, puckering her lips and narrowing her eyes like she wants to devour Dorian whole.

"Good," Dorian says. "Nice."

"Fuck you mean by *nice*? You think *nice* is gonna get me a train of dudes so I can make rent and pay for that bounce house for my boy's birthday?"

Dorian knows this game. "Kathy, you look like one badass sexy bitch."

Kathy snaps her compact shut. "That's what I fucking thought." She combs her fingers through her short bleached curls and shoulders her bag. At the back entrance to the fish shack she stops. "You gonna do something about those birds? I don't feel safe eating where someone's murdering fucking hummingbirds."

"Like what?" Dorian asks.

"Least Jermaine what's-his-face's mother is raising hell. Least she's getting heard."

"You want me to *raise hell* about some dead birds?"

"I fucking would." And Kathy's gone, taking her game out to Western, lighting up the night with her brilliant blond hair and hard cackle.

Finally the news switches over to a different story—a possible bullet train from Los Angeles to San Francisco. Dorian exhales, letting out the tension that always surges inside her when she hears Idira Holloway's voice.

She stares into the fryer, checking the oil to see how long before she can dump it.

Dear Idira, I know it's hard to talk over the fury because the fury does the talking. But you'll learn eventually. I've got fifteen years on you and there's not a day that I don't want to scream at someone, press my meat cleaver into my hand, punch the wall. The scars I should have in addition to the one on my heart. But there's no point. Over time you let it go. That's what you do. Stop making noise. Or that's all you are. Noise. Nuisance. A problem. You are nothing but your pointless rage.

Dorian claps a hand over her mouth. Who the hell is she talking to in her empty kitchen? How come the past won't stay put?

She turns the oven off, hits the lights, locks up, and says the same lame prayer that feeding Kathy and the rest of them will keep them safe on Western.

It wasn't too long ago that this strip of Western was a hunting ground. Fifteen years back, thirteen young women turned up dead in surrounding alleys, throats slit, bags over their heads. Prostitutes, the police said. Prostitutes, the papers parroted.

Lecia wasn't a hooker, but getting killed the same way as a few hookers seals your fate no matter how much noise your mother might make, how much hell she might raise.

And Dorian had made some noise. Lots. All up and down

Southwest Station and even Parker Center. At the local papers—
the free weekly and the *Times*.

No one listened.

In fact, the mothers of some of the other victims got in her face
about it. *Different 'cause she half white?* they wanted to know.

*Death don't care if you're black or white. Only thing in this world
that don't indiscriminate,* one of the other mothers told her.

Thirteen girls dead. Fifteen years gone. By Dorian's count, and
her count is right, three other serial murderers have been hauled
in, tried, and locked up in Los Angeles in that time. But not a
single arrest for the murder of girls along Western.

The cops got lucky—the killings stopped after Lecia. No need
to revisit old crimes in a city where tensions are always on a sim-
mer. Let sleeping dogs do their thing.

Dorian peers back through the bars on her window, checking that everything's in order. The winds are still ripping through
the city, swirling trash, shaking trees, and sending palm fronds
swirling down. She steps to the curb and checks for the bus, then
figures she might as well walk home.

The air is choked with the sounds of the evening commute—
the idling cars slower now that everyone's distracted by their
phones, the heave and wheeze of buses snarling traffic, the overhead noises, the planes flying too low over West Adams and local
news choppers out pursuing some story for the nightly digest of
other people's misery.

It's early enough that most of the girls are keeping a low profile. The bus pulls to a stop half a block up. Dorian doesn't chase
it. The walk will do her good, clear her lungs of the heavy kitchen
air and maybe get rid of some of the grease smell that clings to
her clothes.

The bus is idling, lowering the plank so a wheelchair can roll off.
The drivers behind it lay on their horns. Dorian arrives at the stop
before the doors close. The driver is fiddling with the controls to

raise the handicap ramp. Dorian reaches into her bag to locate her TAP card. There's a screech of tires from the southbound lane of Western followed by the roar of a powerful engine. Dorian looks up to see a black car—black tinted windows, fat tires with brilliant chrome spinners—thread a needle between the stalled traffic, then pull up to the opposite curb. The passenger door opens, releasing a preposterous amount of white smoke. A woman gets out.

"You getting on?" The bus driver is shouting at Dorian. "You getting on?"

A passenger bangs on a window. "Lady, get on the fucking bus."

Dorian doesn't take her eyes off the woman across the street because it's Lecia climbing from that car. Seventeen, unblemished, beautiful and alive. Her curly golden hair tight to her head and pulled into a high ponytail that swishes over her shoulders.

"Get on the goddamned bus!"

Dorian hears the door swing shut as the bus pulls a few feet away only to be stopped by the traffic light.

"Lecia," she calls, even though she knows it's crazy. "Lecia."

Then she's tearing into the street, zigzagging between cars coming from both directions, summoning a mad chorus of honks and screeches. "Lecia."

As she reaches the middle of the street, she comes to. It's not Lecia, of course—but Julianna. The resemblance between Lecia and the girl she had been babysitting the night she died still surprises Dorian. She stares at Julianna, who's leaning into the passenger window of the car she's just exited. Julianna laughs at whatever the driver just said and steps back onto the sidewalk.

Thefuckoutofthestreetlady.

Getoutthefuckingstreet.

Two cars close in from opposite directions, trapping Dorian. The drivers lay on their horns. The wind charges from the east.

She scrambles to safety. But Julianna has already walked away.

"Julianna," Dorian calls after her. "Julianna."

No response.

"Julianna," she tries again. But her voice is lost as the black car revs its engine and tears off, somehow carving a path for itself through the stalled traffic. Julianna has turned her back and is walking away when Dorian realizes her error. "Jujubee," she calls. Dorian squints, trying to tease Julianna's shape from the dark street, but she's lost her.

She leans against the bus stop on the southbound side. The number 2 is pulling up. When it rolls to a stop, Dorian kicks its bumper. Pain radiates up her leg. "What's your problem, lady?" the driver calls through the open door.

"What's yours?"

The only answer is a gust of wind.

3.

———

SHE CONTINUES NORTH PAST THE ODD ASSORTMENT OF INDE-pendent shops—Martin's Fishing Tackle, Crown & Glory Hair Design, Queen's Way beauty supply, a barbershop, two water refill stations, three Pentecostal churches, and a Laundromat, all surviving between the strip malls that are eating up Western. You'd think there weren't customers enough for another budget cell-phone place, knockoff chain pizzeria, donut shop. But the city, especially south of the 10, seems to have an insatiable appetite for the same stores sloppily reproduced.

It's just over a mile to her house—the last uphill stretch giving the neighborhoods surrounding the 10 the title of *Heights*: Western Heights. Arlington Heights. Harvard Heights. Kinney Heights. The houses grow grander on the incline. Three- to five-thousand-square-foot Craftsman, Victorian, and Beaux Arts homes, not to mention the row of oddball mansions lined up on Adams Boulevard.

From the business corridors like Western it's hard to see the neighborhood's old grandeur. Hard to see how West Adams and all its constituent neighborhoods were once upscale and desirable. That was before Los Angeles lifted restrictions on nonwhite home ownership, moving the city's focus farther north and west. And once blacks moved in, staking their claim in a genteel hood in the middle of town, city planners didn't think twice about where to put the 10 connecting downtown to the beach. They laid it right in the middle of West Adams, creating a five-hundred-foot-wide gully obscuring one part of the neighborhood from the other and tearing down houses like they were razing a rain forest. And as an aftermath, or rather an afterthought, some of the most beautiful houses in Los Angeles have a tidal wave of traffic or a stagnant sea of red and white lights in their backyards.

The houses that remain unsettle Dorian, reminding her of how fast the city can turn its back.

Dorian's not a neighborhood booster. She understands why people don't want to live in West Adams, why they can't envision a life for themselves between Boost Mobile, Cricket Mobile, and Yang's Donuts. Why they don't want to live next to a once beautiful home chopped up into a boardinghouse with too many occupants in a warren of rooms. She knows why folks pass up the opportunity to own a pristine bungalow or a rambling six-bedroom mansion on the wrong side of the 10.

Still, every year there's more and more chatter about the neighborhood coming up, about how it's the last great value in Los Angeles, the last place to buy a substantial house and be part of an actual community. But tell that to the guy who got murdered in front of Moon Pie Pizza on Western and Adams, or the bartender who got shot at Lupillo's on Western by Pico, or the dozens of stray cats flattened by boys drag racing their steroidal Nissans up and down the residential blocks.

Dorian's breathing heavy by the time she reaches the 10. She stops before crossing over the freeway. In the triangular strip between the eastbound on-ramp and the street where the girls have a regular beat someone has opened a nursery. Dorian peers through the chicken wire at the plants in their pots, some woven on three-by-three-foot square trellises and lashed to the fence and choking on freeway exhaust. There are pencil plants and other succulents, a few cacti, some shrubs, roses, as well as California natives—wild geraniums, sages, and asters that will attract birds. Soon, she imagines, finches, hummingbirds, and even orioles will swarm this grim plot next to the 10.

There's a rustle in the air and she braces for a gust of wind. But when she looks up she sees a flock of green parrots tearing through the sky, their wild birdsong cutting through the traffic noise in an unfettered, melodic mania. Dorian cranes her neck, watching the birds swoop low, then rise as one—a multicolored storm funnel in the last light. Ever since she first spotted the swarm of parrots in her neighborhood she's been hoping to lure them to the fish shack or to her house. But the parrots follow no discernible pattern— appearing for days, stirring up the sky and trees, shaking the palm fronds, chattering wildly, then taking their excitement elsewhere.

You'd think it's either random or a panicked response. One goes, so go the others. But there's a method to the flocking—to the great mass of twisting, soaring, wheeling creatures taking to the sky together. It's not the action of a mindless herd but a precise communication, each bird interacting with at least seven neighbors, adjusting, coordinating velocity and individual move- ments, copying angles and vectors and directions so the whole flock moves in graceful lockstep.

Dorian watches the flock disappear to the south, where they will roost in one of the palms and then vanish again. After the par- rots, the crows always follow, bringing a different sort of energy— a stormy menace. Dorian doesn't stick around for their arrival.

It's rush hour and the freeway is eight lanes of traffic going no- where. The wind is roaring overhead, outpacing the stalled cars. To the east the scattershot skyscrapers of downtown are a gray and purple smudge in the hazy sun that's fading in the other di- rection. A few merchant posters—bold black letters on fluorescent paper—are attached to the fence that guards the overpass. "We Buy Houses Cash." "We Buy Houses Quick." Two promote concerts for Ivy Queen and Arcángel. Then there is the smog-stained memorial—a dirty cross made out of plastic flowers, a faded laminated photograph, and a filthy teddy bear—to a young woman who died on the overpass or below on the freeway.

No denying that this strip of Western is grim. Strip malls with hybrid Chinese food/donut shops, budget lingerie boutiques, busted ATMs, chop shops, tire shops, pet stores with sickly animals. She passes Washington, then Venice. At Cambridge she glances east. She can see the house, her legacy from Ricky and his parents—a mustard-colored five-bedroom Craftsman on the corner of Oxford one block down. A family house, able to accommodate the older generation as well as Dorian, Ricky, and Lecia.

Dorian lives there alone.

She pauses before continuing up Western. She wants to hold back the inevitable loneliness of the dusty rooms, the bric-a-brac she can't part with. The skeletons of objects broken in her rage, the faded reminders of everyone who left or was taken.

There's a bar two blocks north. Lupillo's. A neighborhood dive—sticky floor, cheap drinks, broken locks on the bathrooms. Same place the bartender was killed a year back. Shot from the doorway by her ex-boyfriend. Now there is a beefy security guy on duty.

Dorian's heard the owner's planning to rebrand the place Harvard Yard, a nod to the surrounding Harvard Heights neighborhood. A smartass joke that doesn't fit the community.

Dorian's usually the odd person out, neither a heavy-drinking Latino nor a young interloper on her way to a concert or a night out in K-town. The other patrons leave her alone.

She takes a seat on one of the shaky barstools. The bartender's wearing a T-shirt she's cropped and tied over her flat stomach. Dorian orders a Seven and Seven that comes in a flimsy plastic cup. Latin hip-hop blasts from the sound system. The place smells like beer and taco grease from the restaurant that serves the bar through a cutout in the wall.

Dorian sips the cocktail through a straw to ease her way into the sweetness before putting her lips to the cup. The bar is nearly empty. Two middle-aged guys are playing pool. Several young women are huddled by the jukebox. The women are easy with one another, their hips bumping, their hair whipping back and forth.

The door opens and Dorian can see a woman standing on the threshold. Her breath catches on the idea that it's Julianna even though she knows Julianna burns brighter, flies higher than the drop panel ceiling and dirty linoleum of Lupillo's. Still, her mind tricks her into thinking there's a chance for her to catch Julianna, stop her from running off, prevent whatever fate awaits her.

When she enters, Dorian sees that the woman couldn't look less like Julianna. The games her mind can play. She's seen them all.

The woman crosses to the bar, bringing a smell of cigarettes old and new. She sits down in front of a half-empty glass of something brown, which she polishes in one go.

She rattles her empty, then glances over and fixes on Dorian.

Dorian gives her a quick look, wondering if she's one of the women who turns up behind the fish shack for a feed before returning to the stroll.

"Who the fuck are you?"

Dorian turns away. No use tangling with strangers.

"I said, who the fuck are you?" The woman is wearing a low-cut blouse that shows a large scar—a raised purplish-black welt—across the bottom of her throat. "What are you looking at?"

"Nothing," Dorian says.

"Damn right, nothing." The bartender slides the woman a fresh drink. She sips it, keeping an eye on Dorian. "How'd you know I'm here? You follow me? You been following me? You think

I don't see you?" Her hair is cropped close to her head and slicked down with oil.

"I don't know," Dorian says. "I don't know you."

The intensity of the woman's glare is unsettling. She's convinced of something, that much is clear.

Dorian has a new drink but she's not sure she's going to enjoy it.

"'Scuse me? What are you staring at?"

Dorian takes her Seven and Seven down in two gulps and pulls out cash. She's out the door.

She hurries south. The wind is in pursuit, sending cans and paper plates after her. The palms on Western bend at impossible angles.

"You running away now? You spend all this time following me and you run away."

Dorian picks up the pace.

"I'm going to find out where you live."

Dorian pauses at the corner of Cambridge, checking over her shoulder to see how far back the woman is. She spots her down Fifteenth, a block away. For good measure Dorian overshoots her own block, takes a left on Venice, then doubles back on Hobart.

There's no one out on her street, which isn't unusual. Somewhere a car is racing down a side street, screeching and skidding. The wind twisting in the telephone lines sounds like someone's sawing metal.

She opens her gate. The porch light comes on, revealing the messy bougainvillea and the vines that have invaded it. She fumbles in her purse. Her heart is racing. Her last drink hits her hard. She drops her keys. She squats to retrieve them. And there on her front porch by a potted pencil plant are three dead hummingbirds.

4.

———

IT'S LECIA WHO WAKES DORIAN THE MORNING AFTER SHE
fled Lupillo's. She's there, sitting at the foot of the king-size bed,
dressed in jeans and a white T-shirt, the clothes she'd worn the
last night Dorian saw her. The jeans were a little tight but Dorian
hadn't complained. Because look at what some of the other girls
had started wearing back then—midriff shirts that looked like
men's underwear, and pants that barely rose to hip height, anything to show belly and butt and a glimpse of pubic bone without
being arrested for indecency.

And here she is, still wearing those clothes, one leg crossed
over the other, leaning back on her hands, her face angled toward
Dorian at the head of the bed. Dorian tosses a pillow to shoo her
away. She doesn't need this ghostly version coming around. She
rubs her eyes, hoping the vision will go. But Lecia is as stubborn
in death as she was in life. Fifteen years and the same dance, the
same standoff.

"Go away," Dorian says. That's the most she'll say. She refuses
this ghost. But it's insistent. And Dorian has to be vigilant or she'll
lose her grip. She works hard to keep the past in the rearview.

She peeks through her fingers. Lecia's braiding her hair, twisting her wild orange curls into a thick plait just like Dorian used to when she was little.

To talk to Lecia is to be satisfied with spirits and memories. To acknowledge her is to start a dangerous slide, an irreversible descent.

Dorian rolls over and presses her face into the pillow on Ricky's side of the bed. She counts to twenty. Then she counts again, this time to a hundred. When she looks up Lecia is gone.

She sits up and turns on the light. The first thing she sees is the three birds on the bureau.

It's still dark out. The Santa Anas are shaking the windows. Just like back East, the winter sun hides until nearly seven though the sky doesn't have the same frigid menace. She finds a shoebox in the closet, fills it with old socks, and tucks the birds inside.

In the kitchen, she heats yesterday's coffee, then scatters stale biscuits in the backyard for the birds and checks her planters to make sure cats and possums haven't been tearing up her vegetables. She overfills the bird feeder, which doesn't need more seed.

Her feeders attract a strange crowd—not just the birds she wants, the orioles, the warblers, and the finches, but also pigeons too lazy or too refined for the sort of junk they find on the street and even a few seagulls thrown off course on their way to the ocean.

She checks the sky for a sign of the parrots. They usually come around in winter, mostly in late afternoon or early evening. But sometimes in the morning. They've never landed in her yard, only flown overhead and settled in the towering palms one street over.

There's birdsong somewhere in the murky sky. Not parrots but the repetitive *chee-chee* of violet-green swallows singing in the early dawn. Dorian closes her eyes and listens, knowing that the song will die out at first light. This time the song doesn't last even that long. There's a rumble overhead, the sonic groan of an airplane flying too low. With a wild rustle the birds take flight, rising into the sky where they are lost in the dark, leaving Dorian with only the morning sounds of the slow-moving city and the whip-whip of the wind.

She catches the silhouette of a cat slinking along the fence. She watches as it stops and considers the feeder. The airplane drove the birds away so the hunting's no good. But the cat lingers. Dorian follows its gaze. It's not looking at the feeder but at something under a desert sage bush.

Dorian waits. The cat waits.

She listens for a rustle, a shift, a flutter or twitter, some indication of what the cat is hunting.

Then it pounces. In one swift move, it's off the fence and beneath the bush. In a split second it emerges, something in its jaws. Dorian leaps with a shriek that will probably bring her neighbors to their windows. The cat drops its prey and is absorbed into the early dawn gray as if it hadn't been there at all.

Dorian squats to pick up the cat's quarry. It's a scrub jay—long dead, rigor already set. It's possible to feel the substance of its life in her hands. Cradling the bird in her palm, Dorian glances beneath the bush. There's another jay on its side—tipped like an empty bottle.

The dead jays bring Dorian to her knees, a sob trapped in her throat. Unlike other birds, unlike other animals, jays can travel into the past of their own minds. Like humans, scrub jays have memories. She brings the jays inside and places them in the shoebox along with the hummingbirds and puts the box in a shopping bag.

Dear Idira, Once you figure out that no one's going to hear you, you'll still have to listen to the echoes in your head, a funhouse of memories that get distorted with time. That place will spook you. I could go on about the things that will remind you of your kid, the things that will never let you sleep. A dead bird for instance. But these things should be a caution to you, a warning about the senselessness of rage. Because in the end it's just you. It will always be you. So it's a waste of energy sending

all that venom and anger out into the world because the return is nothing.
It's a one-way ticket. You give and give your anger and get nothing in
return except more anger, leaving nothing behind.

THE SKY IS SOFTENING. It's Saturday so traffic is light on Western. Still the girls are out, pulling their coats tight against the
strong gusts—some working hard to snag a last customer before
the hour gets too polite, others being collected by their pimps.

It's a twenty-minute walk to the fish shack to grab the two
boxes of birds stashed in the kitchen, then another twenty-five to
Southwest Station. About a decade ago Dorian was a regular at
the precinct, so well known that she was used to the detectives
busying themselves with inconsequential tasks when she arrived.

She got used to being ignored. But she spoke anyway, her voice
angry and insistent. Her fury unnerved even herself. It was as if her
voice belonged to someone else. She hated saying Lecia's name in
the stale precinct. She hated summoning her daughter's memory
under the cold fluorescent lights between the static of radio calls
and the clatter of ringing phones.

It's pretty much what you would expect in the station early
on a Saturday—the aftermath of the previous night, the angry,
the drunk, the lost, the violent, the wronged, the insane. Dorian
checks in at the desk. She wants to file a report: someone has been
poisoning birds behind her business and now her house.

The sergeant gives her the once-over, sniffing for a whiff of
crazy. Then he pages someone in the back.

Dorian drums her fingers on the shoeboxes as she waits. It
takes twenty minutes but eventually the door behind the desk
opens. "You're in luck," the sergeant says to the person stepping
out from the back. "Caught a poisoning case."

Dorian looks up to see a short female detective. She's clearly

Latina but she's dyed her dark hair blond, giving her skin a pasty pallor. "Not my beat," the detective says. "Vice, remember?"

"You want it or not?"

The detective doesn't reply. She just holds the door open for Dorian to follow her.

"But don't get too excited," the sergeant adds. "It's only birds."

Dorian pretends she doesn't know every inch of the station's ground floor—every desk, every interrogation room. She's been in all of them. She's been listened to, taken seriously, consoled, indulged, told to leave, escorted out.

Let the professionals do their job.

I hope you're not suggesting we are doing a third-rate investigation.

How well did you really know your daughter?

Spend enough time on my side of the desk and you'll learn all about the things children keep from their parents.

I asked you, how well did you really know your daughter?

The short detective leads her to a far corner of the floor unfamiliar to Dorian—to a desk crammed between two filing cabinets. Away from the action.

Dorian sits with the shoeboxes in her lap. The detective hasn't said a word. The dregs of last night's makeup are visible on her face, the faded paint of a day at the office. Dorian can see that her dye job needs a touch-up. There's a furrow of half-inch roots framing her face. This sort of maintenance is the reason Dorian let her own hair go gray.

But this detective, she's a different story. It's as if she's trying to be someone else with hair and makeup suited to a person with a different complexion. And yet she's a cop. In Dorian's experience cops don't try to be other people. They just try to be cops.

Dorian glances over the desk to a nameplate: Det. E. Perry.

The woman sitting in front of her sure doesn't look like a *Perry.*

"What does the *E* stand for, Detective?"

The woman looks up as if she's only noticed Dorian for the first time. "Esmerelda. You?"

It takes a moment before Dorian realizes what she's asking. "Dorian Parkhurst."

Detective Perry takes a piece of gum from its wrapper and pops it in her mouth. She doesn't take her eyes off the workhorse computer monitor. "So, birds," she says after a moment. She's typing furiously, her gaze never meeting Dorian's.

Dorian places the boxes on the desk. "Thirty-one hummingbirds and now two Western scrub jays," she says.

With no encouragement from Detective Perry, she launches into the story—the birds she's found behind the fish shack and now the ones in her yard. "I'm being targeted."

To her surprise, Detective Perry seems to be writing it all down. Her fingers are racing across her noisy keyboard, clicking and backspacing.

Dorian takes this as a sign to continue. She goes into more detail—describing the mental prowess of scrub jays, how they seem to know what other birds are thinking. How they hide food but only if they have stolen it from another bird. She talks about the navigational genius of hummingbirds.

Detective Perry's fingers freeze above the keyboard. The snap and clack of her gum ceases. "Dorian Williams, right?"

Dorian's certain she gave her maiden name. "Parkhurst?"

"But you are Dorian Williams," the detective says, meeting her eye for the first time. "Says it here." She taps her computer screen. "Simple background check."

"Why?"

"Why not," Detective Perry says. She resumes typing. "It's a health code violation. Dead animals in a commercial kitchen is a health code violation." She lays off the keyboard and squints at her monitor. "Why do you think someone stops killing after thirteen victims? You think he finds God or some other kind of redemption?"

For a moment Dorian thinks she's misheard the detective. "Excuse me?"

Detective Perry doesn't look away from her monitor.

For twenty-four hours Lecia's death hasn't given her a moment's peace. And now here it is again, unbidden. Dorian shakes her head, trying to stick with the present, trying to hold on to her equilibrium. "I'm here about the birds," she says.

"Birds?"

Dorian holds up the boxes. "Thirty-one hummingbirds and two jays."

The detective rubs the corner of one of her eyes. "What's this about birds?"

Dorian's not sure she has the energy to go into it all again.

"Someone's poisoning them? That's what you said?"

"Right," Dorian says, relieved not to have to repeat herself.

Detective Perry snaps her gum. "There's a reason they never caught the guy."

"What guy?" Dorian says. And here it is again.

"The one who killed all those women back then."

All those women back then. Dorian takes a deep breath. "Lecia wasn't like the other women."

Detective Perry leans closer to her monitor. "What matters is who killed her, not who she was."

"Both of those things matter."

"Why?"

"Because Lecia was a mistake. I told you she wasn't like the other women. He made a mistake killing her. That's why he stopped."

Detective Perry glances up from her computer. "Someone told you this?"

"No," Dorian says. "It's just the only thing that makes sense."

"The only thing that makes sense to you."

Dorian tries to hold her stare but the detective looks away. Who else should it make sense to? Who else matters besides Dorian? Who else cares?

"Do you ever think about the person who killed your daughter?" Dorian opens her mouth to reply but Detective Perry cuts her off. "I mean as a person, not as a killer. Like what does he do? How does he spend his days? Does he like hamburgers or tacos? Does he watch baseball or football or maybe soccer? Does he drive a sedan? Is he in good shape? Does he put sugar in his coffee? Does he drink beer or liquor? Does he listen to the radio? What's his email address? Does he recycle? What supermarket does he use?" She pauses to pat her brassy blond hair. "Or when you think about him, do you think about some kind of faceless evil incarnate? Some criminal mastermind who stole something from you and got away with it? A sociopath cobbled together from the nightmares of pro-filers and psychologists to satisfy their own shortcomings because they can't find him?"

"I stopped thinking about him years ago," Dorian says. "What he's like doesn't matter. Not to me. Clearly not to the LAPD. All that matters is Lecia." And all that matters is that the past stays put. All that matters is that it not gate-crash her every day. But these last few days that has seemed impossible, as if that whole history is out to get her, as if her mind is threatening to shake off its delicate reality.

"This guy, you wouldn't notice him on the bus." The detective returns to her monitor, still punishing her gum. "It's a guy thing, that way of thinking. They need their foe to be their equal. All the detectives you talked to back then were male?"

Dorian doesn't want to reach back to the countless interviews, the endless appeals to the Southwest Station, the frustrations and dead ends. "Yes," she says, "all men. Not one cared that Lecia was different."

"You keep saying that."

"She was his last victim. She had to be different."

"You keep the birds," Detective Perry says.

The swing catches Dorian off guard.

Detective Perry taps the topmost box with a pencil. "In there," she prompts.

"Yes," Dorian says, snapping back to the present day. "They're in there."

The detective doesn't seem to think that there's anything odd about thirty-three dead birds on her desk. She taps the box with her pencil again, then peers at her monitor. "Hummingbirds and jays?"

"Exactly," Dorian replies. "Mostly at my restaurant but now at my house, too. I think someone is trying to send me a message."

"Why would anyone want to send you a message?"

Dorian fumbles for a reply.

"Leave them." Detective Perry spits out her gum and unwraps another piece. She stands and holds out her hands for the shoeboxes. She opens the bottom drawer of her desk and places them inside. Dorian winces, waiting for her to bang the drawer shut, but she slides it in place carefully. "We'll be in touch," the detective says. She doesn't offer Dorian her hand. She doesn't meet her eye. She's already back in her seat, lost in her monitor.

Dorian glances around the station.

Dear Idira, Let me tell you something that I know from experience. You're going to keep shouting, but no one's going to listen. It's their job not to listen. To listen would mean that you matter, but you don't. You're just a problem, one that will eventually go away. I did. I went away. I made myself scarce, because I couldn't take the do-nothingness, the brush-offs, the anger at my own anger. I had become a problem on top of the problem of my daughter's death. So I shut up. You think it will be difficult, impossible. You think you'll never get used to it. But you do, because all that rage is exhausting. You need something left for yourself when it's over.

She clears her throat. "I suppose it's going to be the same old thing," she says. "Hear my story but don't listen to it." Her voice is louder than she expected. "Take the easy way out, hope this blows over, goes away. Hope there's nothing you have to do about it." She's on her feet. "And hope whoever's killing these birds will just stop. Or be hauled in for something else. Or even better, maybe I'll just stop caring that they're dead and that it's okay you're not doing your job." She bangs a hand on the metal desk.

Detective Perry looks up, a strange expression on her face like she'd been somewhere else. "I heard you. Lecia wasn't a prostitute," she says.

Dorian stares at her. But the detective is back at her computer screen, her brow furrowed. When Dorian walks off, she doesn't even look up.

THE SHIFT IS CHANGING—cops coming and going. Radios crackle. Someone is brewing a pot of coffee that already smells burned. It looks like it was a bad night in Southwest. Several officers from the late show are still wrapping up business—their eyes bloodshot, their faces heavy. Dorian's almost at the door that leads to the sergeant's desk when she hears her name, or thinks she does.

"Dorian Williams?"

She turns. It takes her a moment to realize what she's seeing. For the second time in twenty-four hours, it's Lecia in front of her, in the flesh, not returned as a ghost. The feeling upends her. She grabs for the nearest desk and steadies herself.

"Dorian, you okay?"

Julianna again. Right there. Right in front of her. Her long orange hair—Lecia's hair—tumbled over her shoulders as she slumps on the bad side of a booking desk.

"Julianna?"

Julianna's wearing last night's clothes, tight, high-waisted black jeans, a stretchy teal crop top, shoes that you wouldn't think you could walk a city block in. On her lap she's holding a shiny pink bomber jacket made out of some kind of flammable-looking material.

"You're up early," Julianna says in her singsong lilt that's a little slurred.

"And you're up late."

"Had my choice, I'd have been home in bed hours ago, fuzzy pajamas and all," Julianna says. "Maybe a little TV. Some hot cocoa. But that *pendejo* had other plans."

She gestures at a detective crossing the room with two cups of coffee. She's still a little high. That's pretty clear from the way she widens her eyes and bobs her head at the end of her sentences.

"They think they can keep me here all night just for trying to enjoy myself."

"Is that what you were doing?" Dorian asks.

Julianna gives her a wide smile. She's so beautiful Dorian wants to smack her for all the crap she's done to herself—the dyed hair, the cartoonish makeup, the ridiculous clothes. "What else would I be doing?" There's a challenge in the question. Julianna nods her head a few times, waiting for Dorian to rise to it.

The detective with the coffee reaches the desk.

Julianna takes her cup. Her nails are done in an array of pinks with tiny purple flowers. There is a minuscule gold ring dangling from the tip of her index finger. Tattoos are inked on her arms—a broken heart, a zodiac sign, a couple of words in Spanish, a few names, and a rose.

"With three sugars, how I like it?" she asks.

"You'll like it how I make it," the detective says. Then he notices Dorian. "This a friend of yours?"

"We go way back," Julianna says.

The officer looks at Dorian. "You're taking her home?"

"I didn't even know she was here," Dorian says.

"She's lucky she's not being booked for an overnight in Seventy-Seventh Street with the rest of her friends," the detective says.

Dorian knows Seventy-Seventh Street. It catches the overflow from the stations that don't have their own jails as well as from Southwest Station, which can't accommodate women in its lockup.

"What friends are these?" Dorian asks.

Julianna shakes her head and lets out a slow, nasty laugh. "No, no, no. Don't mother me. Don't start thinking I need anyone's help. That I need yours. Don't go thinking like I know you're thinking. It was just a little *llelo*. Keeps it real. Keeps me on my feet all night."

Dorian doesn't want to ask, but she can't help herself. "And why do you need to be on your feet?"

"Because I was at a party." Julianna snaps her fingers and sways her head side to side. "I needed to cut loose, you know. I needed to dance. And sometimes, I need a little help. It makes the music jump."

"Just under a half gram of help," the detective says. "Anything more and you'd be joining your girls over at the jail."

"How come you arrested my girls and none of the other messed-up bitches at the party? All those USC sorority chicas were rolling and you just tell them to get home safe. Probably called them a cab. Bet you would have given them a police escort if you weren't too busy dragging me and my girls in."

"You and your girls are on our radar," the detective says.

"Because we're nasty bitches who know how to party?"

"Something like that."

"Come on, Detective, we're just a couple of cocktail waitresses having some fun. Last time I checked, that wasn't a crime."

"Cocktail waitresses," the detective says.

"Detective, do you have a problem with how I make my living?"

"You know I do."

"Come on down to the Fast Rabbit. First round's on the house," Julianna says.

The detective blows on his coffee and glances at Dorian. "She can leave with you if you want. Otherwise she'll have to stay until she's sober."

"So you're calling me a babysitter."

"Do you want to leave or not?" the detective says.

Julianna looks around the room like there actually might be something worth sticking around for, then shakes her head. "I wouldn't want to waste the day, now."

She stands up, makes a show of putting on her jacket, tossing and retying her hair. The detective hands her a slip of paper. "Don't forget to show up. Miss your court date, this misdemeanor is going to get a whole lot worse."

"It's a date," Julianna says, blowing him a kiss.

She saunters past Dorian and out the door.

Outside, Dorian has to blink several times to adjust to the sun.

Julianna pulls a pair of sunglasses from her purse, then keeps riffling through the bag. "I guess smoking's a crime now too." She dumps her bag out onto the station's steps. "Took my Newports."

"It's not a crime but it's a bad habit."

Julianna squats and scrapes her stuff back into her purse. "You think I need a lecture on top of all that shit in there?" She zips the bag and flings it over her shoulder. But she doesn't stand. The effort seems to have exhausted her. Instead she rests her head on her knees, her sass and venom gone.

Dorian sits next to her and places a hand on her back. She closes her eyes and for a moment allows herself to imagine it's Lecia's back beneath her palm, not Julianna's.

Dorian can smell the late night on Julianna—the sweat mixed with baby powder, perfume, cigarettes, booze, and the strange sweet smell that leaks from the pores of people who use too many speedy drugs, a chemical sugary tang.

Julianna coughs and Dorian feels the rattle in her lungs.

What happened to the little girl Lecia would bring over after school and plop on the carpet while she got out her old toys? The little girl she introduced to her scratched dolls, her chipped tea set, her windup television that played "Row Row Row Your Boat"? What happened to the kid Lecia and Dorian taught all the games and songs that they'd played for years? She was somewhere inside this hard-partying Jujubee, hidden behind the makeup and the tattoos—the little girl Lecia started babysitting for next to nothing after discovering her playing alone in a playground one summer afternoon.

Julianna coughs again and slides forward a little more.

Dorian keeps rubbing her back anyway, trying to buff away last night and all the others that came before it.

"Julianna."

Julianna stands up, knocking away Dorian's hand. "I need to get some new smokes. I need a shower and a Diet Coke."

"How about breakfast?"

5.

———

JACK'S FAMILY KITCHEN IS JUST AROUND THE CORNER FROM the station on Western. Julianna's all sass and swagger, tossing her hair and strutting the short distance to the restaurant. But when she takes off her sunglasses at the table, Dorian can see the weariness in her eyes—the whites tinged with red, the dark shadows underneath.

Dorian's not really hungry, but she orders large to inspire Julianna—eggs, chicken sausage, biscuits, salmon croquettes, and chicken wings. The waitress brings her a coffee and a water for Julianna.

Julianna scans the restaurant, seeing no one she knows or no one of interest. "You're hanging out at the station now?"

"Julianna, you're a beautiful woman, you need to be careful."

Julianna rolls her eyes. "Not this shit again."

"When was the last time anyone told you to be careful?" Dorian says.

"Who says I'm not careful?" The last hint of brassy energy has vanished from Julianna's voice. She sounds plain worn. "I'm not the one who lost a kid." Dorian imagines Julianna would be ashamed of her words, but she holds Dorian's stare, challenging her for the reprimand.

Dear Idira.

"What's that?"

Had Dorian said it aloud?

Dear Idira, They'll try to tell you you were careless. They will say the most hurtful things because you've already been through the worst. They think you can handle it, that you need to hear it. That you are either tough enough because of what happened or that you need to get tougher, hear the hard truths. But there's nothing you can do. You just listen. You ignore. You turn in and away.

"Where are you living now?" Dorian asks.

"What's it to you?"

"Do you ever go home?"

"Fuck that shit. Some girls and I have a place down by the Rabbit, down on Forty-Seventh. But it's hectic. Too many ladies. So I move around. Here, there. Home, if you really need to know. Can't be tied down."

There's a second when Dorian envies Julianna's attitude. Because if there's one thing Dorian is, it's tied down. Tied to the fish shack. Tied to Lecia's memory. Tied to the women on Western she needs to feed.

"I know," Dorian says.

But Dorian also knows the Fast Rabbit—a cocktail bar down Western from the Snooty Fox and the Mustang Motel where the luckier girls take their customers. The bar is rumored to have a back room where the cocktail waitresses make big tips.

"Life's too short to be tied down by bills and rent and all that shit."

Dorian's certain that Julianna has no idea how short life can really be, and if she does, she's not paying attention. One day you can be getting dressed for work, slicking your hair, tightening your curls, lining your lips, and quarreling with your girlfriends over who's going to wear the pink halter top. One day you can be heading out the door for your weekly babysitting gig. And the next you're lying in an alley or worse.

"Too short," Dorian says. "For sure."

If Julianna catches her meaning, she doesn't show it.

Their food comes—too many plates for the table. Dorian digs in, although fried food apart from hers never appeals. Julianna picks at her plate, eating like someone who's hungry but whose stomach is troubled. She takes a bite of a salmon croquette, then pushes it away.

"Something wrong?" Dorian asks.

"It just can't hold a candle to yours. Your fish is the best on Western. Everyone knows."

"Do they?" Dorian can't remember the last time Julianna had been in the fish shack.

"I tell everyone, I've been going to the R&C since I was too little to see over the counter."

"So how come you don't come by anymore?"

"Life," Julianna says, "it gets mad busy." She glances around the restaurant. "I need a cigarette."

Dorian opens her mouth to object.

"Did I say I need a cigarette or a lecture?" Julianna asks. She gathers her bag and steps out onto Western. Dorian watches her glance up and down the street. There's a gas station and a minimart on the corner. But Julianna stays put, waiting.

Dorian signals for the check and drops forty bucks without doing the math.

Julianna flags a middle-aged man passing by. Dorian can guess at their exchange—Julianna flirting, asking for a cigarette, asking for a light, giving the man the time of day for a second, then sending him on his way so she can smoke in peace.

The waitress is at Dorian's side. "You want change?"

Julianna steps closer to the curb to smoke. The wind lifts her curls, making them fly back from her head like a cape. From a distance, last night doesn't show.

"You want change?"

Dorian nods, waves her hand, a noncommittal gesture.

"Yes or no?" The waitress leaves.

A car approaches, slowing as it passes Julianna. The window rolls down. Julianna tosses her smoke.

"Here you go." The waitress is back with a pile of ones and a heap of loose change. "I was out of bigger bills," she says. "And now I'm almost out of singles. Excuse the coins." She puts the tray with the check and the money on the table. A handful of change tumbles onto Dorian's lap and then ricochets onto the floor. She stoops, colliding with the waitress on her way down.

She gathers the change and rights herself. The car and Julianna are gone.

Dorian had her and she lost her. She bolts from the table to the street and looks south where a sedan is speeding off—too far for the make, model, and license. She's alone with the wind on Western.

6.

———

WEEKENDS ARE FOR LARGE PARTIES—BIRTHDAYS, QUINCEA-
ñeras, baby showers, family get-togethers, postchurch meals, and
lazy suppers—which means Dorian can lose herself in the all-day
routine of battering, frying, baking. It takes her mind off Julianna.
Because Julianna was there one minute, smoking her bummed
cigarette, tapping her impossible heels on the sidewalk, and the
next she was gone, vanished into a passing car like she'd been
waiting for it all along.

The kitchen is a comfort, a place to hide. By the time the first
lunch orders come in, the fryer is bubbling. There's a rhythm to
it—the dip, shake, and fry. The way the chicken or fish spins to
the surface of the oil when it's battered perfectly and the temperature is just right. Dorian can lose herself in the details, the ideal
cut of the fish to make it curve slightly when crisped, the uniform
golden brown of each strip of chicken, the way to make shrimp
retain their shape when battered.

At six o'clock Willie, who helps her out on the weekends, sticks
his head into the kitchen. "Time to get the big one going."

For nearly as long as the fish shack has been running, or as
long as Dorian has been working it, an order has come in on Sat-

urdays for a long-standing dice game. Twenty dinners, shrimp, catfish, whiting, sand dabs, and chicken with assorted sides. Everything except french fries, because everyone knows they don't travel.

Willie cocks his head. "You forgot?"

Instead of responding, Dorian pulls down twenty Styrofoam containers.

Willie taps the doorframe. "I'll tell 'em food's gonna be late."

"Don't you dare," Dorian says.

She works hard. It's tempting to crowd the oil to get the fish done faster. Dorian knows adding even one extra piece will result in a mess as the fillets bump against each other and the breading falls off. Eventually, with loose coating and fish overcrowding the fryer, the temperature of the oil will fall and she'll have to clear the whole thing out, change the oil, and start over. So she works slow, one dinner order at a time in the four fryers. Everyone knows fried food is better hot, but for nearly two decades the dice game hasn't complained about delivery.

It takes Dorian half an hour to prep all the meals. Willie helps her pack up the sides family style. Together they load everything into the wheeled cart that Willie uses for the delivery.

The rush of cooking over, the anxious feeling that Dorian has been sidestepping all day is back. She feels jumpy. She needs to do something, to somehow rewind to the morning and instead of letting Julianna vanish, chase her, or even better, keep her at the table, forbid her from getting that smoke. She looks down at the cart full of food.

"I'll take it," she says.

Willie raises an eyebrow. "How's that?"

"I'll take this." Dorian grabs the cart. "What's the address?"

"How long they've been ordering this dinner?" Willie asks. "And you don't know the address."

"I cook it," Dorian says, "I don't walk it."

He scribbles something on the back of a grease-stained receipt. Dorian squints at his scratchy writing. "Twenty-Ninth Place?"

"Between Cimarron and St. Andrews."

"You sure it's place not street?"

"Who's been making this delivery for the last seventeen years?" Willie looks down at the containers loaded into the cart.

"But you're sure it's place?" Dorian asks again.

"Place," Willie says. "Place."

Dorian's staring at him, not because she doesn't trust him, but because she doesn't trust herself. Because here's the past coming charging in, destabilizing her.

"Dorian? Dorian?"

Twenty-Ninth Place between Cimarron and St. Andrews is Julianna's block, the house where Lecia used to babysit. The last place she was seen alive.

Willie's shaking her arm. "Dorian, where'd you go?"

Julianna. Reborn as Jujubee. Julianna whom Dorian lost to the driver of a strange car. A man she chose over Dorian. Danger over safety. Unknown over known. The things that happened on her watch.

"Why don't you let me take it," Willie says.

"I'm going." Dorian grips the cart. "I was just thinking it tastes better fresh out of the fryer." She can already sense the perfectly battered fish going limp.

"They don't complain. But they will if you don't get moving." Willie holds the gate open so she can wheel the cart out.

"How come we never got a delivery bike?" she asks.

"Now you want to ride a bike?" He lets the gate close.

As Dorian wheels the cart to the corner of Western at Thirty-First she wonders, not for the first time, if Lecia's death had something to do with Julianna's transformation from little girl who hid behind stuffed animals into a firecracker bursting high and bright in the night. Not that Dorian knew exactly what Julianna got up to. She'd heard the rumors. She asked around, even knocking on Julianna's parents' door once a few years back only to be told by her father, Armando, "She's gone downtown."

Like that was an explanation.

It's nearly dark when Dorian turns onto Twenty-Ninth Place. With the light goes the warmth. Thirty-five years in Los Angeles and she still can't get used to the temperature swings of a SoCal winter day—83 at lunch, 53 by dinner. A city that just can't make up its mind about anything.

Only one block off Western and it's a different world—quiet residential streets lined with colorful Craftsman bungalows cast into shadow by the final stand of the sun. Look close and you can see the change everyone's been going on about. A few new family cars—silver SUVs and minivans. Freshly landscaped yards in the drought-resistant style that's both trendy and necessary. New paint jobs and repointed brick porches.

It's not as if Jefferson Park was derelict. People here might not have the cash to restore their houses according to historic standard, but for the most part the houses have always looked neat.

From the end of the block she can see the red house where Julianna grew up, made all the more visible by its treeless front yard surrounded by a motorized iron fence painted cream.

Dorian slows as she passes it. Like many families who lived here before the riots, Julianna's parents still have bars on their windows and a metal gate in front of their door. This must look ugly to the newcomers, who probably think the bars are a sign of bad taste and a bad attitude. But the recently arrived weren't around for the chaos that tore down Western in the aftermath of Rodney King, or for the mistrust and suspicion that settled in after the fires and gunshots died away. They can't imagine that this bungalow community was adjacent to a six-day war zone.

And they can't quite see the lingering signs of gang activity that once surged through these seemingly quiet streets.

Dorian stops in front of the red house. Paint is peeling on the siding and window frames. Strands of Christmas lights sag from the eaves. Unlike the houses on either side, the yard is untidy—there's a Ford Pinto up on blocks in the driveway and another car behind it that looks stripped bare. There are rusted tools, auto parts, and car mags scattered on the ground. Three folding chairs form a semicircle around a wooden box strewn with beer cans.

The wind has picked up—a resurgence of the Santa Anas that have been raging all week—knocking the empties to the pavement and turning the pages of the magazines. Dorian cranes her neck, trying to see if there's any movement in the dark windows behind the bars.

Someone is approaching from up the block—a light shuffle step. Dorian moves away from the gate. She waits, but no one approaches. She strains to hear—nothing.

The palms creak overhead.

There's a burst of noise from a nearby yard—a group of men ribbing one another in Spanish.

"Julianna?"

A radio cranks up, filling the street with classic soul music.

"Julianna?"

Something rustles in the tangle of vines and bushes between the faded red house and the one next door. Dorian's breath catches.

"Jujubee?"

A cat dashes out over the uneven sidewalk and into the street.

Dorian puts a hand to her chest as if to catch her pounding heart. "Jesus."

Maybe she is getting old. Maybe too much time alone has made her jumpy. Maybe there's something in this house that still gets to her. Or maybe she's started that descent for real, her mind heading for free fall.

She tugs the cart, jump-starting it over a crack in the pavement. By the time she arrives at the house next door the music has been lowered to a tolerable level.

The house is on a corner lot with a wraparound porch. It's well maintained with a fresh coat of dark green paint on the siding. The eaves and trim are sage with red accents on the window frames. The clinker brick on the porch columns is in good condition. If there were once bars on the windows, they are now gone.

Dorian opens the gate, bumps her cart up the steps, and knocks. She can hear the party going on in the back—waves of Spanish and English mingling with the music. There's no answer. The door is solid wood with a small window that shows a dark hall. Dorian checks the large picture window; it's heavily curtained. She knocks again.

The curtain shifts and a woman looks out. She's white, about Dorian's age with a thin face and elegant features. But there's something disdainful in her eyes. She scowls. The curtain drops.

Dorian knocks again.

"Around back. Go around back."

If this was the drill, why hadn't Willie told her?

Dorian knocks once more. The door swings open.

"I'm here with the food," she says.

"I can see that."

Two white women in Jefferson Park—two old-timers. But Dorian's certain they've never met. The woman is wearing a nurse's uniform, perfectly starched.

"I'm Dorian," she says.

"The food goes around back."

"It would be easier if I could bring it through the house."

"Lots of things would be easier," the woman says.

Dorian has no interest in bumping the cart down the steps and then dragging it over the driveway to the backyard. "The food's going to get cold."

The woman holds the door open. "Since you insist. But normally it goes around back."

"You never told me your name," Dorian says.

"I didn't know that was required. Anneke."

Dorian eases the cart over the doorstep. The interior of the house is pristine. It has the original built-in cabinetry and even what look like several original light fixtures.

The furniture is all period, Mission and Arts & Crafts reproductions or perhaps the real thing.

Anneke eyes the cart as Dorian heads down the hall toward the kitchen.

"I was studying to be a nurse once," Dorian says.

"It's not a job for everyone."

"I had planned to go back to school, but my husband died and I took over the restaurant."

"What you learn about nursing is that many people don't want to be properly cared for."

"I guess it's lucky I stuck with cooking."

"Lucky for who?" Anneke says.

Dorian stops wheeling the cart, causing Anneke to bump into it. She turns so they are face-to-face over the stacked Styrofoam boxes. Anneke's face is pulled into a pucker. Her eyes narrow as if she's sucking on something sour.

"Is there a problem?" Dorian says.

"I keep my house clean," Anneke replies. "I tend not to open it to strangers."

"I'm not a stranger. I'm delivering food. You called me."

"I didn't call you. My husband called you. Next time around back, please."

Dorian continues into the kitchen. Like the dining room and the living room that she'd glimpsed on her way down the hall, it's pristine. There are few personal touches.

She opens the door to the garden, eager to get out of the house.

"Let me tell you something," Anneke says, as Dorian edges the cart through the doorway. "There's no such thing as luck. There's only responsibility."

"Noted," Dorian says.

"You think you are doing something important, cooking for the neighborhood, right? That you are helping the community."

"No," Dorian says. "I just think I'm getting by."

Then she yanks the cart out of the kitchen, down the porch steps to the garden. She stands at the foot of the porch for a minute before anyone notices.

It's a mixed crowd—white, black, Latino. All men. Some are Dorian's age, others in their thirties, and a few just out of their teens. There's a washtub with beer off to one side next to an empty table, which must be for the food. A boom box is making it difficult for anyone to be heard without shouting. Some of the guys are passing a bottle, others are throwing dice.

"Yo! Food's here." It's one of the younger guys who flags her down. "Bring it on through."

The game stops as Dorian drags the cart to the table. She's halfway there when a man takes the cart from her. He's white with a dark beard and hair peppered with gray. He stares at her. One of his eyes is smaller than the other. She knows this man from somewhere. Or perhaps from nowhere in particular besides around. The two of them—white faces from the days when Jefferson Park was predominantly black, just respectful acquaintances— the four-sentence-exchange-at-the-store type, the remark-on-the-weather type, the allied-against-too-much-change type. "Roger, right?" Dorian says, relinquishing the cart. She's seen his name on the order for years, but never put it to a face until now.

"Indeed," Roger says, rattling the cart across the yard. "He sent a woman to do his job today?" There's an odd formality to the way he talks.

"I make the food," Dorian says. "Willie brings it. Today we switched things up."

"He made the food?"

Dorian has to laugh. Willie could take the reins in a pinch—but he'd be drowning in an order this size. "I cooked it and I brought it." She begins to unload the containers onto a folding table at the far side of the yard. "You know it tastes better right from the kitchen," she says. She can't help herself. She's proud of her food. It wasn't what she expected she'd bring to the world but she does a damn good job.

Roger places a hand on her shoulder. "All these years, have you heard a complaint? But maybe it's time you get a car."

"Maybe," Dorian says, trying to shake off his hand. She glances around the yard, then up to the second story of the house, where one of the curtains has been pulled back.

Her eyes meet Anneke's.

"You should come around more often," Roger says. "Old-timers and all."

Dorian's still looking over his shoulder at the window. Roger follows her gaze. Anneke steps back.

"My wife," Roger says. "She doesn't like gambling."

"So that's her problem," Dorian says. "I thought she didn't like me."

"She's seen a lot in her life. Her exterior is hard." He holds out the dice. "You want a turn? If you call the roll, you keep what's on the floor."

Dorian looks at the ground, where there's about forty bucks in singles and fives. She takes the dice. Ricky had been a dice player—a habit he picked up in the army. "Deuces," she says. She shakes and tosses. Up comes an easy eight.

Roger puts a hand on her shoulder. "Better luck next time."

7.

———

MONDAY AFTER WORK DORIAN CALLS THE FAST RABBIT AND
asks for Jujubee. The woman who answers has to shout above
the music to be understood. *No Jujubee here.*

"When was the last time you saw her?"

What's that? Whatchu sayin'?

"Jujubee—when did she work last?"

I'm telling you, no Jujubee here.

"How about Julianna?"

No Julianna. No Jujubee.

"Now or ever?" Dorian asks.

Come down and search the place.

Dorian hangs up. Maybe it's her night off. Maybe she quit.
Maybe she never worked there at all.

After work on Tuesday she drives Western from the 10 down
to Seventy-Seventh and back. She makes the loop four times.

Wednesday crawls. Only four lunch orders. She keeps checking the clock to see if it's time to start closing up.

On Thursday, still no sign of Julianna, not that Dorian knows
where to look.

Just before closing, Kathy appears at the back door. She accepts a plate of fried shrimp and some fish trim.

"How come you care about fucking Julianna all of a sudden?" Kathy's wearing a plastic raincoat over a dress that looks like a long tank top. No bra. She's rebleached her hair so it's the color of corn silk. "Bitch thinks she's too good for us. I knew her back when."

"Me too," Dorian says.

"Oh yeah? *You* knew her?"

"She used to eat here when she was little."

"Fucking small world," Kathy says. "So, what, she owes you money or something?"

"Not exactly."

Kathy reaches for the cup of iced tea Dorian's poured her. "Shit," she says, "that's motherfucking sweet."

Dorian senses Kathy's eyes on her.

"You think something messed up happened to Jujubee."

Messed up. Funny how Kathy can't say the words, make them real. Invite the danger closer.

"I don't know what I think," Dorian says.

"Tell you what," Kathy says. "Julianna probably found some dude, holed up with him. Bet she found a rich one. Taking a few days for herself. Let me tell you, sometimes you need that. You motherfucking need that. New place, new guy. Time out of mind, you know what I mean?" She shakes her head. "And more power to her. Doing a thing like that. Matter of fact, that's what I need to do. Find some dude with a big old house out of the city, in Upland or San Pedro. Get out of town for a few. Make some cash. Get some sleep. Take care of myself instead of the rest of them." She tosses the empty cup. "Bet you anything a few days from now you'll find her at the Rabbit, pockets full, well slept." She reaches for the empty cup again. "Actually, lemme get a refill."

Dorian fills the cup from the four-gallon tub, then watches as Kathy takes a half pint of SoCo out of her purse and tips it into the tea. "One for the road," she says. She takes a sip. "You start worrying about what can happen out there, it's a one-way ticket."

"Julianna's different."

Kathy snorts, blowing bubbles through the straw. "Every girl thinks she's different."

Outside someone's honking a horn.

Kathy squints through the kitchen out the front window. "I'm gonna miss my shift."

"I'll walk you out," Dorian says.

They go out the front. Dorian locks the gate behind them. They head south on Western.

Kathy's like a snake shedding a skin or perhaps growing a thicker one the farther they get from the fish shack. Her voice changes, grows harder, colder as she arms herself against the night. She stares down a woman who's standing on the wrong corner, taunts a driver for looking too long. She stomps the sidewalk, side-eyeing the civilians.

At Thirty-Seventh she turns to Dorian. "You gonna walk with me forever?"

"I'm just headed this way."

"You think I need watching over like some fucking Julianna."

"Kathy, I'm just walking."

"You think because we eat your food you're some kinda saint. Bitch, please."

"Kathy—" Dorian begins.

"Just let me do my fucking job. This shit isn't your business. None of it." She whirls around and presses a hand into Dorian's chest, holding her back, as she storms off.

Dorian watches her cross the street, trying her luck southbound.

The sky is ribboned with a few strips of pink. The palms are waving. The wind nags.

Two northbound buses pass. Dorian doesn't get on. She keeps

heading south, not admitting where she's going until she's standing in front of the Fast Rabbit.

It's seven thirty. Probably too early for the real action. She stands back and waits. The door opens more frequently than she'd expected. Single men. Pairs and groups. Some walk in proud. Others slink through the door.

Dorian circles the block. She buys a few tacos from a street vendor. Then heads for the door of the Fast Rabbit.

The bouncer looks more fat than strong. But you still wouldn't want to tangle with him. "Have a good evening," he says, holding the door open.

The interior is dark, lit by pink and blue strobe lights and a smudged disco ball. There's a small dance floor and a black lacquered bar. Dorian waits for her eyes to adjust to the light before taking a seat on a vinyl stool.

The bartender gives her a look like he's never seen a middle-aged woman before. Like after thirty, women cease to exist. "You want a drink?"

"I'm looking for someone."

"Does he know that?"

"She."

The bartender raises his eyebrows.

"I'll have a Seven and Seven," Dorian says.

The drink comes in a cup just like the ones at Lupillo's. Dorian sips it through the straw and watches as a door at the far end of the dance floor opens. A man strides out, takes a look around, then heads for the exit. A few moments later, a woman about Julianna's age emerges. She's got a wild, leonine mane of hair and a heart-shaped face. Her eyebrows look as if they're drawn with Magic Marker.

She takes a seat at the bar. She has a tiger claw tattoo ripping the skin of each breast. "Fuck. We're banging and it's hardly nighttime. Gonna wear out my damn thighs by midnight."

The bartender pours her a green drink the color of a science experiment. "You complaining about getting work?"

"I'm just working the work," the woman says. Then she glances at Dorian. "You new here?"

"She's looking for someone," the bartender says.

"She's not here." The woman winks at Dorian. "You buying?"

"Excuse me?"

"Most people who sit there buy me a drink."

"That's okay," Dorian says.

"You nervous? This your first time?" The woman slides her stool closer. Dorian can smell her perfume and something else— maybe someone else, a musky, murky odor. "Come on, baby, buy me a drink."

"You have a drink," Dorian says.

"Damn, lady, you don't know how the game is played."

Dorian sips her cocktail. "I'm not playing."

The woman runs her hand down Dorian's thigh. "Then get the fuck off that stool." The bartender snaps his fingers, directs the woman's attention to the other end of the bar, where two young guys are appraising her like she's a test car at an auto show. She slides off her stool and heads their way. Dorian watches her slip between them, somehow commanding the attention of both at once.

"A woman's got to work," the bartender says.

The back door becomes a turnstile. Women and men in together. Men out first. Then the women. Dorian keeps her eyes on it in case Julianna appears.

"Hey, lady, you still taking up space?"

The woman with claw tattoos is back. "I'm having a good night," she says, "and it's barely night. So I could give you one on the house. Ramon will let it slide." She winks at the bartender. "Come on," she says, slipping an arm around Dorian's waist, "when was the last time you got a little something-something?"

Years and years. Decades. Time beyond imagining.

"Bet it's all cobwebs up in there," the woman says. "Bet you need someone to shake you loose." She pulls Dorian tighter. "Come on, what do you say? What are you waiting for?"

Dorian feels her body tense in the woman's half embrace, as if by stiffening she can increase the distance between them. "I'm not waiting for anything."

"Don't tell me that. Everyone is waiting for something." She's breathing into Dorian's ear. "Come on, you can tell me. You can tell me anything."

"I'm not—" Dorian begins. But then she realizes the woman's right. She has been waiting. Waiting for something, anything, to release her.

The woman puts a hand on Dorian's chin and pivots it so they are face-to-face. "I'm right," the woman says. Her voice is baby soft, deceptive and slippery like black ice. "I know I'm right. I know what you want better than you do."

And then her mouth is on Dorian's. Her lips are a wet crush, her tongue—all muscle.

It takes a moment for Dorian to realize what's happening. Then she springs back, jumps off her stool, crashes to the ground.

"Get the fuck out," the woman says. "You ain't interested in shit."

8.

———

FRIDAY NIGHT—NO WOMEN SHOW AT DORIAN'S BACK DOOR.
Saturday the same. It's as if someone warned them off.

Even two days after her experience at the Rabbit, Dorian can still taste the woman's mouth. Still smell her. The taste lingers—salty, liquor-sweet. But something else too. Her words.

What are you waiting for?

Dorian takes another swallow of tea to erase this woman and her question. But it won't go.

The fish shack is slow.

When the clock hits five, Willie ducks into the kitchen.

"I know," Dorian says, "time to get the big one going."

She's pulling down twenty Styrofoam containers when the front door opens.

She hears Willie's voice. "Anneke, right? You here to pick up for Roger?"

"No." The reply is curt.

Dorian looks through the kitchen window and sees Roger's wife. "I want to talk to Dorian."

Dorian pokes her head out. Anneke's standing in the doorway, as if she can't bear to enter the restaurant.

"Can I help you?"

"Not anymore," Anneke says. "I'm here to cancel Roger's order. We won't be needing your food at his game."

Dorian sighs and takes off her apron. "You could have called," she said.

"I just want to be clear." The corner of Anneke's eye is twitching. "I'm canceling it permanently."

"I always said fried food doesn't travel," Dorian says. "But it didn't seem to bother you for more than a decade."

"Tastes change." She has an accent Dorian can't place. Clipped and pinched.

Dorian dips into the kitchen and switches off the fryer. When she returns, Anneke is still there.

"Anything else?" Dorian says.

Anneke is craning her neck, staring into the kitchen and through the back door. "It's a health hazard. Those women. The ones who eat back there. Everyone knows."

"Do they?" Dorian asks.

"If they don't, they will. People are trying to clean up this neighborhood."

"I bet they are." Dorian holds Anneke's stare, watching her eyelid flutter like an incensed butterfly. Finally, Anneke turns. "Nothing for the road?" Dorian asks.

The door shuts without a reply.

She puts her hands on the counter. "Bitch."

"Go on," Willie says. "Get out of here. I'll clean up."

She doesn't argue. There's no sense in waiting for the girls. If she passes any of them, she'll reassure them that they're always welcome at her back door.

The wind has picked up again, sending more desiccated palm fronds down to the street with a loud rip and rustle. Empty cans and bottles are rolling down Western. They're in for another wind event—a dangerous, dry howling gale that will send sparks into the arid hills and ignite a wildfire if folks aren't careful.

Dorian figures there's still about half an hour of light left, which gives her just enough time to walk to the Rosedale Cemetery up on Normandie and Washington if she hurries.

Western is slow. Light on traffic, low on girls. Maybe it's the incessant wind from the desert or maybe it's the threat of cold that's keeping the girls away. But the street is empty. Only Dorian is on foot. At Twenty-Eighth she catches the bus that takes her to Washington. From there it's a ten-minute walk east.

It's a shame about the streets surrounding the cemetery—dirty, trash strewn, smeared with pepper tree buds and dog shit, and more often than not now home to a scattershot collection of homeless.

But the cemetery is pleasant. Fifteen years on and Dorian's still surprised each time she walks up the slight hill from Washington to find her daughter's spot. The place is carpeted with a well-maintained lawn even in the dry summer months. Towering palms line several of the wide, circular drives ringing the main lawn, offering shade and secrecy—a refuge from the city.

There are uniform rows dedicated to soldiers from the Spanish-American War with life-size angels bowed over ornate headstones or standing atop looming columns. There are two family mausoleums in the shape of pyramids as well as obelisks and a jumble of neoclassical structures. Look closely and you can find the names of Los Angeles's vanguard families—Slauson, Glassell, Burbank, and Banning. Dorian used to linger there but now she makes straight for Lecia's grave, closer to Venice than Dorian had wanted, but still sheltered from the street noise.

Rosedale is empty. There are never many visitors, and the few who do come freshen up the more modest gravesites with flowers, food offerings, and from time to time, a radio set to a favorite station. Lecia's headstone is across from this section—an area of old and new graves with a few shiny headstones amid the nondescript markers.

The sun is gone but there's still a purple glow in the sky. A gust of wind sweeps through the cemetery. She hears the sound of broken crockery, offerings scattered and strewn.

Then she hears something else. "Give that back!"

Dorian sees a man she recognizes as one of the caretakers hurrying toward the custodial house, his arms cradling carnations in a plastic vase, a couple of teddy bears, a balloon.

"Give that back!"

Dorian steps to the side just as a wiry black woman about her age pounces on the caretaker from behind.

"That's mine. Give it back to me."

The caretaker shakes her off. "You're lucky I'm too close to the end of my shift to bother calling the police."

The woman darts in front of the custodian, blocking his path. Her features are sharp, her skin scarred and thin—the signs of past addiction. "Are you telling me it's a crime now to leave what I need to on my daughter's grave? That seems more like sacrilege than criminal. I'm just doing what the Lord commands. I'm just honoring the dead."

The custodian adjusts the objects in his arms, trying to get a better grip. "If your daughter was buried here, you could leave what you want. But what you're doing is vandalism. You can't just dump your stuff on someone else's plot. You can't—"

"Now that too seems sacrilegious. Seems like a sin to tell me I can't honor the dead. My dead. What's more, I don't hear anyone complaining. Do you hear anyone complaining?" The woman tilts her head back, opens her mouth wide. "Should we ask any of these dead souls if they've taken issue with me leaving stuff on a grave? I suspect they appreciate it." The woman wheels around and sees Dorian standing on the path. "Do you have people here?"

"I do," Dorian says.

"Now that's a blessing. You know what I had to do? I had to cremate my girl. I had to burn her like a dead Christmas tree just because the dirt in this place is saved for folks with deep pockets. Doesn't matter that I'm God-fearing. Doesn't matter that I recommitted myself to the Lord, that I love him even though he took my baby away." She lowers her voice and draws closer to Dorian. "But my girl deserved the best. She deserves to be here with all the stone angels watching over her. So I scattered her ashes all up in that meadow, right up by the grave with a woman on top with her head in a tree. A heavenly lookout."

Dorian knows it well. A perfect vantage over the gentle hill. But private, too—its own little sanctuary sheltered by the overhanging oak. Before the woman winds up again, Dorian hurries off to Lecia's plot.

The wind comes in waves. You hear it first tangling in the trees above before it descends to the ground. The cemetery is a mess of the day's offerings rattling through the headstones and rolling down the paths. She finds Lecia's spot and kneels down. She's never sure what to say to Lecia, never sure what to do at her grave. In fact, sitting at Lecia's headstone is when she finds it hardest to think about her daughter at all. Because there's no real connection between Lecia and this place, no memories. So Dorian's mind wanders, back to Kathy, to Julianna, to the razor's-edge life beyond the cemetery walls.

Across the drive is the large meadow where the woman berating the custodian claims she scattered her daughter's ashes. The meadow is dominated by a massive grave Dorian remembers belonging to someone named Ruddock—the name engraved on the base of a tiered pedestal that rises up supported by four short Corinthian columns. On top of this is another pedestal with Gothic arches, which rises into a third pedestal. On top of that a statue of a woman holds a garland of flowers, her head partially obscured by the overhanging oak.

In the last light, Dorian watches Ruddock's angel presiding over her meadow. There's movement in the shadow of the grave's columns.

Dorian crosses to the meadow and arrives at the Ruddock grave in time to see the angry woman wielding a can of spray paint. Even in the faded light she can make out what is already written on the marble. "JAZMIN FREEMO—".

Dorian watches the woman finish the name to read *Freemont*.

Jazmin's mother turns and sees Dorian. "You got a problem?" She cocks her head to one side, waiting for Dorian to challenge her. "No one visits any of these damn graves. I claimed my spot. What are you going to do about it?"

"Nothing," Dorian says.

The woman takes a step back, then gives Dorian a look. "Nothing? Bad enough my daughter was murdered. I don't need you and that caretaker snooping on my business."

"My daughter was murdered too."

"You want a prize or something?"

"It doesn't get better."

"Do I look like I expect it to? Do I look like I expect the Lord or anyone to take this off my shoulders? I might pray to ease the pain, but I'm no fool. This is a violent world, and to expect it won't touch you is madness." She puts away her can of spray paint. "I did my best with her. You want them to be part of you but they're not."

There's a noise from above, a chaotic rustling. Together they glance up and see the green parrots swooping through the air, bringing their hectic song. It's a quick flyover—no stopping or roosting. After the birds are gone, Dorian's still craning her neck, trying to follow.

"Crazy birds," Jazmin's mother says. "They can go anywhere in the world and they stay here. My choice, I'd go to Hawaii or Mexico."

"Maybe they like it," Dorian says.

"Maybe they just don't have any sense in their heads. Maybe they expect the world is going to change for them. That this place is going to get better. Or maybe they just don't care." She shakes her head at the insanity of it all. She takes a cigarette out of her purse.

Dorian kneads her hands together. She feels the same tightening in her chest that she does whenever Idira Holloway comes on the radio—the strangulating proximity of another mother's grief. Because this can't be happening again—another reminder, another hand creeping from the past to reach around her throat.

"You good?" the woman asks.

Dorian doesn't reply. Because she's not good. And never will be.

The woman kneels down and presses her lips to her freshly painted daughter's name. "Bless you, baby," she says.

Headlights are coming up the hill. The custodian is on his way in his golf cart. Before he pulls into view, Jazmin's mother hurries off in the opposite direction. Dorian watches her go, slipping away into the night.

She exhales, shakes her limbs, breaking free of the claustrophobia of another's sorrow. But this time, she doesn't let memory disappear. She turns around, taking in all the graves, the dead, the reminders of violence and tragedy that surround her. It was she who'd been the fool, burying her head in the sand whenever the past tapped her on the shoulder, thinking that because she'd tried and failed to make things right for Lecia it was over and done.

But it continues. Always. For her and for the rest of the mothers who've lost their children. To expect a reprieve, to expect to be released—that's the true insanity. Because it's everywhere, this violence. It reaches forward and back.

Dear Idira, I need you to do something for me. I need you to keep shouting as loud as you can because there is tragedy everywhere. I need you to raise your voice against this endless night. You need to illuminate it. You need to root it out and expose it. Because it's there. It's everywhere. There's violence all around us.

Dorian heads home. West on Washington to Western, then south across the 10 into Jefferson Park. If the winds die out, she thinks the parrots might return tomorrow, filling her trees with their antic song, allowing her to watch the fireworks of electric green rise into the sky. The wind is fierce but at least it's at her back, pushing her home, hurrying her down the hill.

She passes the first bungalows of Jefferson Park, planning to stick to Western until she comes to the fish shack, where she'll grab some leftovers and check her inventory before heading home. Just before Twenty-Seventh Place she notices a commotion on the east side of the street—a couple of police cruisers and an ambulance with lights on, sirens silent. She recognizes the riveted stance of the silhouetted onlookers and crosses the street.

Crime scene tape.

Something—someone—on the ground, twisted, motionless.

She steps up to the tape that blocks the entrance to an empty lot. There's a body on the dirt bathed in red lights that circle—circle and circle and go nowhere.

Dorian doesn't want to look, but she does, she has to. She sees a woman tossed, her throat slit, a plastic bag over her face. She looks exactly as Lecia had. Exactly.

Then Dorian screams. She screams herself hoarse. Screams until someone leads her away, until her heart settles, her mind stops raging, until she finds the words she needs.

FEELIA 1999

YOU'RE NOT GONNA COME GET THE DOOR? YOU'RE NOT GONNA open the motherfucking door? You're not— Well, thank you. No, I don't have luggage. You think I packed a bag before some mother-fucker tried to straight up murder me? You think I was, like, hold on, I need to get my nightgown in case that knife doesn't do its job? You think I packed my toiletries and some shit?

Yeah, I got money. You think I'd call a cab I can't pay for?

Calm down? Do I not seem calm to you? I got my throat slit, motherfucker. How've you been?

Ten days. That's how long. You'd think it would be longer. But they tell me I'm good to go, get out the door. Didn't even wheel me down in one of them chairs. Just handed me my bloody clothes in this plastic bag here.

Take the 105 to the 110. I don't care you don't have a FasTrak. I don't feel like herky-jerking through all of South L.A.

You wanna roll down this window? Don't mind if I smoke, right?

That's the one thing my daughter, Aurora, did right. Came and dropped off a few packs of Newports. Girl's not all bad. Lazy. Head so far up her own ass, she forgets about her mom in the hospital. But at least she brought me enough smokes. Probably show up at my place tonight like nothing at all. *Hello* and *how the fuck are you* type shit and *can I get some cash* or *mind if I crash here.*

Least she has a job. So she says.

Only other visitors I had were the police.

Two detectives. Cheap suits and all. *Ma'am, can you tell us what happened?*

What's it look like happened?

Ma'am, can you take a look at these photos, see if you can identify anyone in them?

Hand me a sheet of pictures of black dudes.

One thing I can tell you for sure, the man wasn't black. The detectives give me a look, like I lost my mind along with all that blood came pouring out my neck.

You sure? Take another look.

Am I sure? Am I motherfucking sure? Did he slit you ear to ear, assholes?

Are you a sex worker, Mrs. Jefferies?

That one made me laugh. How many hookers you know go by *Mrs.* anything?

A sex worker, I say, in my best white-lady voice. *What exactly are you asking?*

Cops give each other another look, then give me one as well. One of them clears his throat like he's a first-timer asking for a full ride. *Mrs. Jefferies, are you a prostitute?*

There he goes with the Mrs. Jefferies shit again. If I hadn't been so goddamn worn, if it didn't hurt to move every muscle, I would have slapped him. Mrs. Jefferies isn't any prostitute. Ask me about Pookie. She's a different story.

But I don't say that. Instead what I tell him is: *What the fuck does it matter? As far as I can see all that matters is that I'm lying in this bed nearly slit ear to ear. I could be an accountant. I could be the president of*

Mexico. I could be the queen of the motherfucking Nile for all that what I do matters.

It matters is what they tell me.

I don't have to ask why.

Hey, watch yourself. You got to hit every bump in this god-damn road? It's like I'm getting stabbed all over again. It's like the damn 110 is running right through these stitches in my neck.

Now that's gonna leave one hell of a scar—one ugly mother-fucking necklace.

Hold up? What are you asking? Did I ash on your seat? No, I did not ash on your motherfucking seat. Shit isn't even leather. And don't you slow down right in the middle of the goddamn freeway.

You don't listen to the news? You don't have your ear glued to the radio? You don't listen to the traffic? You want to be one of those incidents on the news—cab rear-ended on the 110 because a woman ashed her cigarette on the seat?

Where are we now? Manchester? Take the next exit. Head to Western. It's to the west. You know that? Well, don't mind me.

Want to know where to go on Western? Can I tell you that at least? Corner of Sixty-Second.

Fucking cops. Fuc-king cops. Not like they offered me protection or anything. They didn't even offer me a ride home. Shit—that motherfucker could be waiting for me for all I know. Could be sitting outside my house. Ready to finish the job.

Hold up. I said hold up. That means slow the hell down. Take a right. Take a goddamned right. I know I said it was straight up Western. But I need you to take a right. Now. I don't care it's one way.

Shit.

What's wrong? You want to know what's wrong? Lemme tell you.

That's where it happened. Right there. That convenience store. That's where— I told you to turn, didn't I?

How long's this light got to be? You want me to relive this shit?

His car was pulled up just there at the edge of the parking lot. Just behind the thing for the free papers. That's where I like to smoke and mind my own.

Might as well keep going straight now. I've already seen it. Still. The fuck was I thinking? The fuck— Nothing in this world worth trusting. That's the truth. Nothing. That's the heartbreak of it all.

I'm only three blocks up. White apartment on the right. Just behind the hedge or whatever you call it. It's not bad. Could be worse. Home is home, you know. You make it what you make it.

Right here. Just over by that white delivery van.

You know what? You want to keep going a little more.

Don't give me that look. I'm good for the fare.

Maybe just a bit farther up Western. Or maybe don't take Western at all. Just anywhere. Just not here. Not right now.

PART II

JULIANNA

2014

1.

———

CLICK.

There's Kathy sitting on a dirty leather couch with the stuffing popping through. There she is, leaning back, arms thrust out like she's beckoning the world, turning that couch into her throne. There she is, five years younger, skin good, hair sleek, skirt so short you can quick-glimpse her red thong. There she is—cigarette in one hand, glass of something, maybe Hennessy, in the other. There she is, wildcat eyes, snake mouth. There she is frozen in time, preserved perfect, in five megapixels.

It was Kathy the Ragin' Cajun who first took Julianna downtown and showed her the bars and illegal clubs just off Olympic, who introduced her to the man who said Julianna was pretty enough to model, the man who promised he'd turn her into South L.A.'s Cindy Crawford. (He didn't know, and Julianna didn't tell him, she liked the other side of the camera.) It was Kathy who helped Julianna get her first job—waiting tables at Sam's Hofbräu, which turned out not to be a beer hall but a strip club. It was Kathy who encouraged Julianna to try out dancing, encouraged her to get onstage. Kathy who turned Julianna into Jujubee.

Jujubee is a nice name when you're high. Nice to say quickly.

Nice to call out across a club. Nice to let buzz around inside your
head. Nice to tell the guy who wants more than a lap dance. It's a
nice name that allows you to escape who you really are—a name
that allows you to do things that a Julianna wouldn't do.

A few years after Julianna started dancing at Sam's, Kathy took
a turn into a rougher line of work. Tried her luck on the streets
instead of the bars. She said she needed more cash for her habit,
her kids, her brother locked up somewhere, and *his* kids. And she
and Julianna went their separate ways.

It's been twenty-four hours since the news rolled down Western
that Kathy was dead up in an empty lot on Twenty-Seventh Place.
Julianna had been getting ready for work at the Fast Rabbit when
she got a call from Coco who'd heard from Reyna who'd heard
from Marisol who'd heard from Sandra whose mom worked at
Moon Pie Pizza a block from Twenty-Seventh, so it had to be true.
Kathy had her throat slit, was suffocated and tossed. The news
was like a punch in the stomach—so hard and fast it knocked
Julianna to the couch. More than a day later she still hasn't left the
apartment.

She hasn't slept and it's coming up on evening again. It started
as an informal wake for Kathy—a gathering of Coco and the rest
of the girls who'd been taken down to the Seventy-Seventh the
night Julianna wound up at Southwest and was surrendered to
Dorian. (And how the fuck *Dorian* had turned up at that particular
moment is a mystery Julianna can't quite puzzle. The woman has
a knack—she'll grant her that.) The girls swarmed the apartment
where several of them crashed from time to time. They'd told
Julianna since she'd escaped being locked up, the *llelo* was on her.
And in no time Rackelle was there with the goods. Then it was
two A.M., then four A.M. Then most of the girls had gone home or
gone to bed. Only Julianna stayed awake.

The sun came up a lifetime ago and now it's already sliding
away. A whole day has unfurled on the TV. The winds started a

fire up on Mulholland that is sweeping down the hills near the Ca-
huenga Pass. People had to drive through a tunnel of fire on the
405 to get to work—the sky black with smoke, the hills lava red.
The pictures on TV looked like something from Mars—an alien
invasion. Julianna thought she'd been tripping.

At noon Coco emerged from her room—her bleached hair
wild around her heart-shaped face, making her look like a mama
lion. When she saw Julianna sitting on the couch, tearing up the
last baggie, she made a *tsk tsk* sound like a teacher at the Catholic school Julianna hadn't much cared for. "Chica, you're taking it
hard. When was the last time you even talked to Kathy?"

It had been a year at least. Maybe more. But Julianna didn't tell
Coco that. And she didn't tell her the real reason she was unwill-
ing to lay off the shit and take something that would make passing
out inevitable.

She might not have actually seen Kathy's body, trash strewn
and contorted, bloated and blue, but she couldn't shake the image.
It would be there if she slept. It would be there no matter how long
she stared at that tunnel of fire on the 405. But instead of coming clean about what was bugging her, she'd just asked Coco how
much cash she had because she wanted to call Rackelle to come
back with more shit to get her through the night.

Coco found some grubby twenties and told Julianna to tell
Rackelle to bring some Molly as well because if she was going to
work the back room at the Fast Rabbit, she sure as shit was going
to get high so it didn't half matter whose hands were where and
what her mouth and the rest of her was doing all night.

It's been a few hours since Rackelle made the delivery and all
Julianna wants is to get up, get clean, go anywhere else. But by early
evening she still can't move, pinned to the couch by Kathy's death.

She yanks her purse open and digs out her cell phone again—
the latest model, an indulgence way beyond the indulgences of
the other girls. Each time a new phone comes out Julianna finds

the money. It's the camera that drives her—more pixels, more saturation, a more perfect eye on her imperfect world.

She scrolls through her pictures, her long pink nail tap, tap, tapping against the glass.

How many selfies you gotta take, the girls tease her. *You think you're becoming an Instagram star? Think someone's gonna buy your low-rent Maybelline?* Julianna doesn't correct them. A while back she figured out how to fake them and everyone else out—pretend she was taking a picture of herself, but really turning the lens around. Using the camera how it was meant to be—looking out not in.

It started as a slim rectangle to hide behind. But soon she began looking at the pictures she was taking. Each night she examined the who, where, and why of the previous day. She used it to see behind the fronts the girls put up for one another—the rough talk, the layers of makeup.

She's scrolling back the years. Rewinding time. Erasing the lines and wrinkles. Doing away with almost a decade of late nights. Removing all the men who have left their marks. And she finds another one.

"Fucking Kathy."

Because there she is again, this time sitting at one of the bright plastic tables at Chabelita Tacos, the twenty-four-hour joint up over the 10 on Western. She's wearing a black cropped halter with three silver buttons. Her hair is bobbed and bleached and looking a little fried. Her head is tipped back so her mouth is in focus and her nose and eyes are slipping away. A gasp of smoke has just escaped her lips and hovers above her like a spirit. There's a man visible just over her left shoulder. He's looked up from his food, drawn by Kathy's laughter.

Julianna swipes the screen again. There's another. This time Kathy's mostly turned away from the camera so that only the edge of the right side of her face is visible. She's either teasing the man or telling him off—Julianna can't remember. In fact, she can barely remember the night, what they were doing at Chabelita and what happened next.

"Fucking Kathy," she says again. "The Ragin' Cajun."

Coco looks up from what she's doing and when she does Julianna can see she's crushing a bag of Molly into a fine powder that she's rolling in wads of rolling paper for later. "Girl wasn't Cajun. She was straight-up Texas. I've been to her mother-in-law's place down somewhere in Inglewood and there must have been five generations eating that sweet-ass barbecue. Cajuns eat that blackened spice shit, not B-B-Q." She shakes the small balls of paper in her palm, then dumps them into an empty tin of breath mints. "You're working, right?" Coco asks, tucking the breath mint tin into the secret compartment in her purse where she hides drugs and extra cash. "Because you miss another shift, you'll be slipped out of the rotation."

This would be the second time Julianna skipped out on work this week. The first time was the night after she'd left Dorian at Jack's Family Kitchen to grab a ride with the first guy who passed, pretending that she was working, but then bait-and-switching him, letting him know that all she wanted was to drive around until she outran the memory of Lecia that Dorian always conjured. If that meant she had to give him a taste, she would. As luck would have it she didn't. She'd crashed at his apartment in Vermont Harbor and slept through work.

First Dorian, now Kathy. It's like the world wants to drag Julianna back to the day the cops turned up asking questions about her babysitter—what she was wearing, what time she left the house, who she hung out with, where Julianna thought she might be going. *She put me to bed*, Julianna told them. Like always. Put her to bed after letting her listen to the hip-hop station her parents hated and watch an R-rated movie on Cinemax. Put her to bed, blew her a kiss from the door—*sleep tight, princess*. And then what? The cops wanted to know. That's when one of them stupidly showed her the photo before his partner could slap his hand down. Julianna saw Lecia's dead eyes behind the plastic bag pulled tight over her face, swollen like she'd been under water, her lips pale and cracked, a choke collar of blood on her neck.

Coco's making faces in the mirror, trying to figure out what she wants to look like tonight.

"Maybe I'll just go back to serving drinks," Julianna says.

Coco raises an arched eyebrow. "Girl."

They both know that Julianna's just talking out of her ass. Because minimum wage plus the shitty tips from guys who want to save their money for the Fast Rabbit's real action can't hold a candle to the cash you can make working the bar's back room. Lap dances and a whole lot more.

"I don't need it," Julianna says.

"The money? How come you don't need the money?"

"There's places I could go I don't have to pay rent."

Coco purses her lips in disbelief, shakes her head, then leans into the smudged mirror propped up on the dresser and starts in on her makeup.

"What?" Julianna says. Because there are ways. She could move back in with Derrick or Dom. Crash with them for a bit. But that would only last until one of them decided she needed to earn her keep and she knows how that would go, a few "dates," followed by the inevitable return to the Fast Rabbit or somewhere like it.

Then, of course, she could go home. She's not like some of these girls who burned their bridges, got thrown out, or didn't have families in the first place. Julianna's got a house—not too far away. She's got a bedroom and a place at the dinner table should she want.

She dips her long pink pinkie nail into the baggie, takes out a half-moon of white powder, and sniffs—a motion so swift and practiced it's like it didn't happen. The drugs hit her with the dull, unsatisfying punch that comes after a night of partying when her body is already so ravaged and buzzed that *llelo* only makes her aware of how fucked up she is and how much she wishes she'd slept. She takes a sharp inhale, trying to heighten the effect so she doesn't have to double dip.

She drums her nails on her thighs and taps her toes. Home. Home. Home.

"Home," she says.

"How's that?" Coco asks.

"Nada," Julianna says. "Nothing. Nothing." She drums her nails harder. Taps her foot faster.

"Jujubee?" Coco says. "If you're gonna keep sniffing that shit, you better quit your twitching. Unless you want me to kill you first."

Julianna opens the bag, dips her pinkie in again. Another swift inhale and she tucks the bag back into her bra. Why the hell shouldn't she go home? She doesn't need this crap—doesn't need to get higher, to get dressed only to get undressed at work, to pretend she's doing this shit—all this shit—until something better comes along.

"Keep up like that, you'll be out before work." Coco checks the time on her phone. "There's, like, eight hours before you get off."

Julianna folds her nails toward her palms to stop her tapping. "Maybe, just fuck it," she says.

Coco's drawing a set of cartoon eyebrows over her tweezed ones. "Fuck what? This isn't some more shit about Kathy?"

Julianna lifts her phone, covers her face.

Click. She catches Coco leaning closer to the mirror, her head cocked to one side, admiring her handiwork by giving herself a *don't fuck with me* look. Coco swivels around at the sound of the camera and mugs for Julianna.

Julianna's already put her phone away.

Her purse is open on the couch, stuffed to overflowing with wipes, lotions and potions, things to make her look prettier or less tired, things to make her feel better or worse, depending. There's a scrap of paper, too, torn from a copy of *Los Angeles Magazine* that Julianna read in the waiting room at Planned Parenthood last week. She takes it out, unfolds it.

"You ever heard of some dude called Larry Sultan?"

Coco looks as if she's really thinking about it. "The dude with the sick purple car who hangs at the Easy Time?"

"No," Julianna says.

"The motherfucker looks like a sultan of somewhere-the-fuck."

Julianna looks at the paper in her hand. It's a photo of a photograph—a woman, clearly a porn actress, between takes on a shoot. She's wearing a cheap satin robe and white platform heels too high even for Julianna and her crew. She's walking away from a skanky-looking pool. Behind her are four gnarly boxer dogs, visible ribs and knots on their skin, all bowed down like they're praying. "Boxers, Mission Hills, Larry Sultan."

She holds out the scrap of paper to Coco. "What do you think of this picture?"

Coco turns from the mirror and squints across the small room.

"I think that bitch is fixing to get gangbanged."

Bitch. Gangbanged. There's no skill to running someone down.

"But what do you think of the *photo?*"

"It's whatever," Coco says. "It's not, like, fucking art."

Julianna folds that paper away. *So how come it's hanging in a fucking museum?* she doesn't say. What she does say is "No way I'm fucking some Z-list ballers tonight for any amount of cash."

Coco fumbles in her purse for the tin of mints. "A teaspoon of sugar?"

Julianna waves her off.

"Guess you're not planning on paying rent next month."

"Mind your business about what I'm planning."

Coco points her eyebrow pencil at Julianna's bra strap. "That shit's messing you up."

Julianna taps the baggie in the cup of her bra, feels it stick to her sweaty skin. "It's not the shit."

"What then?" Coco's leaning in close to the mirror, still painting a face over her face.

What then, what? Julianna wants to ask. *Who isn't messed up doing what we do, seeing what we see? Partying to pretend that none of it matters. Acting like there's no difference between us and that posse of USC sorority chicks rolling into that South Central house party like they had a right to be anywhere, do anything.*

"Who you think did Kathy?"

"Kathy was a straight-up street ho last I checked. You and me, we do classy," Coco says.

Street ho. Corner bitch. Crack whore. Names. Ranks. Distinctions. Anything to make yourself feel better, make yourself feel higher up.

Ask them, Jujubee and Coco are dancers—exotic dancers, private dancers, stick-their-hand-down-your-pants-and-make-you-feel-better-about-yourself dancers. That's what they are. They're not back-alley girls—all-the-way girls, do-anything girls. They've got limits. At least that's what they say.

Coco walks over to the couch and takes Julianna's hands. "Get in the shower. Then I'll make your face. I'll make you pretty-pretty Jujubee."

Julianna lets herself be pulled to her feet, led to the bathroom, pushed inside. She turns on the water but leaves the door open while the shower heats up. Coco's back at the mirror. She's put on music, swaying her wide hips, popping out her round butt as she polishes her makeup. She finishes her lips—a cartoonish bow that nearly doubles the size of her mouth. She tips her head to one side and gives herself her sexy gangster pout once more, testing out the strength of her armor. Then her face falls, her eyebrows and mouth sag, her cheeks droop. The exhaustion and anger and frustration break through. She closes her eyes, stays like that—resting, hiding. Julianna pulls out her camera.

Click.

2.

———

IT'S ONLY ONE NIGHT OF NO SLEEP, WHICH ISN'T THAT BAD.
It's been worse. One night—you can think your way around, put
yourself outside your fatigue, separate yourself from yourself so
you can get through it. The drugs help. That's exactly what they
do—split you in half.

The music at the Fast Rabbit helps, too—loud enough that it
doesn't exactly matter what you say, more how you say it and how
you look when you do. It's a Monday so the crowd is thin but com-
mitted. Julianna recognizes several of them. She's doing her best,
making eye contact but not intruding. Her game isn't up in your
face. She's the kind of girl who makes the guys come to her, let her
know what they want. But it's not working and Julianna's been
spinning her swizzle stick round and round her Midori sour alone.
Her energy's bad—that's what Coco tells her. She needs to lighten
up. Coco pulls out her breath mint tin. "Freshen up?"

Julianna points at her bright green drink. "I'm good." She pulls
out her phone, busies herself like she doesn't need this.

There's a man in the corner near the back door sitting alone at
one of the high tops. He's large, light-skinned, with a mustache
and thinning hair. He's got his arms folded over his chest. He's

been staring at Julianna with eyes that are either wild with drink or just wild. He looks hungry and angry—like the world owes him.

"Who's your friend?" Coco says.

Julianna casts an eye over her shoulder. "No friend of mine."

"Now you're picky as well as bitchy."

"He'll come if that's what he wants," she says as Coco stalks off to find someone to buy her a drink. She pulls out her phone and turns her back on the guy.

She scrolls through her photos, finding the snaps of girls last night. Marisol splayed on the couch. Coco ashing a cigarette into the sink while Sandra bumps and grinds her from behind. Sandra searching for a song on her phone. Rackelle coming in the door. She rewinds the night, so the ladies sober up, the apartment gets clean, the night grows young, and the party has yet to begin.

From across the room she can feel the man staring at her.

She tosses her hair and rounds her shoulders, lowers her head over her phone.

Tap, tap, tap back to a week ago when Kathy was still alive. Tap, tap, tap through a week of parties and people and cruises up Western. *Tap, tap.* And there centered on Julianna's screen is a photo she doesn't remember taking—Dorian framed in the window of Jack's Family Kitchen.

Julianna had stepped out to the street to smoke. She knew it would annoy Dorian but the woman didn't own her. Anyway, she needed something to chill her nerves and erase the taste of food she hadn't wanted.

She'd looked back and seen Dorian staring at her, her face full of that longing Julianna can't stand, that need for Julianna to be Lecia or to pretend to be Lecia or at least not to be the person she's become, to be some little girl she can take care of, freeze in time. In the split second that Dorian had looked away, Julianna had pulled out her phone. *Click.* Dorian in profile, slightly blurred behind the smeared glass window. A lonely woman eating breakfast.

She stares at the picture on her phone—the first time she's looked at it since she snapped it. With Dorian's face angled the way it is, Julianna can't see the need, the frustration. Can't hear the questions and the silent demands.

Like Lecia, Dorian must have been beautiful. Unlike Lecia, Julianna guesses she never knew it. But Lecia, she sure knew. Julianna loved to tag along when her babysitter went to the corner market, listening to the men catcall from their cars, and the locals whistle from their porches. She stood next to Lecia, a shy but proud smile on her face when the guy at the *carnicería* refused to take Lecia's cash or slipped her something extra with her order. Like some of Lecia's glow rubbed off on her—like she was part of the package in her knockoff Disney T-shirts and rubber sandals.

Julianna's eyelids flutter. Her head nods back. And for a moment the music is gone, the lights are still, and both Julianna and Jujubee are sucked into the past, standing next to Lecia on Western, three men leaning out of a souped-up sedan telling Lecia to jump in. Lecia's about to pull away from her. Julianna feels Lecia let go of her hand—

"You good?"

The bartender's got a hand on her wrist, pulling her back to the bar.

"Good like gold," Julianna says, sliding off the barstool.

The bartender gives her a look that says she'd better get it together. Which is exactly why she's headed for the bathroom—a pick-me-up to drag her back to the present and keep her gliding along.

Everyone's eyes are on her as she goes. No way to deflect attention, no way to hide as she walks right down the center of the Fast Rabbit. She locks the bathroom door behind her. She pulls out the baggie and her keys from her purse. She does one bump. Then two. Then one more for good luck. She leans toward the mirror, checking her nostrils. She inhales deeply, drawing the ammonia burn high into her sinuses. She pops her eyes wide, staring at the woman who stares back. She's fucking beautiful is what she is.

She checks her makeup—her lips, eyes, a little more bronzer on her cheekbones sending them sky high. She puckers, blows herself a kiss. She tosses her hair—makes it loose and wild. Then Jujubee unlocks the bathroom door, leaving Julianna behind.

The Fast Rabbit is her runway—the show is her. Fuck all those other girls trying too hard. Fuck Coco and her attitude. No one gets attention like Jujubee. At the bar she spins around so she's leaning back on the rail facing out, her gaze flying over the customers— *Come and get it if you dare.*

And in no time someone does. A thirtysomething dude who tells her his name is Carlos and *Where you been hiding all night?* Jujubee winks, draws her finger down his jawbone.

Came out just for you.

Carlos signals to the bartender and Jujubee points at the back room. *You want these to go, right?*

And just like that she's leading Carlos across the bar, his hands on her waist as she carries their drinks.

Dean is guarding the door as always. He reads Carlos his rights—only things you can do back there are exactly what the lady says you can do. Then he tells Jujubee the third room is empty.

She takes Carlos to Room 3, pulls back the curtain to reveal a space not much bigger than a half bath. She pushes him into a chair, lets him have a sip of his drink. Then she goes to work. The thing is—guys always want everything even if they don't know it. You have to guide them, teach them, make them open their wallets wider.

Dance for me, chica.

There's a knob in the wall that raises the music loud. Jujubee makes it near deafening so she needs to press her lips into Carlos's ear to be heard.

How you like it, baby?

She doesn't need to wait for a response because it's already on. He reaches for her breasts, but she wags a finger at him. *Not so fast.*

She disappears into the music, pulls it around her like a large velour blanket in which she can wriggle and writhe. She straddles Carlos, bouncing on his lap. She feels electric, invincible, in control.

She's down to her panties—teal and lacy. And doesn't it feel good to be free of her clothes, to be moving, her arms and legs exposed, her belly tight? Doesn't it feel good to be Jujubee?

It's Jujubee who undoes Carlos's belt.

It's Jujubee who reaches for the zipper of his pants.

It's Jujubee who takes out his wallet to cover this additional expense.

It's Jujubee who uses her mouth and hands until Carlos is collapsed in his chair.

It's Jujubee who tells him to get himself together because the night is young and she has work to do.

It's Jujubee who strides back out to the bar, tipping Dean on the way for keeping guard.

It's Jujubee who takes her place at the bar, facing the room again. *Come and get me*, she says.

She owns this place. She owns everyone except for the man still sitting alone at the high top in the back, glaring at her like she's just cheated on him. She gives him a smirk, waves him away. *I don't need you*, she says.

He only stares harder. His eyes burn angry.

She rubs her thumb across her index and middle finger. *All it takes is money, baby.*

Another guy approaches—young, soaked in cheap cologne. He smells like a taxicab. It could be worse, Jujubee thinks as she tells him, "Don't you smell fine?"

He's never done this before, it's clear. His boys are cheering him on from across the bar. He wants to talk money but that's

not how it works. Deals are made in the back. She takes his hand.
"We'll work it out."

But before they leave the bar, there's a palm on the guy's shoulder, yanking him back. "Sit down, *niñito*."

The man who'd been sitting at the high top puts himself between the kid and Jujubee. Up close, Jujubee can see that one of his eyes wanders.

"He wouldn't know what to do with you," the man says.

Before Jujubee can object, the younger dude has slunk off to his friends.

"Let's go," the man says. "I want to see the show."

"Buy me a drink," Julianna says, then takes him toward the back room.

Dean holds the door open for Jujubee and her new customer. "Things are picking up."

The man pushes past him with a grunt. He doesn't want to be led. Jujubee follows him into one of the curtained rooms.

He takes a seat. "Dance."

Jujubee turns up the music. The edge is coming off the coke—the moment when you are still on the shit but becoming aware of its transience. The awful realization that the drugs can't carry you forever. She should do a little tick, but it's too late, because this guy is staring at her and she knows she has to start moving.

And she does. The same routine as last time, but this time it feels just that—routine. She's going through the motions and it shows. He pats his lap, telling her to sit.

But that's not how it works. This is her room, her rules. Her order of business.

"Sit, baby."

She tosses her head side to side, trying to take back the game. Trying to take control.

"You're too good to sit?"

Jujubee winks, wags a finger.

"Don't play."

He reaches for her arm. He grabs her wrist. Not hard.

Jujubee stares at his hand on her skin.

The lights go out. She can't hear the music. The Fast Rabbit fades away. And she sees Kathy's face bloated and bagged just like Lecia's in the photo the cop accidentally showed her. She sees Kathy in the lot near her parents' house—discarded, battered. She sees her lying on the ground, her body twisted.

It's as if she can feel Kathy's struggle, just like she used to think she could feel Lecia's. She can feel the man grabbing her, restraining her, wrapping whatever it is around her neck to strangle her. She can feel the plastic bag go over her face.

She can feel Kathy bite, kick, claw. She can feel her raw, ragged desperation, her frantic need to escape.

"What the fuck, Jujubee." Julianna opens her eyes. Dean's got her by the waist and has dragged her into the hall. She looks at her hand and sees several of her nails are broken.

"Don't you fucking move," he says.

He pulls back the curtain to the room. The man with the wild eyes is pressed against the far wall. There are scratches on his face and arms.

"She's fucking *loco*. I didn't even touch the—"

Dean holds up his hand. But the man keeps talking, stuttering about how Julianna wouldn't do her job, was half-assing it, then straight up attacked him, clawed him like the *puta* she is.

Dean turns to Jujubee. "Ju—what's your side?"

"He wanted to do me like Kathy. He wanted to do me like he did her. He wanted—" Julianna can hear the hysteria in her voice. It's as if she's standing outside herself watching this scene. And then, crash, she's back together.

"He did what?" Dean asks. "He did who?"

"Nothing," Julianna says. "Nothing." They're all the same. All the fucking same.

"What do you mean nothing?" The warning in Dean's voice is unmistakable.

She shrugs. What does it matter who put his hand where and what he meant by it? They're all a bunch of pigs. Rapists and killers and whatever the fuck. Their dirty hands, their dirty minds. Their appetites. Their sweat and breath. Their smell. Their—

She stands and spits at the guy.

Dean yanks her arm. "Out. Now."

She fumbles for her purse. The contents scatter across the floor. She rakes it all back in. Except for her phone, which she holds up, points at the man still cowering in the private room—his face rigid and angry.

Click.

3.

————

JULIANNA PINWHEELS OUT OF THE FAST RABBIT, TOSSED BY Dean. She catches herself before she stumbles out onto Western.

The street is dead. It smells like smoke and ash. She checks her phone. It's almost one A.M. The only business is back at the Fast Rabbit or at one of the two motels the street girls work. But there's nothing for her in these places—nothing keeping her in this stretch of Western. Time to go home. Not to the apartment where Coco or Marisol or whoever else will return cash heavy and ready to party, but home to her own house on Twenty-Ninth Place.

Julianna's left all her tips. There's a split second when she thinks of getting the bouncer or one of the girls to retrieve them for her. But the smell of the place—the perfumed antiseptic spray that covers the stench of other people's sex and hunger—turns her stomach. She has no cash for a cab, so she's on foot.

She takes out the baggie and polishes it off in one go, then turns north.

Twenty blocks. Just about two miles. With the *llelo* running through her system she can knock it out quick. The smoke from the fires up in the hills hangs in the air.

Julianna knows what she looks like out here in her white heels, tight jeans, pink halter. She knows why the few cars that pass, pass slow.

She approaches Martin Luther King, where cars are pulling in and out of the Snooty Fox Motor Inn, taking advantage of the three-hour rate. She keeps her eyes ahead, trying to block out the action.

At the corner a car pulls to a stop along the curb—a gray Honda Accord. Its windows are tinted. The light changes. She crosses MLK, but the car hangs back.

She's at the far edge of her own neighborhood now. Not too far from Jack's Family Kitchen, where she'd ditched Dorian. She's working her lower lip as she walks, chewing it hard. She's ashamed of her own nerves.

Not that Julianna works the same beat as Kathy, but she plays by the same rules. If you think too hard about danger, there's no going to work, there's no getting the job done. There's no strapping on your heels and putting yourself out there.

Danger is what happens to other people.

Danger comes when you acknowledge it.

The Honda's back, creeping alongside Julianna, even-wheeling her. She casts a quick glance to let it know she's not interested, she's not what the driver thinks she is. Whoever's behind the wheel has gotten her mixed up with a different sort of woman.

At the next corner the light is red and a few cars are moving east-west so she has to wait. She can feel the Honda alongside her. She waves it away. When she crosses the street, the car doesn't follow.

There are a handful of girls out. They meet Julianna's eyes as she passes, give her the nasty once-over. Julianna doesn't tell them they're welcome to their corners. Doesn't dare say the game is all theirs. But she's glad they're out—more distraction for the Honda driver, who's back on her heels again.

She glances over her shoulder. The car flashes its headlights. Then it peels away, speeding past her, squealing right on Fortieth.

She runs a hand over her lips, which are chewed and swollen. A good thing she's done with this shit—a good thing she's not working tomorrow or ever again.

Her feet are starting to ache. A mile is about her limit in these heels. She's going slower, limping. Another busted girl on the walk home.

It's ten blocks now through the landmarks of her childhood— the shuttered salons, pupuserias, strip malls. Julianna pauses in the doorway of an empty storefront to give her feet a break. She wedges her finger between her shoe and her heel, freeing the skin from the clammy lining.

She finishes adjusting her shoe. She can feel the blisters and the trickle of blood pooling below her heel. She steps out of the doorway. There's one car heading south on Western.

She steps onto the street. There's a flash and a squeal of rubber on concrete. She looks to her left to see a set of headlights bearing down on her. She leaps back to the curb, scrambling for safety. But the car doesn't give ground, chasing her right onto the sidewalk, pinning her in the doorway.

The headlights blind her. The engine rumbles. Julianna hears the door open. She shades her eyes as a man steps out—all backlit and shadow.

Her heart, already racing from the coke, is quickstepping in her chest, rising in her throat. She feels as if someone's choking her.

"You bitch."

Julianna cowers. She slinks back into the doorway even though she knows she's only trapping herself.

"*Puta.*"

She puts her hands over her head. The chemical taste of the *llelo* rising in her throat is making her gag.

"You stupid fucking whore."

The man's face emerges from shadow and Julianna's heart thumps as she recognizes his wild, wandering eye and the ribbons of blood she left on his cheeks. The man from the Fast Rabbit raises an arm above his head. He's holding something dark and round.

Julianna has enough time to close her eyes before the bottle connects with her forehead and she spins into black.

4.

_____

CLICK.

Julianna's face stares back at her, startled by the flash—lips chewed, pupils bugged and black swamping her irises. There's a nasty cut above her right eye that's going to swell. She wipes blood from her lashes and squints at the screen. The woman she sees looks savage and raw—not Julianna, not Jujubee, but someone unfamiliar. A person who's been scraped from the inside out. Now she can see that there's dirt in the gash on her forehead from where she hit the sidewalk. She'll be lucky if it's not infected. She swipes the image away and looks at the clock readout. By her count ten minutes have passed since she hit the ground.

It takes her fifteen minutes to reach her parents' house. She takes the smaller streets, away from Western, away from the supposed safety of streetlights and reliable traffic. There's no one on Gramercy or Cimarron to see her staggered approach, no one to wonder at the way she shields her face from the empty block.

She reaches Twenty-Ninth Place and stands across the street from her house under the canopy of a magnolia tree. She stares into the darkened windows, watching for signs that anyone is awake. She wants to make sure she enters unseen, slips up the stairs, into the shower, and into her bed without meeting her family.

Because they can see them on you, they can smell them on you. No matter how many times you wash, no matter how much time has passed, every man has left his mark, every man has left his fingerprints, imprinted himself. The best you can do is clean yourself up, scrub down and pretend. Which is what Julianna needs to do.

Kathy wasn't afforded that luxury. Discarded dirty, not just with the grime from the alley, but with the filth of her clients. A dead hooker, not a dead mom, not a dead woman. A disrespect almost worse than murder.

Julianna waits, peering in the windows to double-check that her mother isn't in the kitchen and that her father hasn't fallen asleep in front of the television in the front room, that Hector isn't smoking weed out back with Isobel, his forever girlfriend.

From down the block comes the sound of grinding metal as a car hits the cracked pavement hard, then jolts on. It screeches past Julianna and squeals to a stop before running the stop sign—nose partway into the intersection. Then it reverses, weaving back in an unsteady line until it stops in front of her house. The car is shaking with bass and reverb.

The passenger-side door opens and a large man hauls himself out—a soft, bulbous profile silhouetted against the weak light over the dash. He staggers to the back door and yanks it open. There's a pile of bodies slumped on the seat, the wreckage of a long night.

The man reaches into the car and pulls someone out— Armando.

Julianna's father stands unsteadily. There's stirring in the car— two women come to life, talking over each other in a mix of Spanish and English. One bangs on the driver's seat, the other half falls out the open door.

Armando's trying to pull himself together but it's not working, so the big man has to help him around the car and through the gate to the house. Julianna's focus isn't on her father, though, it's on the two women in back. They're full figured, curves that have become rolls. The one closer to Julianna is wearing a skirt so short Julianna can see the tattoos snaking down her upper thigh. She dangles her feet in their strappy heels out the door and lights a cigarette.

This is what happens. One day you're fine and fierce and still able to pretend you're in control, that men want you because they want you, not because anything can be had at a price. Next thing, you're big and battered, lying in the back of a shitty town car, rolling around with dudes like Julianna's dad or worse. Dudes who think that because they have jobs, families, something steady somewhere else, they are better than you, they have a right to you. Dudes who think that because they have enough cash to pay for you or your drinks or your dinner, they have every right.

Julianna can see how it will go. She'll get straight for a bit, take a job outside the life but the money won't work, won't make anything come together for her. Then one of her friends will invite her to a party and next thing she'll be back with the old crowd, breaking dawn and living hard. Soon she'll take a second job, something for tips, and eventually she'll be playing in the shadow of the game—not a street hooker, never that, but someone invited to motel parties where the line between party girls and paid girls gets fuzzier as dawn creeps in.

And eventually the better part of the game will pass her by. She'll age, lose her looks, grow soft and heavy with too many years of sweet booze and cheap meals. She'll never work the streets, but she'll grow dependent on guys like her father for a good time. Soon she'll be waiting for them, needing them, hoping they'll come to call.

Julianna hears the rusted hinges followed by the bang of the gate to her house slamming shut. The woman in the back of the car brushes ash from her leg. Her head lolls back. "Where the fuck are we?" she asks.

The driver dismisses her with a wave of his hand.

Soon the big guy who dragged Armando home is back. "Get your ass back in the car," he says, kicking the woman's feet. "Move your *colita*."

She tosses her cigarette at him. He gets in the shotgun seat. The car sags under his weight. The door slams and they speed off, leaving Julianna staring at her father passed out on the steps, his arms splayed like he's on the cross.

She opens the gate and sits at his side. "Papi? Papi?"

Armando smells like cheap car air freshener and even cheaper booze. And something else—the smell of the changing rooms at Sam's Hofbräu, the Fast Rabbit, even the apartment she shares with Coco and the rest of them. The smell of sweat and women's perfume. Her stomach rises.

"Papi?"

He stirs, mumbles something, and waves a hand in her direction.

"Papi, no way you're sleeping out here for the whole block to see."

"Who the fuck—"

"Didn't anyone never tell you, don't shit where you eat?"

There's no response.

"Papi!" She digs a finger into the flesh and fat above his ribs—twisting her jagged, broken nail into his shirt.

He groans and tries to roll away.

But here's the thing Julianna's good at—the rough customer, the drunk customer, the one who won't get off, who comes too close, who won't leave, who tries to take what he wants by pressing into you hard. She tosses her heels aside and stands barefoot on the step above her father's head. She squats down and wiggles her hands under his armpits.

She slides him up the two steps toward the front door. She finds her keys, then rolls her father inside.

It's hard work and the drugs raise her pulse so she's panting. She kicks Armando's legs so he's inside the house, then closes the door. The sweat on her forehead makes her cut sting.

Armando looks like he's been dropped from several stories up, splayed and motionless. Julianna wants to get him into the shower, erase the night and the smell of the other women, roll him onto the couch and tuck him in, shield her mother from what she surely knows. But it's too much work and he doesn't deserve it. She takes a pillow and a small blanket from the couch.

She squats down and tucks the pillow under his head and tosses the blanket over his bulk. Then she kicks him in the side. "I should have left you on the street," she says.

Julianna tiptoes through the house, passing her own room. Hector's door is open a crack. She pushes it wider. He and Isobel are sleeping in the king-size bed that takes up most of the room.

Hector is on his back, an arm and a leg hanging toward the floor. He's getting fat, Julianna thinks as she watches his belly rise and fall under his white undershirt. Isobel sleeps on her stomach. She's wearing a pair of Hector's boxers and a large T-shirt. She's flopped over toward Hector, one of her arms stretching across his waist, her long black hair spread across the sheets behind her.

Julianna tiptoes into the room and slides along Hector's side of the bed. She inches open the drawer of his nightstand and feels for his canister of weed. A helicopter passes overhead, its searchlight slicing through the dark.

The helicopter's carving a tight circle—its searchlight bouncing over Julianna's house in one-minute intervals, the hammering of its blades rising and falling. She palms the weed and closes the drawer.

She pauses once more at the door, watching Hector and Isobel. The searchlight skims their sleeping bodies—caressing Isobel's smooth, unblemished skin, her untainted arms, the edge of her jaw, her delicate fingers, the soft curve of her calves.

A fucking miracle, Julianna thinks, *to sleep so goddamned unaware of the chaos outside, the person being chased by the cops and the violent sound of the chopper chewing the air. How amazing to be able to sleep next to someone, peaceful and comfortable and numb to the world around you.*

Julianna takes out her phone.

Click.

5.

———

THE WEED MUST HAVE KNOCKED HER OUT. SHE SLEPT THE whole day, waking in the evening to grab something to eat from the fridge, smoke some more, then crash again. Nearly thirty-six hours pass before she gets up for good. She spends half an hour in the shower, coming close to running out the hot water, scrubbing herself until her skin hurts. She finds a pair of Hector's old boxers and a tank top from when she was in high school, both a tight fit around the curves she didn't have back then.

Armando is sitting at the kitchen table eating a *chuleta* and beans, Alva's specialty and the only thing she cooks with any regularity now that she is managing the car rental at the airport.

The TV is on in the background—a special report about the fires devastating the country from Santa Barbara down to the Hollywood Hills. Sparks and ash are floating over the city like snow, igniting smaller blazes as far south as the 10.

"How you feeling, Papi?"

Armando looks up from his plate, fixing Julianna with his large black eyes, searching her. "*¿Qué es?* An interrogation?"

"I can't ask my father a question?"

"You can if it's a good question."

"I just want to know how you're feeling." Julianna's brain is foggy from so much sleep, her limbs untrustworthy after too many hours in bed.

"It's not me who's been sleeping two days straight." Her father's eyes haven't left her face, like he's appraising her, judging her—like he's shopping her.

"Papi, stop staring."

"I can't look at my daughter? My daughter everyone tells me is so beautiful. I can't look at her so I can see for myself?"

Julianna pulls out the coffeepot and scratches a jagged nail in the brown crust at the bottom of the glass carafe. She takes it to the sink, turns on the water, and begins to scrub.

"So you live here now?"

"This isn't my house?" Julianna says.

Armando drags a slice of *chuleta* through a sludge of refried beans and shoves it in his mouth. "The whole neighborhood knows your business," he says.

Julianna doubts people know everything, but then again the Fast Rabbit is local and now she's seen the crew her father's running with, she can't be too sure. "How come you're not working?"

Armando gestures at the clock with his fork. It's four P.M. He's already returned from his low-cost tax preparation business.

"You going out tonight, Papi?"

Armando drops his fork and pushes his plate away, like someone is going to clear it for him. "What's that mean?"

"I'm saying, do you have plans?"

"I do, baby, but unlike you, I'm the one enjoying the entertainment, not providing it."

In one surprising, swift motion, Julianna reaches across the table and tosses the plate at Armando like a Frisbee. He ducks to one side, toppling the chair, as the plate crashes to the floor.

He picks himself up and laughs.

There's a knock at the door.

"Clean that up," Armando says, pointing at the floor. "Your mother doesn't like a mess." He smooths his polyester dress shirt and pats his hair like he's off to do business. He opens the inner door, then peers through the riot gate. "Can I help you?"

Julianna can't hear the rest. But next thing, her father's pushed the outer gate wide, not caring that she's standing there in her underwear.

There's a woman in the doorway. She's so short Julianna almost mistakes her for a child. But the suit gives her away.

"LAPD," Armando says, moving to the couch and kicking up his feet. "Looks like you got trouble, baby."

Julianna crosses her arms over her chest, trying to compensate for the fact that she's in her pajamas in the late afternoon.

"Detective Perry," the woman says, holding up a badge.

"Perry?" Armando says. "You don't look like a *Perry*, Señora LAPD."

"Julianna, maybe we could talk outside," the detective says.

Julianna knows how news travels, how things get exaggerated, how people trade stories to help themselves out. It would be nothing for someone who might have been swept up at the Fast Rabbit to have filled in the cops on Julianna's tirade—told them she was tricking in the back, told them she was holding, told them she was guilty of assault, told them any number of things that Julianna may or may not have done.

Julianna can feel her father's eyes boring into her—his joyful need to judge.

"You can put on a sweater if you want," the detective says.

Julianna dashes to Hector's room and grabs one of his oversized Lakers sweatshirts. It hits midthigh, covering her boxers. She finds the detective standing on the porch.

The woman is tiny. Like Julianna, she's dyed her dark hair. But it's a cheap job, probably one of those boxes from the drugstore with the light-skinned Latina lady on them. Julianna pays for her color. A couple of hundred every other month to brighten her curls to a fiery orange, to make her look fly.

"I'm going to smoke," Julianna says, taking a seat in one of the plastic chairs and drawing her knees to her chest. She lights a cigarette and takes a deep drag. She notices the detective is chewing gum, working her jaw like she's mad high. "You used to smoke?"

Detective Perry looks at her blankly.

Julianna points her cigarette at the detective's jaw.

"Never smoked," Detective Perry says, removing her phone from her suit pocket and tapping the screen.

Her nails are round and neat, polished in a neutral tone. Her suit is spotless. She's wearing low black heels, sensible shoes for walking or whatever it is detectives do all day. She's even got bangs—the no-nonsense haircut Julianna associates with people who don't give a shit.

Julianna pulls her sweatshirt lower, more aware than ever of the whole inappropriate mess of her. "Is this about the Fast Rabbit?" Julianna says. "Because that shit wasn't my fault. I don't know who told you what but—"

Detective Perry tucks her phone away then gives Julianna a look that makes it pretty clear she hasn't heard a word she's said. "Katherine Sims," she says. "You know her."

It doesn't sound like a question. And Julianna doesn't know a Katherine Sims. "No."

"You were friends." Detective Perry isn't exactly looking at Julianna when she addresses her. She's glancing at something scribbled on a piece of paper. It's like she's in two places at once. Like Julianna is only part of her business.

"I don't know any Katherine."

"Julianna, what is it that you do for work?" The detective looks as if she's thinking about something else. Like she left the stove on or forgot where she parked or missed some other appointment.

"Nothing," Julianna says. Because that's the truth, at least right now. No work. No dancing. No hustle.

"But you used to work."

The way the detective doesn't make eye contact when she talks is starting to bug Julianna. "I guess."

"So Katherine Sims."

"I told you. I don't know a Katherine. I know a Coco, a Marisol, a Princess, a Yessina, a Ruby, a—"

"Katherine Sims. Kathy."

Fucking Kathy. More than a decade later and Julianna never learned her last name.

"You know Kathy Sims." Again it's not a question. It's like the detective turned up on Julianna's porch so Julianna could tell her what she already knew.

"Who told you that? Dorian?"

"Dorian?" The name gets the detective's attention and her eyes meet Julianna's for the first time.

"I bet it was Dorian. That busybody."

"Your face," Detective Perry says, as if she's just noticing Julianna for the first time. As if she's just seeing her. "What happened to your face?"

Julianna's hand flies to the gash above her eyes. "Nothing. Some shit."

"Interesting," Detective Perry says.

"You sure you're not here about the Fast Rabbit?"

"The Fast Rabbit?" The detective repeats the name as if it's the first time she's hearing it. "Is that where you work?"

"I told you, no." If she doesn't know already, Julianna isn't telling her. Let the detective do her job and find shit out.

"Is that where Kathy worked?"

"Hell, no."

"She worked the streets."

"I guess you already knew."

"And you already know she's dead."

"Everyone knows. Everyone knows everything."

"That makes my job easy."

Julianna exhales and grinds her cigarette out on the cement porch. "So what do you want to know about Kathy?"

"There was another woman who died," the detective says, "fifteen years ago."

"Now this shit is about Lecia?"

"This shit. That's an interesting phrase. What do you mean by 'this shit'?" Detective Perry takes out a small notebook and a pen, like she's actually going to write Julianna's answer down. She sits in the other plastic chair on the porch.

"You know," Julianna says, "this. You, me, here, what you're asking."

"So far I've only asked you if you knew Kathy."

"I knew Kathy," Julianna says.

"You were good friends. My partner wrote you up the other day. Then I spotted a picture of you on Kathy's social media."

"Must have been an old-ass picture."

"So, you were friends."

"It sounds like you're telling me the answers to your own questions. But yeah, we were." Because she's not going to lie about the dead, not going to disrespect Kathy to save herself. Kathy was a good friend, a fucking great friend.

Detective Perry clicks her pen, then snaps her gum. "How did you know each other?"

"We worked together. She got me a job."

The detective's pen goes click-click. Her gum snaps. She's waiting for more.

"Dancing at Sam's Hofbräu." What kind of bullshit is this to be sitting on the porch in her pajamas next to this detective in her neat suit and the rest of it? Maybe there was another world where Julianna finished high school, didn't start partying, wasn't the kind of girl Kathy noticed, the kind of girl Kathy read as someone who wanted to get in the game. Maybe there was a world where she could have been the lady in the suit, the one who spent weeknights with a glass of wine and some takeout, whose weekends involved some straight-world shit—dinner, movie, a free concert in a park.

"So you and Kathy started hanging out when?"

"When I was fourteen."

"So after Lecia Williams."

"What's that have to do with it?"

"Did she come around the house?"

"Sometimes," Julianna says. Kathy sure did come around. Always pulling up in a fast car that would roar to a stop in front. Julianna would look out and see Kathy leaning over the driver's lap, laying on the horn until everyone on the block came out and took a look at her ride—Armando included. Julianna thinks half the reason Armando didn't object to her going out with Kathy was the cars—the Camaros, Corvettes, the lowriders, and even the El Caminos.

Detective Perry scribbles something down. "When was the last time you saw her?"

Julianna pulls her hair back, twists and tucks it into a top-knot. "Not for years. Kathy and I turned out different." She pulls out another cigarette but she doesn't light it. She can guess what this detective thinks of her and those like her. Just look at the woman—her bleached hair hiding who she really is. The suit, the basic white-girl makeup. Pretending to be someone else.

How many women like Julianna does Detective Perry come across in a week? How many who are working some part of the game—dancers, strippers, hookers, hos, and bitches? How many does she question, book, dismiss? How many does she discard when she turns the page of her little notebook?

"You were how old when Lecia died?"

The redirection startles her. "What's that?"

"Eleven. You were eleven."

"Something like that."

"You were the last person to see her alive?"

Julianna glances off to the side. Her next-door neighbor, a bitter white woman, thin and pinched like a starved rodent, is watering the front yard in the corner house—a spray of water arcing toward the sidewalk, dropping a rainbow as it falls. Julianna watches her spray the flowers. It's a loveless gesture, as if the flowers are asking too much.

"That's what they said."

"Did they know each other?"

"Kathy and Lecia? Like you said, I was eleven. I didn't know anything about anything."

To talk about Kathy is to reduce her to what the detective needs her to be. A streetwalker, a hooker, a bitch who tricked her life away. Julianna won't do that. Because there was more to Kathy than what she did for cash. There was the woman who always made sure other dancers had money for a cab home, who organized day trips to the beach, the theme park—anything to distract the girls from what they had to be. There was the woman who loved crappy movies, who taught her crew to sneak into the multiplexes for a whole day.

"What was she like?" Detective Perry asks.

"Kathy?"

"Lecia."

"She was fucking beautiful."

Now Detective Perry follows Julianna's gaze, watching the water from the hose rain down. "That's honeysuckle," she says. "Honeysuckle and huckleberry. People plant them to attract hummingbirds. You know, some hummingbirds' wings can beat over five thousand times per minute." The detective pauses and squints, like she wants to summon one of the birds into view. "You can kill them with a swipe of your hand." She takes a slim leather wallet out of her breast pocket and passes Julianna a card. "Call me any-time," she says. "About Kathy or Lecia."

Julianna takes the card and puts it into the pocket of Hector's sweatshirt. No way she's calling because there's only one reason girls like her call people like Detective Perry. A trade. A deal. *I'll give you info, you cut me some slack the next time I'm hauled in.*

She lights her cigarette and watches the detective head off down the steps. Detective Perry opens the gate, then turns and doubles back.

"You're a dancer."

Julianna opens her mouth to object.

"Let's say you're a dancer. What's interesting about the men you perform for?"

"What do you mean?"

"What is memorable about them?"

Julianna looks at the burning cherry of her cigarette. "Nothing, they're a bunch of losers."

The detective has her notepad out and is scrawling some-thing down.

"You give them a lot of power," she says without taking her eyes from her notes.

"That's what they think."

Detective Perry looks up from her pad, then makes one more note before tucking it away in her jacket. Without another word, she opens the gate again.

There's a bike chained to a street sign just down the street. Juli-anna watches her unlock it, then unhook a helmet clipped around the rack on the back and climb on.

"Nice ride," Julianna calls.

She can hear her phone ringing somewhere in the house. She doesn't have to look to know it's probably Coco or Rackelle won-dering where the fuck she is, what the fuck she's doing, and what her problem is. By now, gossip about her show at the Fast Rabbit will have spread, the story exaggerated until Julianna's been turned into a wild, violent crackhead, a dirty, unhinged bitch. She should change her number, get a new phone. That's what she should do. Because she's done with this, them, and the rest of it. Done with Coco and the dudes at the Fast Rabbit and the others who ask for "dates" on her off night, who take her to what they think are fancy restaurants out in Inglewood or near Watts, pay the bill, then take her home for their due. But Julianna knows what a real fancy restaurant is like, knows the menus aren't in plastic sleeves, that the water doesn't come in cafeteria-style cups, that half the food isn't fried, that the wine isn't poured from a box or a jug, and the tablecloths aren't waterproof. She knows it's a poor trade.

She heads inside, passing Armando, who's camped out in front of a Central American soccer game on the television. "What did the lady cop want?"

"Some shit I didn't know anything about."

"She seemed like a bitch."

Julianna's phone is ringing again—the reggaeton tone that used to get her in the groove but now only irritates her. She looks at her chipped nails—her pricey gel extensions that she ruined back at the Fast Rabbit. Maybe she'll swap them out for something understated like the detective's. Maybe she'll change that ringtone too.

"Don't make me ask why the LAPD's after you," Armando says.

Julianna jams her hands in the pouch of her sweatshirt. "I won't."

She goes to Hector's room and slides open the drawer on the nightstand, searching for more weed. But he's empty or he's found a new place for his stash. She rattles her hand around and finds a scrap of one of her brother's preposterously large joints. It's about an inch long but plenty wide. She opens his bedroom window, sparks the tip, and stares at the house next door.

There's a large hedge that obscures much of the yard. Above it, Julianna can see the fresh red paint and perfect siding of the house—nothing like the chipped and splintering exterior of her parents' place. She blows smoke at the hedge as if she can part it and glimpse the tidy lives of her next-door neighbors.

There's someone on the far side of the hedge. She can hear feet on the concrete, the sound of a hose spraying the plants. Even the plants are cared for over there.

There's only about three tokes' worth in the roach. Julianna grinds out the filter on the windowsill and tosses it.

"Isn't it time you get your own weed?"

Julianna starts at the sound of Hector's voice.

"You're out," Julianna says, tapping the top of the nightstand.

"And whose fault is that?"

Julianna shrugs. "Where do you get your shit anyway? You have a card?"

"Cards are for nerds. I use some dude named Peter."

"Peter? You buy weed from a white boy?"

"So the fuck what? He gets medical grade. Anyway, the shit from the dispensaries is mad expensive."

"You want to get me some?"

Hector checks his nightstand to see whether he's really out. "Fuck. You really are a bitch." But he's smiling as he slams the empty drawer. "So you're living here now? Is that the deal? You're crashing all permanent?"

"Why?"

"Because I'll need to find a better hiding place for my shit is why."

"Tell you what," Julianna says. "Give me the address of this Peter and I'll hook us both up."

Hector pulls out his phone and starts clicking through his contacts. "Don't be stingy now. And get the good shit."

6.

THE ADDRESS HECTOR GAVE HER IS A FIFTEEN-MINUTE WALK
from Twenty-Ninth Place—but she might as well have crossed
into another dimension. The house is a giant white mansion on a
row of mostly derelict mansions a block south of the 10 and a few
blocks east of Western. It looks like something out of a movie—an
old horror movie—a crumbling stone exterior with wings, towers, and windows, several of which are broken. Along one side of
the house is a covered archway. There's a whole mess of scaffold-
ing on the exterior and Julianna can't tell whether it's there to fix
the building or hold it up.

Peter meets her in the scraggly garden that wraps around the
house. He's white, of course, and wearing the skinniest pair of
jeans Julianna's ever seen a man wriggle into and a tight plaid
shirt. He sells her the weed from a cigar box. She buys a quarter.
It's packaged like it comes from a hospital or pharmacy—RX and
the name of whatever strain printed like a prescription label.

Julianna tucks it into her purse.

"Want to check out the party?" Peter asks. "No charge for customers."

She gives him a look that tells him she's not sure why anyone would pay to enter the run-down mansion.

"It's like a fund-raiser. We're trying to restore the place. So normally we'd charge. But since you already paid." Peter taps the cigar box.

"I'll check it out," Julianna says.

She follows Peter up a crumbling staircase. She's all too familiar with what goes on a few steps from here on the side alley she could probably hit with a rock if she aimed it right, the place where Kathy and her crew worked their freeway business. But here on Harvard and La Salle it's a whole other party. A type of party Julianna can't quite figure.

If they are planning to make the mansion habitable, they sure have a strange way of going about it. The entire place is covered in graffiti, floor to ceiling. And not just random graffiti but the shit Julianna's heard the local taggers dismiss as "street art." Murals and stencils and paper transfers. Pictures of famous people she should recognize, political figures she would never recognize.

Julianna looks out of place and feels it too. She had dressed down—superdown, not wanting to be confused with the girls she knew she'd pass on her way here. She'd put on an old pair of jeans that don't fit as high and tight as the ones she usually prefers. Her shirt is a souvenir from the Santa Monica Pier—a pastel California sunset splashed across her chest with the pier disappearing toward the horizon.

Even in loose clothing she's a rolling wave in a flat sea of skinny women who are dressed like moms in old TV shows—pleated jeans, fuzzy, boxy sweaters, fussy blouses, and the kind of glasses her school nurse wore. Julianna's built for a different world—a world of jiggling and taunting, of sauntering and displaying.

Julianna pulls in her stomach, rounds her shoulders, tucks herself into herself as she walks through the party. There are people everywhere drinking beer and wine out of red plastic cups. The staircase wobbles under their weight. On the second floor the wallpaper is artfully stripped away and made to look as if shadowy figures are climbing through the walls to join the action.

There's art everywhere. In one of the back bedrooms a young man with tufted dreads is working on a mural. People have gathered to watch him paint a strange version of Los Angeles where the main boulevards are replaced by rivers that seem to be moving along the plaster. He works oblivious to the chatter around him.

He's painted a man's face in the center of the mural. Julianna recognizes it as the kid on TV, the one the cops killed in Brooklyn. She can't quite grasp the name. But then she sees it painted on a ribbon below the kid's neck: Jermaine Holloway. The story is everywhere. Pulled from his cousin's car, kicked black and blue, then shot for good measure.

Julianna tilts her head side to side. The artist did a bang-up job capturing the dead kid's good looks—his soft brown eyes, high round cheekbones.

From what she's seen on TV, Jermaine Holloway had wild, kinky hair, corkscrew curls that sprang from his head in all directions. But on the mural something totally different is taking place. There's another type of explosion happening on the kid's crown—a woman bursts from his head, breaking through his brain, full-formed and regal. She's emerging, arms raised, circled in golden light and bolts of blue energy. There's a ribbon around this woman's chest like a pageant queen: Idira.

Julianna moves on down the hall where people are leaning on a railing they shouldn't lean on, pushing past each other and craning their necks to see what they're missing, commenting on everything.

She comes to an enormous room at the back of the house—the only room where the walls are untouched by graffiti. There's a crowd and it takes a moment for Julianna to figure out what they are looking at.

She can't see past the people blocking the doorway so she elbows her way in. There's a woman standing in the middle of the room. She's naked. Her body is painted blue—lighter at the top, darker at the bottom. There's an enormous bucket at the woman's feet and every so often she fills a ladle with water and dumps it on her head, letting the paint run down.

The crowd shifts. People watch the woman dump two or three ladles of water, then move on. But Julianna is transfixed.

There are people out there who would consider this woman hot. She's skinny with good enough breasts and long hair. Her butt curves nicely and her stomach is tight. If she were in Julianna's business, she'd have to do something about that bush between her legs. But no one's looking at her that way—or if they are, they're keeping it to themselves.

It's not the crowd's response that interests Julianna, it's the woman herself, the way she's standing there, letting herself be looked at but not giving herself away. Even with it all hanging out, it's like she's holding some part of herself back.

Julianna finds a place near the window. She's been around naked women for years. She's checked them out, compared, found faults—so many faults—but she's never admired them.

A couple has moved into the space next to Julianna. They're drunk or stoned or whatever it is that sets their voices at speaker volume. They stumble back and forth, rocked by their own laughter.

Julianna tries to see if the naked woman hears this but her face shows nothing. She just dumps another ladle of water.

"I know you're not supposed to say what's the point," the woman says. "But what's the point?"

"Power." The answer flies from Julianna's mouth before she can stop it.

The couple turn and stare at her, then back at each other. "Sure," the man says. "Power."

"I like your shirt," the woman says, pointing at the sunset on Julianna's chest.

Julianna gives her the kind of look she gives men who can't pay.

"No, for real," the woman says. "Where'd you get it?"

"The Santa Monica Pier," Julianna says.

The couple leaves. The crowd changes. The naked woman has nearly run out of water. Her face, breasts, and torso are almost entirely cleaned of paint. The floor around her feet is streaked with blue.

She dumps two or three more ladles.

Soon Julianna is the only one watching. The woman rolls her neck to one side, picks up the towel from behind the bucket, and dries her hair, her face. She rubs her shoulders and stretches her back from side to side.

Julianna pulls out her phone.

Click.

The woman lifts her face from the towel and looks at Julianna.

Julianna tucks the phone away. "Sorry."

"I just stood naked in a room for two hours. It's not like I mind if you take a picture." She wraps the towel around her chest and spins her hair into a topknot. "You're into performance art?"

"Kinda," Julianna says. Because she could be. You could call what she does, or did, *performance art.*

"Most people think it's pointless."

Julianna inclines her head, hoping that the woman won't elaborate, won't explain any further. Because Julianna knows what this means to her and she doesn't want to be told different.

"I know you, don't I?" the woman says.

"I don't think so," Julianna says.

"We're neighbors."

"On Forty-Seventh?" A lot of women come and go in the

apartment building where Julianna used to crash, where her old life unfolded deep into the night. But she's pretty sure she's never seen this skinny white girl.

"You're Julianna, right? I grew up next door on Twenty-Ninth Place."

It takes Julianna a moment. "In the nice red house with all the plants."

The woman taps the towel on her chest. "Marella—you don't remember me, do you? I used to watch you from my window when I was little. You were always—"

She doesn't finish. She doesn't need to. They both know what Julianna was always doing.

Julianna does remember, kind of. A girl next door was a year or two younger. The fence between their houses must have been more like a fortress.

"As early as they could my parents sent me away for school, so I wasn't around much. They were supercautious, borderline paranoid," Marella says. "Pretty odd for people who moved from one war-torn country to the next before I was born."

"Your mom doesn't like me."

"Anneke? She doesn't like anyone." Marella squeezes water from her hair.

"You live at home?"

"For now. Me and some of the other artists around here are looking for a studio or something. You should swing by some-time. You know, neighbors."

"Maybe," Julianna says. "Sure."

"I got to wash this blue crap off," Marella says. "Just knock on the door."

Julianna watches Marella go, walking out into the party wrapped in her towel like she's dressed to kill.

7.

———

JULIANNA'S STILL THINKING ABOUT THE PARTY—ABOUT THE mural with the flowing river and naked Marella dripping blue paint, her body getting cleaner and clearer as the party progressed. She's on autopilot as she heads home, paying no attention to the streets as she wends her way from Harvard toward Western.

She catches herself before she almost trips on a paint bucket filled with flowers. A few dried bouquets lie next to the bucket. A shrine. Julianna doesn't have to cast the light from her phone over the photo in the plastic frame to know that she's standing in front of the lot where Kathy was discarded.

She squats down and runs a hand over the flowers in the bucket, sending a cascade of petals into the dirty water. She picks up the photo. It's a blurry shot, pixelated, blown up from a low-res image that shows Kathy and her three kids dressed for a holiday. A mother, not a hooker, but still not the Kathy that Julianna remembers. The woman in the photo looks remote, drained, not filled with the crazed energy and wild laughter that Julianna caught in her own photos.

"You knew her, right?"

Julianna drops the photo.

There's an arm on her shoulder. "I didn't mean to scare you."

Dorian. Of course. Always Dorian.

"What are you doing here?" Julianna asks.

"Same as you."

"Not me. I'm not doing anything." Because she wasn't. She was just passing by. Kathy had nothing to do with it. "I'm just on my way back from somewhere."

Dorian stoops to replace the photo next to the bucket. "But you're here."

"By accident. There was a party." Julianna waves her hand in the direction of Harvard. "This artist thing."

Dorian picks up the photo again and wipes the plastic frame with the hem of her shirt. "I used to see the two of you together. A long time ago."

"No you didn't." That was a different Julianna. That was a young Jujubee.

"I did," Dorian says. "She was wild, she made you wilder."

Julianna runs her fingers through her hair. "So, I knew her."

She knows what's coming next—the questions, the suspicions, the connections.

Julianna holds up a hand to stop Dorian before she starts. "I knew her way back. But that's it. Kathy and I danced together. And for your information, that's what I do. I'm a dancer. Or I was a dancer. Because, well, that's another story." Julianna takes a breath, trying to catch up with her own thoughts. "Kathy—she was a street girl. It's a different life."

"Kathy and Lecia are both dead. And you knew them."

"You think that's something more than coincidence? I know lots of people. And lots of them have died. Not just Kathy and Lecia, but also Marianna who ODed and Stacy who had some kind of cancer and Little Juan who wrecked his car on the 10 and Jimmie who got knifed and—"

Dorian puts a hand on Julianna's wrist to silence her. "Julianna, please."

"Please what?"

"You need to be careful."

Julianna laughs. She can't help herself. Who is this woman who couldn't even protect her own daughter to tell her to be careful?

Dorian tightens her grip on Julianna's wrist. "He's still out there."

"Who?"

"The man who killed Kathy. The one who killed Lecia."

Julianna jerks away, making Dorian stagger back. She's startled by the violence of her own reaction. "Who says I'm not careful? Who says I'm any which way at all? I told you I'm a dancer. Was. How come you think otherwise? How come you think there's something I need to be careful about?"

"Julianna, please."

"Please what?" She cocks her head to one side. "Was it you who put that lady detective on me?"

"Lady detective?"

Julianna holds her hand to chest height. "This one."

"Detective Perry?"

"Yeah, her. You sent her my way? Because I don't like that shit. I don't like LAPD messing with my business." It's easy to be hard with Dorian. It's as if the woman demands it with her pained looks, her pathetic pleading eyes.

"No," Dorian says.

"Bullshit," Julianna says. It's too much of a coincidence to be otherwise. Dorian down at the Southwest. That lady cop showing up at her place. "Let me make a suggestion. Mind your own business." Dorian couldn't help solve her own kid's murder. There's no way she should be nosing around Kathy's.

"This is my business."

God, the pain in Dorian's voice. The fucking desperation. And underneath it all the same goddamned echo—if Lecia had lived, Julianna wouldn't have gone wrong. Even worse—that Julianna had gone wrong, needed saving, and couldn't save herself.

"Kathy was crazy. She worked crazy. And she picked up the wrong dude. Occupational hazard. Comes with working the streets. Don't watch yourself you wind up dead in a place like that." She nods toward the empty lot.

"Lecia didn't *work the streets*."

This is the moment when Julianna should apologize. But what she really wants to do is slap the pain off Dorian's face. Instead she runs. And for once she's wearing sneakers. She flees Kathy's memorial, the dirty lot where she was either killed or tossed. This is a life to be left behind, a life gone, dusted.

But Dorian's on her. Chasing her. Calling her name.

What a scene the two of them must be making running down Twenty-Seventh Place toward Western. A young Latina woman pursued by a middle-aged white lady. Not your average South Central commotion.

"Julianna!"

Julianna runs faster. So easy to escape in sneakers. The things street girls do to stack the deck against them—the alleys they work, the hours, and the shoes.

Was it the shoes that brought Kathy down? Or was she careless in another way?

Dorian is closing in. But Julianna's got one final burst left. She accelerates. There's a bus pulling out of a stop on Western. She flags it. The door opens and scoops her up, leaving Dorian on the sidewalk, panting.

Julianna doesn't have change for the bus or a TAP card. What she does have she uses, tossing her hair, rolling her shoulders, sticking out her chest. She knows what the driver likes, what's going to excuse her from paying her fare.

The bus climbs the incline from Adams toward the freeway, then rumbles over the 10 and farther north out of West Adams into Koreatown. Julianna has no plan, no place to go other than away from Dorian. She rides until Wilshire, then gets off, winking at the driver as she goes.

She crosses the street to the southbound bus stop. The usual banners hang from the streetlights, advertising various cultural events Julianna has never paid attention to—museums, plays, stuff that takes place in a whole other city. But this time, they catch her eye. Because the picture hanging above Western is the same Larry Sultan photograph she tore out of *LA Magazine* and stashed in her purse. She steps out into the street to get a better look.

A car swerves, barely missing her.

Getthefuckout of the way, bitch.

Normally Julianna gives the driver a little bit of *whothefuckare-youcalling bitch, bitch? Get back here and say it to my face.*

But she doesn't care. She's staring at the streetlight on the eastern side of Western—another Larry Sultan photo of a porn set. Two women who've just finished with each other, tangled on the couch and laughing with the director. Julianna turns and looks south. The banners line both sides of Western, images of women and men in the downtime between takes.

She follows the photos south. The pictures of women not too different from her crew—their working lives made into art and displayed not just on these streets but in a museum. A whole exhibition of these women for the city to see and maybe even to admire.

The sickly smell of the fire hangs in the air. Particles of ash swirl like moths.

She walks home beneath the banners, crossing against lights, making cars squeal and honk. Ash from the wildfires is blowing down Western. Her neck aches from looking up at the scenes the photographer captured, the moments when the women are themselves—the stolen moments where the self slithers in. The very same moments that Julianna saves on her phone.

She comes to the final set of banners at the intersection of Western and Washington. She takes out her phone and turns the camera around. She puts on the flash and crouches down so the banner above is in the frame.

Click.

8.

———

HER PHONE IS GOING, BUZZING AND JUMPING ON THE dresser. Coco again. She's been calling nonstop for forty-eight hours, which lets Julianna know exactly what her crew's been up to and why she shouldn't pick up.

Her head is pot-hazy. In one day she'd run through half of what she and Hector had split, rolling fat joints and blowing smoke into the concrete yard behind her parents' house. She'd kept her phone on vibrate, only glancing at it every so often to see the missed calls and texts from Coco and Marisol—*What the fuck happened to you, bitch? You caused mad trouble at the Rabbit. How come you don't answer, bitch? You got yourself done like Kathy? Don't make me worry, bitch. You too good to party with your girls?*

There were even a few messages from Rackelle. *Hit me up for the weekend if you want to hang with Miss Molly. She's in town.* And, *Ju—if you want to go skiing make sure you get here before the snow melts.*

Julianna picks up her phone and turns the vibrate function off so there will be no alert, no temptation. She opens her photos, scrolling through her time machine to the old life.

There's Hector and Isobel asleep on the bed. *Click.* A blurry image of the back room of the Fast Rabbit—the walleyed customer splayed against one of the booths, the tracks of Julianna's nails on his face. There's Coco getting dressed, the apple of her ass front and center, her face visible in the mirror, lips puckered in a gangsta pout.

Julianna holds the phone away from her, tilts it to the side. She closes her eyes, tries to imagine the picture blown up, museum size, tries to imagine it as art.

Tap, tap, tap. Back through the photos. Back in time. Again and again. Some of the pictures jump out at her, something about them, the way they are put together, the story they tell, elevates them above the rest.

"Hector," Julianna calls. "Could you come in here for a moment?"

She hears the heavy tread of her brother in the hall. She scrolls back to the photo of Coco looking in the mirror. She holds out the phone. "What do you think of this?"

Hector appraises it. "She's got an ass."

"I mean what do you think of the picture?"

"Like how?"

"Is it art?"

Hector folds his arms across his chest. He'll be able to rest them on his belly soon if he isn't careful. "Is it supposed to be?"

Julianna swipes her brother across the cheek. "Fuck yes it is," she says.

"I like it," he says, taking the phone from her. Soon he's scrolling and clicking, zooming in and taking a longer look from time to time.

Julianna flutters her fingers. "Give it back."

Hector turns so the phone is out of her reach. "Hold up."

"I said give it—"

Hector looks up from the phone, looks Julianna right in the eyes, looks at her like he's never seen her before. "This your life, Ju?"

"What?"

"This is your life? This?" He holds up the phone. Julianna can't quite make out the exact image. All she can see is a mess of bodies, flesh and lace and smoke and what's probably a coffee table strewn with powder or pills.

"No, Hector, it's my art." She yanks the phone from his grasp and shoves him out the door.

What the hell does he know? And if this shit gets blown up, hung on a wall, on display for everyone to see, no one's going to be criticizing her. Her life could be what she makes it. Her life could be a life instead of something that just happens.

She's out the door in an instant, the riot gate banging into place behind her. Before she's second-guessed her own crazy idea, she's already knocking on the door of the house next door. For a moment she's filled with the fiery confidence that she usually gets from *llelo*, the magic that turns her from Julianna into Jujubee.

Marella's mother, Anneke, opens the door. Her eyes narrow and her mouth puckers when she sees Julianna. "Yes?"

"I live next door?"

"I know," Marella's mother says. "I've seen you."

Julianna stands silently, not quite sure what she's doing anymore. She looks past Anneke. She can see that the house is laid out exactly like her parents'. But unlike next door, where Armando and Alva painted all the woodwork white, the interior of Marella's house is dark wood. It even has the glass cabinets and built-ins that Julianna remembers Armando stripping out of their living and dining rooms and tossing on the street. Marella's family has a sofa done up in some dark fabric and a set of matching chairs. Through the sliding doors, she can see a dining room table that seems built to match the rest of the house.

"Is there a reason you're here?" Anneke asks.

A man has emerged in the hallway, middle aged and white with a graying beard.

Anneke turns. "I'm taking care of it, Roger."

"I live next door," Julianna repeats.

"We know that already," Anneke says.

Her husband is still standing behind her.

"I'm looking for Marella," Julianna says.

"How do you know my daughter?"

"She said I could stop by."

"She's not here."

"I wanted to ask her something," Julianna says. "She's an artist and I have these photos—" She holds out her phone.

Anneke begins to close the door. "I said she's not here."

"Can you let her know I stopped by? She could just ring my bell or something?"

"Maybe," Anneke says.

Marella's father clears his throat. "She's—" he begins.

Anneke holds up her hand.

"We'll let her know," he says.

Julianna's about to reply when Anneke closes the door, leaving her standing on the porch. She crosses the street and lights a cigarette. She glances over at her house. She can see Armando and Hector on the sofa watching a soccer replay. Alva is at the airport car rental working the late shift because one of her employees called in sick.

Then she sees movement on the second story of Marella's house. A curtain is pulled back. Marella appears at the window. Julianna watches her until the light goes out. Then she grinds out her butt.

Now Marella is coming down the stairs. Julianna sees her pass the small window in the front door and disappear down the hall. The front curtains are cracked slightly. She can see the family preparing to sit down to dinner. It's like a dance. Marella carries a serving bowl. Her mother follows with bread. The father with a bottle of wine.

The family sits. They look to be eating without talking. Their movements are precise, like they've rehearsed them, like they're performing this meal rather than enjoying it. It's nothing like the chaos at Julianna's table—Alva berating Hector for eating too much, berating Armando for storming off to watch soccer, berating Julianna for being unable to eat at all.

Marella's invitation was easy and careless. Julianna will never knock on their door again. She's worlds away. Lifetimes.

She fumbles in her purse. She's out of cigarettes. She might as well walk to the liquor store on Western, grab some smokes. She turns and heads off.

She doesn't see Marella's mom leave the table.

She doesn't see Marella rush to close the curtains.

9.

IT'S THE USUAL CREW AT THE WESTERN LIQUOR—MEN DRINK-
ing sweet wine and forties until they pass out in the parking lot.
Julianna ignores their slurred Spanish come-ons, their demands
she slow down and let them take a look. She buys a pack of men-
thols and a wine cooler, then sits on the low wall of the strip
mall parking lot just down from Dorian's fish shack.

She glances north. She can't see the fire in the hills but she can
smell smoke. She inhales deeply, letting her menthol mix with the
ashy L.A. air. A bus passes before stopping halfway up the block.
On the back is an ad for the Larry Sultan show. She can't remember the last time she was in a museum, probably a school trip that
she ducked out of midway.

"Julianna?"

An inch-long ash is dangling from the tip of her cigarette.
Julianna flicks it away and looks at a young woman who's suddenly standing in front of her.

"Yeah?"

"You don't recognize me?"

The woman is twenty, if that. Copper skin. Pretty enough

with straightened ebony hair streaked magenta. A baby face with hard eyes. "You don't know me? It's been a while."

She's too fresh faced for the streets, a little too young for the Fast Rabbit.

"Jessica."

The name means nothing to Julianna.

"Kathy's eldest."

Julianna can feel her eyes widen despite herself. Jessica was in the picture by the shrine, blurry and younger, stuffed into a holiday dress that was supposed to hide the heartache of having Kathy as a mother. "Your mom—that's messed up."

Why can't she say the words? Why can't she let her grief loose? Why does she have to be hard?

Jessica shrugs, like worse things have happened. And maybe they have. Maybe she'd been waiting for the day that Kathy didn't make it home.

"You're okay?"

"I'm whatever," Jessica says.

Julianna tosses her cigarette and fishes for another.

Jessica holds out her hand. "I can get one of those?"

It's not that Julianna doesn't want to give her a cigarette. She just doesn't want to have to stick around while they smoke together. But it's too late. Jessica's already waiting for her to pass the lighter.

They both exhale toward Western.

"So your family is holding up?"

"It's not like Kathy was around much," Jessica says. "She was always working or out somewhere. She was getting high or coming down or sleeping or getting ready to go back out. You know." It's not a question.

Julianna does.

"She was a bitch. But she brought in cash."

Is this the kind of mother Julianna would become? Coming down and cranky in the mornings. Spending herself at night.

"She worked mad hard," Jessica says. "Now it's just me and my two brothers. Both of them still in high school. My dad's who the fuck knows where."

"What about your grandma?"

"Dead. We live at her place. Some shit with her stomach. Killed her quick."

"Sorry," Julianna says.

"Everyone's sorry. But no one does anything. I work at the Carl's Jr. And it gets me a whole bunch of nothing."

Julianna takes a long drag. "Anything I can do?"

Jessica turns and looks square at her. "Yeah," she says, "there is. You work at the Fast Rabbit, right?"

"Not anymore."

"But you did."

"So?"

"You could hook me up?"

"Hook you up?"

"Like a job. A good job. Like the shit you do."

The shit you do. Why doesn't she come out and say it? Call it what it is. What her mother did. "How the fuck old are you?" Julianna asks.

"Twenty-one."

"Bullshit." Not that it matters. Ramon and Dean and the rest of them would take her. Fresh and clean and ready to work. "Sorry," Julianna says. "I can't help you."

"Can't or won't?"

"I said I don't work there anymore." There's no way she's introducing this girl into that life, doing to Jessica what Kathy did to her. Telling her it's all fun and drinks and late nights and parties. A few hours waiting tables. Then a few trips to the back rooms, line your pockets, like no big deal. And soon nothing will be a big deal, nothing will be taking it too far.

"You asked if you could help. I got two brothers to take care of. And myself."

"That's no way to take care of anyone."

"You got a better way of pulling in cash? 'Cause I don't. Anyway, it's just dancing and a little extra. No matter."

"Sorry," Julianna says again. There's no fucking way. She rummages in her purse, looking for something that will distract her from the handprints that will mark up Jessica's smooth arms, the streaks of someone else's sweat that will roll down her chest.

"My mother always said she helped you out."

"Is that what she said?"

"She said she looked out for you."

Julianna tosses her cigarette into the street. "You have no fucking idea what you're saying."

"Fuck you, bitch," Jessica says.

"You have no fucking idea about anything." Julianna wants to hurt her, scare her, anything to keep her away from this mess.

For a moment Julianna thinks Jessica is going to slap her. But she marches away, north on Western without a word.

Julianna watches her go—a young woman walking into the night. But a moment later she's chasing after her. She catches Jessica, yanking her back by the shoulder. "Where you going?"

Jessica shakes her off. There's wildfire in her eyes. "Get the fuck away from me."

Julianna's been around enough to know how to be tough, how to dominate one of these junior bitches who dream they have the drop on you because they're young and pretty and think they know it all. She places herself in front of Jessica, grabs her wrist. "I said, where are you going?"

Jessica stops walking. "I'm going to find Brandy or Big Pete, if you want to know. Get their help, since you won't. Or maybe I'll find what's-his-name, Carlo? Carlos? CC?"

Julianna lets go of Jessica's wrist. She doesn't have to know Big Pete or Carlo/Carlos/CC to know who they are. Brandy too. This late on Western it's obvious who the girl is looking for. And she has no idea what's in store if she finds one of these people—how quickly they will introduce her to a rougher life than she'd ever imagined.

"Fuck it," Julianna says, taking out her phone, click-click-clicking until she finds Coco's number. She shows it to Jessica. "Call her. She's my girl. I'll give her the heads-up. She'll get you into the Fast Rabbit if she can. But I want to see you get on a bus right the fuck now. I don't want you looking for Big Pete or Brandy or whoever the fuck else. I want you to cross the street. Get on the bus. And when you do, I'm going to call Coco and tell her you'll be by ASAP. And you better not disappoint her."

The look on Jessica's face is a mix of shock and surprise. She opens her mouth but Julianna beats her to it. "And don't thank me. Don't you ever fucking thank me. Now cross the street and get on the bus."

Jessica obeys. Julianna watches her dart through traffic and waits until the bus takes her away. Then she collapses against a shuttered storefront.

Before she knows what she's doing she's texted Rackelle. And before she can second-guess herself, Rackelle's there because she was just around the corner. And when she sees Julianna looking all beat up and undone, she throws in a little extra baggie, telling her *don't be a stranger and come party with the girls again.* And Julianna's thanked her and before Rackelle's back in her car, she's cracked one of the baggies and scooped up some *llelo* with her pinkie and now the world is buzzing in Technicolor.

Without realizing it, she's done half the bag and been pacing

Western for an hour or more in her sneakers and shorts, no party to go to, no job. Nothing. And she's walking home, because she doesn't want to go to Coco's apartment and see Jessica again.

Up north she thinks she can see the fires sparked on the hills again, little electrodes of red in the dark. Or maybe her eyes are playing with her.

She feels hot and cold.

She's saved a girl from the life for a minute, deflected her, sent her elsewhere and bought her time until the streets come calling. They will. They always do. They'll want their piece, take their due.

She dips her pinkie again.

Jessica will find her way to Big Pete or CC one way or the other. Or she'll find her way elsewhere. It's only a matter of time.

Julianna's head is spinning. Western is streaked with tail-lights and headlights. Men on the crawl, prowling for women like Jessica. Women like Julianna. The need is endless. It's never satisfied. Men are always hungry for more and the streets will provide.

She's closing in on her block.

Who is she fooling that the Fast Rabbit is any better than things up here—somehow more tasteful or respectable? Who is she kidding that she did something noble by sending Jessica that way?

There's a car coming down Twenty-Ninth. It's slowing. She can feel the driver watching her. Shopping. Appraising.

The car's windows are tinted. She can feel darkness looking out at her from behind the windshield.

She knows what the driver wants. She knows what he thinks she is. He's right. Doesn't matter that she's not dressed for the game. The game is in her. She is the game.

She took a girl from the streets temporarily. And she must give herself in return. Because if not her, he'll find someone else. Julianna tosses her hair. She rolls her shoulders, sticking out her chest and ass, summoning Jujubee. Because Jujubee's hard. Jujubee's not scared of the person she can feel looking at her from behind the tinted window

Jujubee won't let the streets get her. She's got armor. She's superhero tough.

Jujubee licks her lips.

It was inevitable.

She was always going to wind up here.

This was Kathy's doing.

And now.

The car rolls over. The passenger window goes down.

Jujubee leans into the darkness. At first she sees nothing. All she can hear is him breathing behind the wheel.

"Hey," he says.

She thinks she knows the voice. She opens the door. Slides into the shotgun seat.

"Oh . . ." she says. "I didn't realize."

"Neither did I," he says.

"Don't worry," she says. "I'm working."

"I'm not worried," he says. "Not at all."

FEELIA 1999

WAIT. HOLD UP. I SEE YOU. I SAW YOU. THE FUCK ARE YOU DO-
ing standing outside my window? Don't think I didn't see. Like I
don't notice shit. I said hold up. Don't you run away before I can
get a look at you. Don't you—

Damn.

Where the fuck did you go? You get back here, you got something to say, say it to my face.

Hey, any of you fools down there see someone standing by that
dead-ass tree across the way?

Don't give me, *no*. I saw. Some dude's watching me. I can
motherfucking *feel* him, you know what I mean?

Paranoid? Like hell I am. I know what I see. Paranoid? Fuck.

Are you telling me to keep my voice down? You keep your
voice down.

Shit. He was there last night. Swear to it. I know when someone's watching me. I know.

Can't motherfucking sleep, I'm telling you. Can't do goddamn
anything. Feel like there's something on my back. That's what I
said—something on my back. Like watching me. Everywhere, no
matter.

You just go about your business like what I say don't matter. Yeah, go on.

You know what it's like, walking down the street and think your own shadow is chasing you? That your own goddamn shadow is out to get you? Makes me feel like a damn junkie, is what. Like one of those women having a full-on argument with herself for everyone to see.

Except I'm not crazy. I feel what I feel.

The other day, let me tell you what happened. I'm walking to the store. Just to get a few necessities. Stuck inside all day, I need food. Something to keep my strength up. You know. Last I checked it should be possible to go to the minimart without feeling like someone was following you—like someone was gonna jump out from every dumpster.

Where I really wanted to go was the liquor store down on Sixty-Fifth, get some Hennessy and my Pall Mall—my regular, you know. My supplies. But fuck if I'm ever going there again. Gonna have to walk halfway to Jefferson Park to get my booze now.

So no booze for me, because I'm not gonna risk that place. Not after what happened.

Don't make me tell you what happened. I'm not going into that shit.

So this time, all I was after was some rice and shit. Some soup. Something soft. Because it goddamn hurts to chew. So that's what I'm doing. But I'm getting this feeling that there's something following me. No, more than feel. I know. I know.

And I'm starting to sweat. It's like, pouring down. Like I'm some kinda professional basketball player. It's raining off my head. I'm motherfucking making it rain.

And my heart—let me tell you about my heart. It's like someone took a needle full of speed and shot it right in there. It's beating so fast I think it's gonna outrun my body. I can feel it in my fingers.

And I can't breathe, you know. My throat, it's closing.

A panic attack? You think I don't know it was a panic attack? Shit.

You going to let me finish or you going to keep telling me things I already know?

So I'm sweating and shaking—can barely walk down Western. And I can feel this person behind me. Like he's gonna stab me all over again. But I can't keep walking, because I'm going to collapse. Like my heart is going to fall right out on the street. And I can feel this person coming closer. But I can't move. No fucking way. It's like my heart is beating so fast it's all I can do to stand up.

So I double over, right there on the sidewalk, like I'm having a heart attack or some shit.

And what happens? Some goddamned white lady walks on past. Some old, skinny bitch.

That's what I was afraid of. Old white lady walking down Western. Tell you what—she's the one should be scared. She was way out of her playpen.

But it goes to show—my mind is scrambled. I'm seeing things I shouldn't. Hearing and feeling them too.

It's like the whole world's out to get me. Every goddamn shadow's got murder on its mind.

It's a burden to even go outside.

Okay. Sounds like you've heard enough. And I'm going. I'm going up to my place. Gonna keep watch from my window. But keep an eye out, you hear. You see someone you let me know.

YOU! GET THE HELL AWAY from the tree. Might be dark, but I can see you. You're motherfucking watching me. Don't make me feel like I'm crazy. Now, go on. Get.

Don't make me open up this window wide. Don't make me lean out farther. I'm banged up enough already. Got my throat slit to ribbons. I don't need to go falling out this motherfucker as well.

Fall out my own goddamn window. Now that would be a way to go. Survived nearly getting murdered, then break my neck on Western.

Folks will think I got all suicidal after my ordeal.

I'm talking to you.

Yo. I'm talking to you. I saw you over by that tree. Now you're in the carport across the way. Can't fool me. You motherfucking can't.

Don't make me keep screaming at you. You know what it feels like to talk after you get your throat slit? Can you even try and imagine that shit?

How long you gonna watch me for?

I can't see your face, but I know you're there.

You come to finish the job? That's who you are? You're pissed that I'm still breathing. You mad at yourself not being able to carry through. Disappointed. Well, shit.

NoIwillnotshutthefuckup. Somebodyouttherestalkingme. Youshutthefuckup.

Next time I see you out there, I'm gonna call LAPD. Matter of fact, I'm calling them now, let them know I'm being harassed. Let them know the man who tried to kill me is trying to finish what he started. Hell, I'm gonna do their job for them. I'm going to catch you myself.

You just wait up.

You got something to say, say it to my face. You've already done your worst.

I'm coming.

I said wait up. Took me a minute to get down the stairs. Can't move so fast with these stitches in my throat and all.

You still there? Come over here and show yourself.

Okay, so you're gonna run away. You some kinda lurker? Had the balls to slit my throat, but now you're hiding? Shit.

NoIwillnotkeepitdown. Gottherighttoraisemydamnvoice.

Excuse me? And who are you now? Lady, you have something

to say? You just here to watch the show? Oh, you're just passing by? Well, be my guest. Pass on by. Don't mind me. There you go. Quick now.

Hold up. Lady, I said hold up. HOLD UP.

Don't I know you?

I feel like I know you.

Come back so I can place it.

You're not gonna come back?

Wait. I saw you the other day. Right when I was having that attack. Right when I was doubled up on Western. You were passing by.

You new in the hood? Is that what it is?

You new?

Am I supposed to know you or some shit?

Lady, let me give you a piece of advice—there's a stalker out there. Watching me. I'm just doing you a neighborly kindness letting you know. Wouldn't want you to get hurt or nothing. No ma'am.

Hey, lady! Don't run off like that. I got one more thing to tell you. Listen up. I got one more thing to say and it's goddamned important. Mind your own business.

PART III

ESSIE

2014

1.

THERE IS AN ANSWER FOR EVERYTHING. IT'S USUALLY SIMPLE. It's people who complicate things. It makes them feel important, smarter. It's easy to impose your intellect on simple problems you can't solve. Blow them out of proportion.

Take cops for instance. Always on about motive. But motive is a distraction. At the end of the day all that matters is who did it.

Here's a clue: *Honey Bunch.* Answer: Bees or Hive. There can be more than one choice but only one right answer.

Crime isn't much different from a crossword. There's always a solution. The catch is finding it.

You have to be on the lookout for a small trick. A distraction. Either intentional or accidental.

See that guy over up the block? Slept in his car in front of his house?

Why?

Fight with his wife? Possible.

Came home drunk and fell asleep?

The answer: locked out and couldn't afford a locksmith.

See. Simple. And usually less interesting than you thought.

Don't complicate. Don't overthink. The answer is there.

Now how about this: last name *Perry*. Essie Perry. Everyone thinks she's a big mystery because she doesn't look like an Essie Perry. So people look at her funny, as if she's a puzzle. As if she's trying to fool them. Like there's some great mystery to why a Latina woman has a white-lady name. A name like a woman from a country club. Your doubles partner. The chair of the garden committee. They imagine there's some big complicated answer.

It's her husband's name of course. Just ask. And Essie? Well, Esmerelda's a mouthful, a bad name for a cop.

She'll tell you. Not everything. Essie's not in the habit of keeping secrets. She just doesn't think everyone needs to know the entire truth. It's good to keep something to yourself. You never know when you'll need it.

Why did she keep her husband's last name after everything? Simple. It's her work name. It's on her badge. Changing it would have meant starting over. It would have implied she was hiding something.

Here's another question. What has Mark Perry been doing all night? Did he sleep? Essie can hear him in the small study downstairs. Even if she didn't hear him, she knows he's there. She can't remember the last time he left the house.

Here's a final one: When are the rest of Southwest Station going to see the pattern? Three dead women tossed near Western in less than a year? She can't be the only one who's made the connection. But there's more, not just these recent killings but the ones that came before, especially Dorian Williams's daughter. Either Essie's mind is playing tricks (which she's been told it does) or there's not just a coincidence here, there's a pattern.

Serial means more work.

It means press and headache and tip lines.

Perhaps they are intentionally blind. Or perhaps it's the sort of women who've been killed that make their deaths irrelevant. One more and Southwest won't have that luxury. It almost makes

Essie want her old job in Homicide back. But she knows that's not going to happen.

Before getting out of bed, she finishes the Friday *New York Times* crossword. It takes her twenty minutes—the *L.A. Times* takes ten. *Rubber from the Middle East?* Aladdin. A dumb way to begin the morning. But reassuring. Answers. Solutions.

The radio is on, local news. The tail end of a press conference with the mayor about a Black Lives Matter protest in downtown L.A. in the wake of the Jermaine Holloway killing. Opposite coast but a nationwide problem. Then cut to Morgan Tillett, local activist from Power Through Protest, a BLM splinter organization, who says she's calling in from her house. Except she's not home, at least not in Los Angeles as far as Essie can tell. In the background is the aboveground rattle of a train like the El in Chicago or the New York subway. It has a different pitch than the L.A. Metro, a roar not a rumble. She's telling the host that the recent protest is only the beginning. That there's going to be more actions unless the cops and the nation start to pay attention.

The host asks her about the climate in Los Angeles, whether racial tensions are reaching Rodney King levels. She laughs and says, "From where I'm sitting it looks like the city is about to explode. They haven't seen anything yet."

Except Morgan Tillett is lying. She's hiding something. Essie doesn't care what. She hears that subway rumble again confirming it. Again, the reason doesn't matter. Just the facts.

She gets out of bed. Gets dressed in one of her suits. Even she can barely tell them apart. She does her makeup—summery colors. Too bright for her complexion, she's been told. She flattens her bangs and checks her roots. She never should have started dyeing her hair when she got out of uniform. Her old partner, Deb Harden, warned her not to—told Essie that her new look would never match the name on her badge. By the time Essie realized Deb was right, it was too late to go back to her natural black. It would have been like admitting she'd made a mistake or, worse, that she was ashamed. Deb saw the lay of the land better, saw into the future, played the angles. She knew what they were up against.

Essie tucks in her rayon blouse and pegs her trousers so they don't snag in her bike chain.

From the hallway she can smell burned coffee on the warmer.

She can hear the monitors whirring in the study. She can see their blue reflection on the wall as she descends the stairs. Japan. Shanghai. London. Switzerland. The US Stock Exchange—they've all been up for hours and Mark's been up with them.

Essie peeks in the door of the study. Her husband's face, bathed in the lights of one of his computers and pale from years without direct sunlight, is a sickly blue.

She watches the numbers scroll by on the screen—signs, codes, cyphers, a world of money and value that is a mystery to her.

Mark trades low—small stakes, not quite micro trades but close.

The accident took away his confidence. He doesn't gamble. Mostly hedges. He brings in a little. With her salary and their small house paid off, they don't need much. No car. No dinners out. There's not much to say anyway.

Seven A.M. in Los Angeles. Ten in New York. The Asia markets are already closed. Six and a half more hours in the trading day. Then Mark will eat a frozen pizza, drink a bottle of Mexican coke, and go to sleep. He'll be in bed when Essie gets home.

Essie pulls out the coffeepot. She can see where the liquid is scalding on the burner. The criticisms she'd face for such a mistake at the station arrive uninvited.

Perry, you burning the coffee again?

You put too much water in the pot?

You the one forgot to hit the on switch?

As if coffee is a woman's job. As if any mistake is her fault.

Her work is checked, even on the most inconsequential details of station business—coffee, light switches in the interrogation

rooms, food left on the counter. And even on the other stuff—
follow-up reports, booking sheets, files. Stuff she does in her sleep.
They never let up on her, always certain she's fallen short.

Perry, you followed up on that, right?

Perry, you filed the report?

Perry, you saved that doc?

Perry, you still bothering everyone about a handful of dead hookers?

Perry, you wasting our time?

Perry, you sticking your nose into Homicide's business?

Like she's a child. Or worse, a rookie. It doesn't help that she's
barely five foot. That's another thing Deb had on her—five inches.

Maybe Katherine Sims will wake them up.

Essie slides the coffeepot back onto the warmer without pouring a cup. Doesn't spill a drop.

She takes her badge from the kitchen drawer where she stores
it alongside rubber bands, her passport, packs of gum, a few older
ID cards, a picture of her and Deb at the LAPL softball game. Her
gun is in a safe in the broom closet though she rarely locks the
safe. If Mark wanted to get the gun, he could, she's pretty sure.

She checks that her phone is on. That's one of the luxuries of
switching from Homicide to Vice. She can turn it off when she
sleeps. Vice cops rarely get called out and only work overnights
on sweeps.

Essie doesn't like living so near her station. Better to bunk elsewhere so the work doesn't come home with you. But she needs
to be close enough to bike or walk, which gives her a three-mile
radius around Southwest.

Between the drag races, road rages, and geriatric buses huffing
and wheezing in the slower lanes, Los Angeles isn't set up for bik-
ing or for pedestrians. No quarter given to someone old or injured
taking his time to make it across the street. Just lay on the horn,
express your annoyance because the world isn't moving at your
chosen speed.

The more time Essie has spent out of cars, the more she's come to resent drivers. All of them. Even before the accident Deb did all the driving. Not driving frees Essie from at least one line of harassment.

Perry, you checked in the cruiser?

Perry, can you see over the wheel?

Perry, you need a booster seat?

No more.

You learn things on foot. You see your beat better on a bike. You catch flak from perps, witnesses, and officers. Worse things have happened.

Jefferson is the best route east-west. It moves slower than Adams and Washington. Then south on St. Andrews one street west of Western for nearly twenty blocks. It's residential. Stop signs instead of stoplights.

Essie's early. She's not on for nearly an hour.

There's a Starbucks on Jefferson and Western with outdoor seating overlooking the intersection. A good place to take in the streets.

She locks her bike. Then buys a small coffee, black.

It's chilly but she sits outside. There's not enough cold in L.A. so you need to take what you can get to remind yourself that things change and the world keeps spinning.

She watches three prostitutes pass. Essie doesn't recognize them. Circuit girls—women who are moved as a unit to different areas of the city even as far as Oceanside or Stockton. Girls who don't get on Southwest's radar. At least they look of age, for what that's worth.

She takes out her phone. Does the mini *Times* crossword in two minutes.

"Detective Perry."

Essie looks up. It's Shelly. She's coming off a long shift it seems

like. Midforties. Handful of convictions for the usual. Pimped by
Jericho. No gang affiliation. Usually works farther north.

"Long night, Detective?"

"Early morning." Essie takes a pack of gum from her suit
pocket. She was never a smoker. The chewing focuses her. Keeps
her in the moment.

"How many johns y'all arrest last week?"

"How long have you been out here, Shelly?"

"Today?"

"Ten years?"

Shelly shrugs and waves her arms, saying *something like that or
even longer.* "So how many you get? How many johns? You're hurt-
ing our bank and when you hurt our bank—"

Essie snaps her gum. "How long have you been working?"

"I'm not going to be working if you keep killing the business.
I'm gonna be doing nothing at all."

"You worked the strip down here?"

Shelly's usual beat is the other side of the 10 as far up as Olympic, even up to the 101 where she's probably fooled herself into
thinking there's a better class of customer than down south.

"All I saw was red and blue," Shelly says.

Essie's not a fan of the sweeps. They're not much more than a
shot across the bow. Let everyone know that the LAPD's got their
eyes out.

"So you changed your beat? You worked this stretch?"

"Fuck yeah," Shelly says. "Did two tours."

Essie glances south on Western. She can see straight down
to the R&C Fish Shack. That woman and her dead birds. As if
the hummingbirds were her real problem. What are the chances
that a woman who shows up at the station with three boxes full
of dead birds had a daughter killed in nearly identical fashion to
three victims found off Western in the last eight months?

What are the reasons someone might stop killing? Jail? Illness? Relocation? Injury? Discovery? Did he age out? Did his hormones change? Did he pivot toward another version of sadism or find release in drugs?

Did he find religion? Did he find a different release? Did someone stop him?

Maybe there wasn't a pause. Maybe he took his game elsewhere.

Or maybe it was as simple as Dorian suggested. Maybe he just made a mistake: Lecia Williams. And that stopped him dead. But if that was the case—and if all of this is linked—why is he back?

"Detective Perry?"

Shelly's leaning over the table. There's a tattoo on her left breast: Jose. And on the right, a cross. Essie's staring straight at them but not seeing them because they're blocking the view down to the fish shack, which is where her mind is reaching.

"So I'm asking are you going to keep doing these john sweeps?"

"You know Katherine Sims? Kathy?"

"That's what this shit is about? Those sweeps are because of what happened to Kathy?"

"Those sweeps are because your business is illegal. So you knew Kathy or not?"

"Bitch was crazy. Lived hard, worked hard. That's all I know."

"Did you see her?"

"Hell, I was on R&R. Checked into a hotel in San Pedro. Left my cares behind. Now let me ask you something. Are these sweeps gonna continue?"

"You want me to broadcast it next time?"

Essie can imagine it.

Perry, you tell the ladies we're sweeping?

Perry, you keeping back, or you giving the game away before we move?

The sound of screeching tires can travel two or three blocks. This is why Essie likes to live as far as she can from any of the major crosstown or north-south thoroughfares. Her house is in a cul-de-sac of sorts at the edge of West Adams past Crenshaw, a dirty dead end.

She hears the tires before she sees them—a sustained shriek of rubber skidding on road. Her heart thumps once. She knocks her coffee over.

Shelly jumps back from the table. "Damn it. That shit's hot."

A Honda Civic has just stopped itself from running the red southbound on Western. It's juddered into the crosswalk. Essie can smell the burn from its tires. She swipes the coffee with a napkin, sloshing it over the table.

"Fuck, Detective, you think someone's gonna pull over now that I smell like a latte?"

"I think it's time you punched out," Essie says, standing up, leaving the coffee to drip on its own.

Shelly flicks some droplets from her thighs. "You need to do your roots, Detective."

It's her job to keep women like Shelly alive. To clean the streets. She does the lengthy stakeouts, analyzes the data, maps the crime. Still the women work. The drugs flow. There are big busts, huge sweeps. But the day-to-day is routine.

After the accident, Essie switched to Vice. She half pretended it was her idea. In fact, it was Deb's. Always Deb working behind the scenes, smoothing things out for Essie, greasing the wheels. And look at Deb now, riding high in charge of Robbery/Homicide for all of L.A., while Essie's chasing down hookers in a hooker hotbed. Not exactly high-policing.

Most women in her detail are put out as bait at least once. The official word from the top is that Essie's too short—regardless of the fact that she wasn't too short for patrol, for knocking on doors in Inglewood, for cuffing dealers, for chasing stick-up artists, before she made detective and moved north. The way she sees it short is an asset, making it less likely for anyone (cops included) to think police.

She knows the real reason: They think she's volatile, that after the accident she cracked. That there's no way she can control her emotions. Or if she can, it's because there's something wrong with her. No matter that she passed the psych eval.

She unlocks her bike, shoulders her backpack, and heads to work.

2.

———

THE SHIFT CHANGE IS OVER. ESSIE HEADS FOR HER DESK, A tanker in the way back. She's got a reputation as a number cruncher. Her partner, Rick Spera, often leaves her to do her own thing and only calls her in for big business.

There's a woman waiting in the empty chair across from Essie's. Black. Middle aged. Heavyset. Essie unwraps a piece of gum as she crosses the room.

"Finally," the woman says as Essie takes her seat. "You kept me waiting."

She's got short hair streaked with magenta that's slicked to her head with a sharp side part. There's a spattering of freckles on her nose and double door-knocker earrings in each ear. She's wearing false eyelashes that widen her already enormous eyes.

Essie clinks her keyboard, waking her computer. COMPSTAT and the *L.A. Times*. "I come on at eight."

"Well, other detectives seem to be here before then, but they told me to see you."

The woman is wearing a loose shirt cut like a peasant blouse with a print of leopard and roses. She's messing with the collar, yanking it up over her neck.

"Detective Perry," Essie says, holding out her hand.

"Orphelia Jefferies."

The woman's hand is soft with lotion.

"You new here?"

"A couple of years," Essie says.

"I never seen you before."

Too old to be looking for help getting off the streets. Too sober to be snitching. There's something there though. Some trouble. Some hard living.

Orphelia Jefferies. Essie searches the name.

"Normally they just shove me off on one of the desk sergeants, take my complaint, and send me the fuck on my way. Sometimes they don't even write that shit down. Last time, for instance, the man was double-tasking me. Taking some kind of phone call in one ear and half hearing my story with the other. The hell I bother with this shit for?" She yanks the collar of her shirt. It falls down again, and Essie glimpses a dark discoloration above her clavicle.

Street name Pookie. Solicitation. Possession. Disturbing the peace. All the usual charges. Essie scrolls down Orphelia's sheet. "Is this a job-related complaint?"

"A job-related what?"

Essie keeps scrolling. The rap sheet ends abruptly. "For instance—did someone rough you up? Did someone steal your turf? Did someone—"

Orphelia holds up her hand, jabbing it toward Essie like she's slamming a busted vending machine. "Who the fuck they send me to?"

Essie looks up from the monitor. Orphelia's blouse is drooping again, showing a raised scar—a jack-o'-lantern smile.

"Sorry?"

"What kinda cop are you?"

"Vice."

"Shit." Orphelia shakes her head side to side. "Let me ask you this. What's my complaint have to do with Vice?"

Essie's about to reply when she glances back at the monitor. Sixteen years ago. The last charge for solicitation. "You're out of the game," she says. See a puzzle. Not a complicated one. A former hooker. Cleaned up for whatever reason.

"Fuck yeah I'm out of the game. You need me to show you some kinda chip like they get in AA? Show you how many years I got?" She cocks her head to one side. "And what I used to do has to do with this I don't know. I should have known the only detective they'd let me see is a Vice cop." Orphelia crosses her arms over her chest, giving Essie a good view of her scar. "I don't ask you how come you have such a white lady name, do I, Detective *Perry*? Who I was has nothing to do with where I am now."

Everything has something to do with something else, Essie thinks. The reason she's in Vice is the reason she left Homicide is the reason she doesn't drive. "What happened to your chest?" It's the reason Orphelia gave up the game that interests her now.

"Got cut."

"When?"

"Fifteen years back, give or take."

Essie checks the rap sheet still open on her desktop. There's a moment you can pinpoint. An event that changes everything. What made you start killing? Start hooking? What made you decide to stay indoors for good? Made you switch jobs? Get off the streets? Get on the streets? Start stealing? Get help? Go to rehab? Stop driving? Stop communicating?

She pushes back from her computer so it's no longer between her and Orphelia. She takes a pen and a pad from her drawer. "So?"

"What do you mean, so?"

"Tell me why you've been waiting for me."

Orphelia rolls her neck, stretching her scar wide. "So now you want to hear my story?"

Essie clicks her pen. "When did I say I didn't?" She looks over her shoulder into the squad room. A few patrol officers and a couple of detectives have their eyes on her. She knows the look— they've played a prank and want to see the outcome.

"Shit," Orphelia says as if that settles it. "Listen, I've been telling this damn story for years. How many goddamn times now?" She counts out on her fingers. "It doesn't matter."

Essie chews her gum hard, trying to stay with this, trying not to let Orphelia's scar drag her mind elsewhere.

She guesses this is a parallel problem like Dorian's, a distraction from the real issue. Figuring out who's killing birds, stop worrying who killed your kid.

She snaps her gum. That's another question, another problem. But one she can't shake.

"You listening at all?" Orphelia's popped her eyes wide to let Essie know she's wandered off.

"Go on."

"Like I said—like I just said to you and to every goddamned motherfucker in this place one time or another—I'm being stalked."

"Do you know him?"

"Now I know you're not even pretending. Do I know him? Lady, there's no him. I just told you it's a woman."

"All right," Essie says, scribbling something on the paper to keep Orphelia talking, "a woman."

"You don't think that's a little fucked up?"

Essie clicks her pen twice. Snaps her gum. "Should I?"

"I don't know," Orphelia says. "Should you? You're the cop around here, not me. You're the one who's all into clues and patterns. Maybe it's normal that some white lady's spying on me. Been spying on me for years."

"Let me ask you something. Do you know Katherine Sims? Kathy Sims?"

Orphelia's eyes widen. "Kathy? That's a nice white-lady name. Is that her?"

"Excuse me?"

"Is that the woman you think is stalking me?"

Essie bites her lip at her own mistake. Her mind had run off on its own. Orphelia can't follow. Hell, Essie's even having trouble keeping up with herself. "No. Someone else. Not white."

"Don't know her. Should I?"

"I just thought," Essie begins.

"Thought because she's a hooker that I'd know her. Like we are all in our own special clique."

"I didn't say she was one thing or another."

Orphelia folds her arms over her chest. "Didn't have to. Now can we get back on my business?"

Essie snaps her gum and clicks her pen twice. "What's she look like, the woman stalking you?"

"White."

"That's it?"

"She doesn't let me see her. I mean up close. Like features and all that. If she did, we wouldn't have a motherfucking problem, because I'd be all over that. Thing is, she's sneaky. I've been telling you all this for years."

"What does she do?" Essie asks.

"What does she do? What do you think? She watches me."

"How long?"

"All night. All motherfucking night. Listen." Orphelia presses her hands onto the desktop. Essie can see the tension in her fingers. "I know you all thinking I'm crazy. There's no white woman hoofing down to Sixty-Fifth to stand across from my goddamned apartment."

"I mean how long has it been going on?"

"Like timewise?"

"Timewise, exactly."

Orphelia closes her eyes like she's counting back the years. But Essie's certain she knows the number without thinking. "Fifteen years."

"You're not going to tell me what happened to your throat?" Essie asks.

"I said I got cut."

"By who?"

"Unsolved motherfucking crime. Open case. You tell me."

It's barely a math problem. The cut. The decision to give up the game. The idea someone was or is stalking her. Trauma revisits in the strangest ways. The mind plays tricks. An attempted murder can return in the form of a white-lady stalker. Easier than focusing on the real danger.

Clue: *Corn Killer.* Answer: Nightstalker.

"It's not like it's every night," Orphelia's saying. "Or not like it's all night when she shows. It's just sometimes. But that's bad-e-fucking-nough. How'd you like to open your eyes and see someone across the street staring into your window?"

"How do you know that's what she's doing?"

"Because I know, I know. I've had years of knowing. Didn't you just ask me how many years this has been going on? You all keep records? Look at them. Or maybe you just write down my complaint and throw it out."

"But you are sure she's watching you?" Essie asks.

"Listen, I'm motherfucking sure. She's keeping tabs on me and don't I know it. It's not just outside my own house. She knows my routine, my goddamn schedule. Go to the store, get some smokes or whatever the fuck. I see her ass passing by the front door. Take myself out for a drink, and who the fuck is parked in the lot behind the bar."

Essie opens her mouth but Orphelia beats her to it.

"It's the same goddamned woman. Boring-white-lady type of lady. Stands out on that part of Western, let me tell you."

"So what brought you here today?"

Orphelia sits back in her chair and crosses her arms over her chest, accidentally pulling her blouse low and revealing her scar. "I thought you'd never ask." She adjusts her shirt and resettles herself.

Essie spits out her gum. Her eyes drift to her monitor. There's a browser window dragged nearly off-screen she didn't notice earlier. *SoCal Birding.* Those hummingbirds.

"Detective Perry? You want to hear this shit or not?"

Essie fumbles for her pack of gum.

"I don't need to be a motherfucking mind reader to know this shit isn't going to make an impression on you, but here I go letting you know anyway." She waits until Essie looks up. "Reason I'm here today is this lady is keeping tabs on me. I can prove it."

Tap. Tap. Essie waits for her to continue.

"So I got a job. A real one. Finally. Can't do a lot thanks to you all giving me enough felonies the city and whoever else won't hire me. But anyway, I cook the meals at a church way the hell down in Inglewood. Two meals a day. And a uniform. So I'm proud. And first day at work, there the hell she is, just passing by like nothing."

"And you're sure—"

Again Orphelia holds up her hand, stopping Essie. "You're gonna ask me how I know it's her when I don't know exactly what she looks like, right? Because I can't draw a goddamn picture of her?"

Essie clicks her pen. How to turn the story back to what's important?

"Maybe I couldn't pick her out of a lineup. I know what she's like. Sneaky. Smart. Keeps her distance. She's like a motherfucking ghost, haunting me. Let me ask you something. You think you could pick a ghost out of a lineup?"

Clue: *Dead Man Walking.* Answer: Ghost.

"No," Essie says. "I don't believe in ghosts."

"I'm not asking you what you believe. What I want to know is what you are going to do. You going to send some patrols down? Sweep my block of Western, scare her off? Because I'm not going through my days with this lady on my back. You know what it's like to wake up in the middle of the night and there's something watching you? Get a bottle of booze and someone just passes by? Start a job and she knows? You know what it's like you all thinking I'm crazy?" She shakes her head. "'Course you don't know what it's like people thinking you're crazy. You're a cop. People think you're the opposite of crazy."

"You'd be surprised," Essie says.

This brings Orphelia up short, breaks her rhythm. She raises her eyebrows and waits for Essie to say more.

But Essie's said enough. She glances around the station. She knows what her fellow officers think, or at least some of them— that she must be at least partly gone after seeing those two girls tossed across the street in separate directions like they were shot from different cannons. Both of them dead, one north-south on Plymouth, the other lying east-west on Sixth. That must have cracked her. At least partially. And those who believe it didn't make her nuts think she's crazy for not having been affected— that there must have been something wrong with her from the start. Too much emotion or too little. Either way, can't win.

"So are you crazy, Detective Perry?"

"I don't think so," Essie says.

"But what matters is what other people think."

"If you let it."

Orphelia points a finger at her. "That's, what-do-you-call-it, privilege right there."

Funny, a black woman telling a Latina cop about privilege.

Essie has no interest in sharing her struggle. She is where she is, that's all that matters. "So," she says, "tell me your address."

"For real?"

"I can't have someone check it out if I don't know where you live."

Orphelia gives her an address ten blocks south on Western. Then she gives Essie a look like Essie might have sold her a bum product. "You sending someone for real? You're taking me serious?"

"I listened to your story, didn't I?"

She can see it now.

Perry, you really sent patrol down Western because some ex-hooker thinks a white lady's stalking her?

Perry, you think this is the way to use departmental time?

Perry, I got a bridge. You got the cash?

Essie sticks out her hand. "I'll take a look." She can feel her mind peeling back to the story on NPR that morning. The activist from Power Through Protest who'd been hiding something. A puzzle that won't let Essie rest. What was her name? What was she up to? Something, Essie's sure. There's some reason she agreed to be on the show, some reason she lied about her location, opened herself up to exposure.

She wheels around so she's facing her monitor. She calls up the website for *Morning Edition*, finds the story. She reads the transcript.

When she looks up, Orphelia is gone.

She clicks through, finds the woman's name. Morgan Tillett. She gets several social media hits and a few newspaper interviews. Essie scrolls through two different social media sites, her mind logging *likes* and *loves* and recent comments. A few names pop out. She cross-references these, looking for people who might live near elevated trains. Finds one: a Chris Jackson in Brooklyn, active in the Gowanus Superfund Site near the aboveground F train.

Doesn't have a girlfriend it seems. Liked two of Morgan's last posts. Looks like they also overlapped in Seattle last spring.

Essie clicks back to Morgan Tillett. Engaged.

The lie. Brooklyn not Los Angeles. Tomorrow she will have forgotten Morgan Tillett's and Chris Jackson's names.

Everyone's hiding something. Her. Orphelia. Half the squad room lies on a regular basis—small, seemingly immaterial things. Pointless fibs. Easy to disprove, which Essie does in a few clicks on the computer, then immediately disregards. Just another puzzle to be solved and put aside.

3.

———

A CATHOLIC GIRLS' SCHOOL AT RECESS. ESSIE TIMES HER lunch break to coincide with the bell that sends the kids outdoors to the grubby playground that she worries is too close to the street. This is her therapy. Better than the mandatory sessions with the counselor ordered by her old captain—the sessions that insist she either had too much empathy or too little.

They assign you to one pole or the other and tear you down. Faking the psych eval was easy. Like everything else: a puzzle with a solution. A game. Pay attention and you'll learn exactly what they want to hear.

The girls wear uniforms, maroon skirts, white polos, blue sweaters. The materials are cheap and pill easily. The younger ones fly down the steps into the playground, racing toward the climbing structures. The upperclassmen take their time, sauntering and performing for one another.

It took a week for Essie to determine the hierarchy—who ruled the roost, who was trying to climb. A couple of overheard conversations gave her enough information that a mindlessly executed social media search—fake names notwithstanding—told her who had a boyfriend from the brother school a few blocks away and which girls were getting involved in stuff out of their league, the kind of stuff that might bring them across Essie's desk in a few years if they're not careful. None of this matters to her. She forgets half of it less than five hours after she uncovers it.

She watches the climbing structure, where the twelve-year-old girls are swinging wildly, daring each other to backflip and catapult from the rungs to the concrete. As they fly through the air—a moment that always seems to occur in slow motion, as if there's a possibility of stopping it, rewinding, pulling back—Essie's nerves spark, a prickle like she's licked a battery that radiates from her stomach to her extremities in anticipation of impact. Boom. They land. A buckle of knees. A moment of silence.

Essie's breath catches.

Then a cheer.

And over again.

As a teenager, Essie was in the hospital when her older sister went into premature labor and Essie watched the complications pile up—internal bleeding, cardiac arrest. She stood by as the doctors held up Gladys's organs, checking them like bruised produce, to see which one was to blame, before tucking them back into place. They sewed Gladys up. She healed. It had given Essie the false sense of security in practical resolutions.

A decade and a half on the force and the human body isn't the kind of puzzle Essie likes. It doesn't have obvious solutions or even solutions at all. From a distance, it looks easy to reassemble. The neck crooked at a horrible angle? Gently put it back. Untwist, realign. Straighten what was bent. Undo the damage.

There's a girl on top of the climbing structure. She stands, balancing on two thin rungs of the jungle gym. She wobbles, pinwheeling her arms to stay upright. The game is to execute the most elaborate jump—the most daring—with a flip or a twist or a straddle or a kick.

The girl is bending her knees deep. She's going to push off hard and soar. Essie watches her close her eyes like she's going to fly blind. The electric jolt hits her stomach again, the anticipation of impact, of a collision and an aftermath that won't have a solution.

She holds her breath.

Her phone rings—her partner's ringtone.

The girl flies. Backward.

Clue: Overstate. Answer: Fly.

It's not the girl on the jungle gym who soars through the air, but the other on Plymouth, the one who flew south, with a grace that seems unlikely in death.

As always, time slows before landing, making room for an avalanche of thoughts.

There's a meeting at two P.M., a task force on human trafficking in Los Angeles that overlaps with Essie's beat. She wants to sit in. Get more intel on what's behind the scene on the streets.

Three days ago on Jefferson, just off Arlington, she answered a call about a message graffitied on a low wall outside the small library. *My name is Jessina Rivera and I'm being held against my will here in Los Angeles. I come from Honduras. Please someone help me.*

The English was good. Too good, Essie thought. But you don't want to write the real thing off as a prank.

She takes the call. "Perry."

The girl lands. Her waist bends. Her chest hits her knees. She sprawls forward.

"Essie, it's Spera."

This formal exchange of names after two years of working together.

"I'm late," Essie says.

The girl lies on the ground for a moment, not moving.

"Not yet," Spera says. He's smoking but hiding it. Essie can tell by how he's not talking into the microphone.

Essie is aware of Spera talking. But the girl hasn't moved.

She hadn't been thinking when she got out of the car on

Plymouth. She'd touched the first body imagining she could just put it back the way it was, no sharp angles, bones all in their proper places.

In a daze the girl gets up and staggers to her friends. She high-fives them.

"You got the address, Perry? You want to repeat it to me?"

It's how Spera keeps her in check. *Repeat it to me.*

"You wandered off before I began, didn't you?"

Essie turns her back to the playground. "One more time," she says.

"Western at Thirty-Eighth," Spera says. "Twentysomething female. They say she might have been our beat."

Our beat. Spera is too well trained, too fresh, to use the old code NHI—no human involved.

"Dead?"

"Didn't I just say that?"

"Not when I was listening."

"Dead."

"Shouldn't this be on Homicide?" Essie knows better than to step on another unit's toes. Although that's exactly what she was doing when she paid that call to Julianna about Kathy. When she brought Kathy up with Shelly and Orphelia.

"They want you down there," Spera says. "I'm on my way."

"They trust me to see a dead body?" Essie asks.

"How's that?"

She lets Spera's question hang and disconnects.

4.

———

THERE'S MORE TO MORGAN TILLETT'S STORY. IT HITS ESSIE AS she bikes down St. Andrews—safer on the side streets—to Thirty-Eighth. Something about the affair solve doesn't sit right. Search for the simple answer, but don't get tricked by the easy one. She called in to the show. Why draw fire? Did she want to be discovered? Was she confident she wouldn't be? There's a game here.

She fumbles for her phone in her pocket. She's about to pull over to the sidewalk, checking databases and travel logs, when Spera's name starts flashing on the screen. Essie tucks the phone away and rides faster.

She turns on Thirty-Eighth. She can see the yellow tape from the end of the block, cordoning off a vacant lot where a bungalow burned a few years back.

A handful of cops are keeping back the locals. The detectives from Southwest are standing around like a still from a TV procedural.

Essie unwraps a piece of gum.

She has a feeling about what she's about to see before she gets there—the fourth in the series of dead women discarded off Western. At the station they've been calling them prostitutes, but there's more to it than that. Some of them are adjacent to the life. Cocktail waitresses, B-girls, as well as streetwalkers. They are linked more closely by location than occupation.

She hadn't seen Katherine Sims's body in person, nor the two that came before that. Homicide had only shown her photos after the fact in case she knew the women, their beat, their clients.

Serial? she'd asked.

Probably not. Just bad luck. Come in threes.

It's serial, Essie had said.

Or three different dissatisfied customers had been Homicide's rationalization.

And that had been the end of it.

At the tape a bald man named Bourke from Homicide hands her a card—her card. "Friend of yours," he says, jerking his head toward the body. "Spera said he booked her the other day. Not sure why she had your card."

Essie ducks under the tape. The detectives tower over her as she peers at the body.

Throat slit. Bag over her head.

This one's not dressed for the stroll or the club. In fact, it looks more like she was dressed for a night in, in shorts and an oversized Lakers hoodie.

"Julianna," Essie says.

"One of your girls?" Bourke asks, like she owns the prostitutes on Western. Like they are people who require ownership.

"Just a contact from the Fast Rabbit. Around the life, not exactly in it." She squats down.

"*Around the life,*" Bourke says, like it's a black-white issue and Essie is complicating things. "The card was in her pocket." He points at the pouch of the sweatshirt where the waterfall of blood from Julianna's neck stopped.

Her orange hair has tumbled out of the bottom of the plastic bag. Some of her curls are matted and clumped in her blood, others are fanned over the weeds and dirt. Her eyes are closed, face turned to the side, like she's looking away from this crap, like she's through.

There's no putting her back together. There's no solution. There isn't even a puzzle.

"I booked her the other day," Spera says. "After a raid on Miss Crystal's on Crenshaw."

Essie takes a glove from one of the techs and puts it on. She reaches out and wraps her hand around Julianna's foot. Her toes are stiff. Through the latex they feel like dried clay.

"She was juiced up on something," Spera continues. "I didn't figure her for a street girl. Too clean. Guess it didn't really matter how she worked. It's all connected, right?"

"It's all something," Bourke says.

There's an eruption overhead, an explosion of birdsong. Essie looks up and sees a flock of green parrots swarm into a nearby palm tree. Their color is a shock. Like the hummingbirds in Dorian's boxes.

Why are people always asking the wrong questions? Who killed the birds? Was she a street girl, a stripper, or a taxi dancer? Just take Dorian and those boxes of birds—all of them nestled in cotton balls like their death was somehow better for it. It doesn't take a genius to figure out why she saves them.

It had only taken a few minutes on the computer to figure out who Dorian was. And a few more to realize that her daughter's death matched the deaths of the three women found just off Western in the last eight months. Two things interested Essie. The murders had stopped after Lecia's, and a name she came across in her quick scan of the file: Julianna Vargas, last person to see Lecia alive. The same Julianna who had been swept up in the raid at Miss Crystal's. The same Julianna who'd been sitting at Spera's desk, half sassy, half worn when Essie was talking to Dorian. The same Julianna whose foot is now in her hand, rigid and clammy against the latex.

After she'd put two and two together, Essie had visited the address on Julianna's booking sheet and her roommate, a woman named Coco on the wrong side of an all-nighter, told her that Julianna had fucked off, pissed about that "street bitch Kathy's death."

A circle. Drawn neat. Dorian—Julianna—Kathy and now back to Julianna.

"It's serial now," Essie says.

There's no response from Bourke or his partner, Mattis.

"It's serial," Essie repeats.

Bourke turns. "How's that?"

"This is number four. When Katherine Sims was murdered, Kenter and Polk showed me two similar vics from a few months back."

"You're not Homicide, Perry," Bourke says.

"I was."

"I don't need your guessing games."

"I'm right," Essie says. "And you know it." She can hear it in his voice. She's not sure whether she broke the news or confirmed it. "The two last year. Then Katherine Sims and now Julianna. You know, don't you."

"Don't work me," Bourke says.

"This is number four," Essie repeats. "Maybe even number seventeen."

"Seventeen?" Bourke's face relaxes. She knows the look. Essie's not ahead of him. She's off the reservation. He doesn't have to worry about her. He doesn't even have to listen to her. "I must have been asleep on the job to have missed all those bodies. Mattis, you seen seventeen of these?" He edges his toes toward Julianna.

"Do you know who this is?" Essie asks, pointing at the ground.

"Julianna Vargas," Bourke says.

But nothing beyond that, Essie thinks. No idea that this woman was the girl Lecia Williams had been babysitting the night she was murdered the same way. No idea that soon too many coincidences are going to yield a pattern.

"She had your card. Why?" Bourke asks.

Essie looks up, snaps her gum. One of the Homicide guys is looming over her. If they can't see it, she's not going to give it to them yet. "She worked the Fast Rabbit," Essie says. "I was hoping she'd keep me up to date on their back rooms. Or you guys still pretending it's just a nice little dance club?"

"You know her address?" Bourke asks.

Spera's like a puppy bounding back with a ball. "It's on the booking sheet."

"She doesn't live there anymore," Essie says. "She's with her folks."

"You want to do the honors? You got that compassion thing down." Bourke sounds like he's doing her a favor, but he's needling.

Essie turns her back to the crime scene. Over her shoulder she can hear Bourke and Mattis laughing. *Seventeen.*

After the accident there had been no need to notify. The girls had been playing outside their house. The impact—Essie can't think about the sound—brought their parents out. There had been no need for the long approach to the door, the death march during which you can't help thinking that until you knock, whoever answers' kin is still alive, that things remain suspended in time.

Out on Plymouth was a different story.

No sense that you held someone else's fate in your fist as you raised it to the door.

Anyway, who the hell lets kids play hopscotch at midnight on the sidewalk in Hancock Park?

5.

_____

IT'S THREE P.M. ESSIE GIVES IT UNTIL THE EVENING NEWS AT
best before the word *serial* goes wide. No matter how hard Bourke
shut her down, he knew she was right. And it didn't matter that
she was right—it's his case, his story to tell, him and Deb, the head
of RHD, side by side. All that matters now is once *serial* is uttered
by a cop, a neighbor, an activist, a relative, it's going to spread like
the wildfire on the hills.

She knows why the department resists the word—the horror
and excitement it summons from the public. The crackpots. The
tips, the theories. The press conferences. The psychics. The talk
shows. The candy-colored news programs, all cartoon outrage
and glossy drama. All the things that distract from the business of
police work. The tabloid horror on a constant loop.

She also knows what the word does to the department, how it
changes the detectives, the way it raises their hackles, draws out
their insecurities and frustrations. Because someone is operating
on their turf—someone blatantly and brutally breaking the law,
but even worse, someone who is one, two, or even more steps
ahead, flaunting his trespasses, taunting the force, maybe even
leaving clues, convinced that they won't find him. It becomes a

behind-the-scenes pissing contest of deduction and wits. And soon the team assigned to the case will have created their foe in their image, made him into their intellectual equal, a mastermind. Because how else could he be eluding them?

Criminals often escape notice not because they're smart, but because they're too dumb or too damaged to worry. It's not about being clever, it's about being numb.

But now it's undeniable. Four women. Two of them found several days apart. More similarities than differences. Serial for sure.

Essie wheels her bike away. She passes the usual crowd of onlookers, wide eyed, excited, hoping to see something, busy making this tragedy into their own story.

There will be meetings tonight. A task force.

Rules will be set. Parameters. Decisions will be made about how much or how little to give to the media. And regardless of that more will be leaked and more will be invented.

Serial is a cottage industry.

Essie figures after this last victim, they'll bring in the profilers and the geoprofilers and the genetic profilers, who will paint a complex picture of an average person. Possibly below average. Just some guy. You wouldn't recognize him. Wouldn't notice him. Not in a crowd. Not sitting on his own porch.

She gets on her bike and pushes off, skirting a bump in the road where a tree root has pushed through the asphalt. She wobbles wide into the street before finding her balance.

Morgan Tillett. Now Essie realizes what she might have missed when she scrolled through the activist's social media. She was looking for the salacious story. The out-of-town affair.

She didn't check the feeds of Morgan's other local Los Angeles friends, other activists. She only looked for a possible outlier. A mistake.

Essie turns right onto Cimarron and collides with someone. Her bike bucks, throwing her on the handlebars.

The moment after a crash seems to exist outside the conventions of space and time—stretching out slow and wide, like a black hole drawing everything inward, containing everything at once. A dead zone, unreachable by the past and the present—an atomic aftermath, a flat sonic ring.

For a moment, she's too stunned to see. Her heart races. Her mind is white, then black. Then there are two girls, one landing east-west, the other north-south.

"Detective Perry?"

Essie opens her eyes, or were they already open?

"Detective Perry?"

A woman has her by the arm. Her face is close to Essie's. Too close.

"Are you all right?"

The corner of Cimarron and Thirty-Eighth. Leaving a crime scene. On her way to notify.

She knows this woman. White. Sixties. No makeup. Frizzy gray bob.

Dorian Williams.

"I'm fine," Essie says. "I hit you?"

"Knocked," Dorian says. "Slightly." Dorian looks over Essie's shoulder toward the crime scene. "Who is it?"

There's a look on Dorian's face that Essie doesn't like. It's the look the mother wore when she flew down Plymouth, past the jackknifed car to reach her daughters.

This isn't Dorian's tragedy.

Essie's not going to give it to her.

"I'm not at liberty to say. The investigation is ongoing." Press conference nonsense. A cut-and-paste brush-off.

"But—" Dorian begins.

There are no *buts*. She'll find out in time. There's no need for her to know immediately.

"Any more dead birds?" Essie asks.

"What?"

"The hummingbirds," Essie says. "Any more?"

Dorian doesn't reply. She's already pushing past Essie toward the crime scene.

FIVE MINUTES LATER Essie's up on Twenty-Ninth Place, bike locked, the chipped gate to Julianna's house behind her. She faces the short set of stairs. They were painted red a long time ago. *I'm a police officer.* That's what she had said to the parents as they ran past her and the sputtering car to their kids.

I'm a police officer. She said it twice as the mother took the girl on the north-south street and the father, the one lying east-west.

As if it would make a difference.

You take a deep breath. You put your mind elsewhere. It's just a job to be done. Just words to be said. There are around three hundred homicides a year in Los Angeles. This is just business.

She unwraps a piece of gum.

The door is opened by a sturdy woman in jeans and a PORTS O'CALL, SAN PEDRO T-shirt. She's wearing slippers. She has half a foot on Essie.

"Yes?"

Her voice is deep and nasal.

I'm a police officer. The words don't change anything. They don't soften blows or bring back the dead. They don't rewind time.

Essie pulls out her badge.

The woman tilts her head to one side. She's been here before. She's opened this door to cops and detectives. People looking for her daughter and possibly her husband.

"Yes?"

The moment before Essie speaks flattens out. Until she opens her mouth, her presence is just an inconvenience, a nuisance, another cop turning up with another problem about another family member.

"Mrs. Vargas? Alva Vargas?"

"Yes."

Julianna's mother sounds impatient.

"I'm an officer at Southwest," Essie says. "You're the mother of Julianna Vargas."

Behind Alva, Essie can see Armando sitting on the couch. The same place he was last time she was here.

Someone is watering the plants next door just like last time, with a spray that reaches into the street.

Alva turns toward the spray. The hose stops and a woman steps out from behind a bush. She's thin and white with a narrow face and pale hair, blond fading to gray.

"Are you coming inside, Detective?"

The riot gate bangs behind Essie. She checks over her shoulder. She can see the woman next door hosing the square of pavement between her house and Julianna's.

This moment has already gone on too long. It's like she's playing a trick on Julianna's parents.

"Mrs. Vargas," Essie says.

"I'm a police officer." *That has nothing to do with what I'm about to say. It just means I'm speaking from a place of authority. I can't undo what was done.* "I regret that I have to inform you that your daughter's body was found earlier today. It appears that she was murdered. I know this is a lot to take in right now. I can call a car to take you to the medical examiner's office so you can make the identification."

If you're there at the scene of your child's death, there's no gray area. No questions. No time when a chance remains that things could be otherwise, that someone made a mistake. That the body in question isn't your child's. There's no drawn-out ride to the morgue or the M.E.'s office. No time for a final round of denial.

I'm a police officer. It was an accident. Essie hadn't been able to stop talking. For a full minute the only sound at the intersection of Plymouth and Sixth had been her voice and the hiss of her car's engine or radiator or whatever was smoking in the aftermath of the collision. She had looked over at Mark, sitting in the car, eyes wide, fixed on nothing, hands rigid on the wheel. Stunned. She'd kept talking and talking, filling the silence until the mother's screams drowned her out. Mark didn't move.

Essie's first mistake was trying to explain away the accident.

Her second was calling Deb.

"Or you can drive yourselves," Essie says.

Alva hasn't taken her eyes off Essie, scrutinizing her like she's trying to catch her in a lie. "Julianna? You're sure it's Julianna?"

"I'm sorry," Essie says.

Alva shakes her head. "I don't believe you."

Twenty to thirty minutes to get to the M.E.'s office. Then maybe another ten to get to the morgue to make the ID. Essie figures Alva has forty minutes max to keep her delusion.

"I understand," Essie says.

Armando hasn't moved from the couch. He's settled back, arms crossed over his chest.

"What makes you sure it's Julianna?" Alva asks.

"The victim was wearing an oversized Lakers sweatshirt and faded shorts. She has curly dyed orange hair."

Alva shrugs. "Could be anyone."

"All right," Essie says. So easy not to believe. "Will you be driving to the station?"

Alva looks at her husband. "You go," he says. "I don't need proof it's Julianna. If that's what the lady detective says, I'll save myself the trip."

Essie pulls out her phone and calls for a cruiser.

"You're not going to tell my wife you were here the other day, already asking questions?" Armando says.

"Detective?" Alva asks.

"Questioning Julianna about some *puta* got killed last week. Lots of questions, no answers."

"Detective?" Alva repeats.

"I was here about Kathy Sims," Essie says.

"You knew she was in trouble?" Alva asks.

See. Alva knows. In her heart she knows. She's accepted it's her daughter. She's just tricking herself into believing otherwise as long as she can.

"You knew and you did nothing?"

"Kathy was a straight-up dirty *puta*," Armando says.

Essie checks her phone. Less than a minute since she called for the squad car. Until it arrives she's going to be shouldering the blame. She's the killer, the bearer of bad news, the one who didn't protect Julianna. The one who didn't clean up the streets.

Alva steps up to Essie and looms over her. "You allowed someone to kill my little girl?"

Stripper. Possibly a sex worker. Drugs. Men. The Fast Rabbit. Sam's Hofbräu. Miss Crystal's. A rap sheet that was a work in progress. And it's Essie's fault.

Armando snorts. "Sounds like you're certain it's Julianna, Mami," he says.

Alva turns, storms in his direction fist raised.

Essie grabs her from behind, pulling her away from him.

"It's LAPD let my little girl get murdered," Armando says. "No reason to be beating on me."

6.

———

THE LINK IS THERE. ESSIE'S NOT SURE WHAT IT MEANS BUT still she sees it. Julianna Vargas was the last person to see Lecia Williams alive and now she's been murdered in the same way. Bourke and his team haven't made the connection to the past murders yet. They're too wrapped up in the present—too eager for a neat solution. They don't want a seventeen-body problem.

What do you do with information? What do you do about certainty? Both are easily stolen and easily corrupted. Release the information the wrong way to the wrong people and it will be distorted, destroyed, misused, or abused. People might co-opt it, making your discovery into their find and cutting you out. Or it could be stashed and shelved for good. Purposefully forgotten.

Break the news poorly and you can be called off the case, made to feel crazy. No matter how certain you are.

Essie's certain. And she doesn't want to lose that.

Which is why she heads straight from the Vargas residence to Robbery/Homicide headquarters downtown, where Deb runs the show.

After the accident, Deb went to bat for Essie, or so Essie thought. She had her back, told everyone that Essie was good, a solid cop, not cracked, still dependable. Little did Essie know she didn't matter at all to Deb. Deb was proving herself. Showing that she was one of the guys, that her blood was blue, that she'd go to the mat for a fellow officer.

Deb said she'd been doing Essie a favor.

Funny favor.

Her star rose. Essie's stuck in Vice in fucking Southwest.

There's commotion and news crews. The word *serial* has already leaked. She'll be lucky to catch Deb.

She's surprised when Deb opens her own office door. She's in uniform and it takes Essie a moment to realize why. There's going to be a press conference. The case is officially serial now. Deb's on prime time.

"Perry," Deb says, shaking her hand.

Partners for five years and Essie gets a formal handshake.

For a while after the accident, after Essie's extended leave of absence while things were being settled, and after she'd stepped down to Vice, she and Deb met for drinks. Once a week, then once a month. Then Deb got promoted. And then again. Soon they were in different orbits.

Deb's hair is perfect. Naturally blond, unlike Essie's. "What a surprise," Deb says. She smooths the front of her immaculate uniform. "Bad timing. Serial, I'm sure you've heard."

"It's my beat," Essie reminds her. She can feel Deb's need to keep this conversation at the threshold. Deb has places to be and needs to keep moving, fearful of getting bogged down by whatever it is Essie's come all this way to tell her. "This is important." She pushes past her old partner into her office.

On a wall is a framed photo of the two of them from when they were partners, a profile in the *L.A. Times* about Hollywood Station's real Cagney and Lacey. Real go-getters. Except now only one of them is.

They used to be so casual with each other, drinking out of

each other's cup, sharing sandwiches, trading makeup. Feet up on their desk, papers and possessions commingling. Now they barely touch.

Deb steps back into her office but doesn't shut the door. "Is this about the serial? Those women were on your beat? You knew them? You want in?"

Efficient. Presenting all the possible answers up front so all Essie has to do is choose.

"I don't want in," she says. Even if she did, she wouldn't get it. Not now. Not even with what she knows. Not even though, as she sees it, she's already in.

"Listen, Perry, I don't have a lot of time. There's five local news crews waiting. Maybe we can grab a drink."

"You're going to be too busy for a drink," Essie says.

"Not after we catch him."

"Confident," Essie says. "Good." Except she knows it's all bluster.

"So what's this visit about, if not the case? I know how you feel about coincidence. Dead women on your patrol about to hit the news. And here you are."

"Listen," Essie says, "remember that spate of killings on Western back when we were in Hollywood? Prostitutes mainly, but also others. All women."

"Yes," Deb says.

"There were protests that LAPD wasn't taking them seriously. A lot of outrage."

"Yes, yes. That's not going to happen if that's what you're worried about. We've got a task force. We are going to make sure that this is handled correctly and publicly. All hands on deck." Deb pats her hair. Runs a finger under each eye.

"You look perfect," Essie says.

She goes on, "Back then the serial killer was never named. The case was hardly publicized."

"Yes," Deb says. "We have this covered. Don't worry."

Essie's tempted to pull out her phone. Distract herself. "I'm not. I'm wondering about those women back then."

"And what about those women?"

Essie unwraps a piece of gum. She needs to stay with this. "Don't you think it's strange that someone just stopped killing them? No real investigation. But the killings stopped?"

"Perry. We have an active serial killer case now. Do you really think this is the right moment to be warming up a case, what, two decades cold?"

"Fifteen years."

"Whatever."

"You see, I found something interesting. A link to the old cases."

"You what—? You're Vice."

"Do you know who your latest vic is?"

Deb exhales. Essie knows she wants to roll her eyes. Instead she holds the door open. "I'm going to make time for that drink. You need to get out more. I know how your mind works. Circles. Patterns."

Essie holds up her hand. "It's the same guy."

"Same as who?"

"Whoever it is you're planning to bring in so quickly with your task force."

Deb steps back into the office and closes the door behind her. "Perry," she says, "I'm going to warn you once. Don't poke your nose into this case. Don't complicate things. Don't overstep."

Essie pulls out her phone, finds a news article about Lecia Williams's death. She zooms in on the detail about the last place she'd been seen alive, babysitting for a girl in Jefferson Park. "That," she says, "was Julianna Vargas."

Deb squints at the phone. "I don't have time for this," she says. "I'm about to go downstairs and announce to the press we have an active serial killer who has killed four women. If you think I'm going to tie this up with some old case that had hundreds of women from South L.A. picketing Parker Center, you are crazier than I thought."

"And why would you ever think I was crazy?"

Deb inhales sharply. "You know."

"I don't."

"Because of what happened."

"And what happened?"

Deb exhales, rearranges her face diplomatically. "Listen, Perry. Solving a whole bunch of cold cases isn't going to fix anything."

Essie snaps her gum. "What needs fixing?" Her mind wants to fly. It wants to race back to Plymouth when Deb appeared and started managing everything. Mismanaging it. Making it into her scene. Her case. Working Essie and Essie didn't even know.

Deb adjusts her lapels. "I know what you're trying to do here."

Her old partner is working her. "I'm not trying to do anything but my job," Essie says. She finds a picture of Lecia Williams on her phone. "You don't think she deserves your attention?"

"Not now I don't," Deb says. "This woman was killed fifteen years ago."

"There's a connection. I can see it."

Deb takes a deep breath. "I know you're not going to give this up."

Essie opens her mouth to reply, but Deb cuts her off. "But there's one thing I'm not going to let you do. I'm not going to let you make another mess I have to clean up. You're lucky to have your job."

"Lucky?" Essie says, holding her former partner's eye.

"I understand that watching those two girls die—" Deb stops and clears her throat for effect. "I mean, I understand how killing those girls might deform the way you see things. But this is a reach. And it's a reach way out of your reach."

"The way I see things?"

"I've got a million questions waiting for me downstairs." Deb turns the handle and opens the door wide. "I know you. Your mind is going to keep turning, looking for connections that will help you make sense of the world. There's nothing I can do to stop you. So go on. Be my guest." She stands aside, letting Essie pass.

Essie walks halfway down the hall, then lets Deb go on ahead.

The way you see things. Deb's words ring in her head. *The way you see things*. As if Essie's view, her way of seeing, had been changed after the accident. As if that made her see things differently or any which way at all.

7.

SOUTHWEST IS BUZZING WHEN ESSIE GETS BACK. A FEW NEWS vans are parked outside. News travels too fast these days. She glances into a conference room and sees four photos of the recent victims on a board: Chriselle Walke, Jazmin Freemont, Katherine Sims, Julianna Vargas.

Deb's right. She's not going to let it go. There's a problem to be solved, a puzzle. And both of them know how Essie's mind works. Maybe Deb is counting on this.

Essie sits down at her desk and flips through her notepad. Her eyes land on the name *Orphelia*.

She puts her own hand to her throat, right where that scar had been smiling at her during their interview that morning. Makes her shiver. She tugs at the collar of her shirt to cover her skin.

Orphelia. What was her last name? Essie searches for her notes. Orphelia Jefferies. At first, she can only locate her rap sheet.

It takes her an hour to find the incident report. Feelia Jefferies. Not Orphelia. Taken to MLK hospital with a wound to her neck. Found on Fifty-Ninth and Western. Interviewed postsurgery. Could not identify attacker—says he was white, possibly Latino. Victim was a prostitute.

Like that excuses it.

Essie pages through the report. There's not much to it. No follow-up.

She doesn't recognize the names of the officers who interviewed Orphelia. Probably transferred or retired. Not worth tracking down. The case didn't matter then. It's dead and gone.

There's a photo of Orphelia in the hospital. The wound is stitched but still fresh. Essie puts her hand to her neck again.

That cut.

Just like Julianna's. Just like—

She goes to records. Requests a file. A photo falls out. A close-up of Lecia's head, bagged, smothered, a six-inch-long crescent wound at the base of her neck. A bib of blood. Just like Julianna's. Just like the other women whose photos Essie has seen. She notes the date. Six months before Orphelia had been attacked.

She flips through Lecia's file, then pulls the file on the rest of the unsolved cases from that period. Tips and leads and dead ends. Arrests and discharges. A whole tangle that went nowhere.

She catches the names of local activists and community organizers who'd demanded the police take action, do something, address the fact that women were being hunted in South L.A. A roster of women picketing the station and the mayor, asking someone to pay attention. Demanding someone—everyone—listen.

Essie knows she doesn't have time to read the whole thing. Only enough time to make a copy, which she tucks into her bag.

Then she checks the incident report for Feelia Jefferies's attack. Six months after Lecia Williams's murder. What if Lecia wasn't the last? What if what Lecia did and who she was really *didn't* matter? What if she had been right and Dorian wrong?

What if the answer was much more simple.

Essie double-checks the address she'd jotted down that morning.

She stops by the desk sergeant on the way out. It's Clemson. An old-timer. Been sitting there for decades.

"This woman came in this morning. I found her waiting for me," Essie says. Clemson hadn't been on when Orphelia had arrived but he checks the log. "You know her?" She shows him a picture from her old sheet. "She got a decade plus on that now."

Clemson puts on his readers and squints. "Yup."

He passes the picture back. Essie wants to slam her hand on his desk. Because why the hell is he making her ask the obvious. "And?"

"Been coming in for years. Always got some complaint or another. I'm surprised they let her see you."

"What kind of complaint?"

"You know what they're like. All the drugs. Makes them paranoid."

"And her paranoia is what exactly?"

He raises his eyebrows like *why bother?* "Thinks some white lady is stalking her. Been going on about it for years. I let her down easy and send her on her way."

"How come you don't believe her?"

Clemson laughs. "Good one, Perry."

IT'S FIVE P.M. The sky is a thin blue. Cloudless. But there's a wash of something, smog or smoke. Traffic is thick on Western, but Essie is able to weave through it on her bike.

Orphelia's apartment is on the corner in a boxy stucco two-story building with no balconies, built over a large carport. The windows are gray with soot from Western.

Clue: *Ditsy SoCal Architecture*. Answer: Dingbat.

Terrible name for a terrible design.

Essie checks the block, looking for possible vantage points a stalker might take. There are several. Other carports, a recessed doorway of a building diagonally across Western. A large ficus.

There are a few faded names next to the doorbells but most are unmarked.

Two men are sitting to the right of the door on camp chairs between two scruffy bushes. "Looking for someone?"

"Orphelia Jefferies."

"No shit," one man says to the other. "You hear that?"

"I did."

"Maybe she isn't crazy after all."

"How's that?" Essie asks.

"You the white lady she says is harassing her?" the first man says.

His friend uncaps a beer. "Always on about it. Screaming out her damn window or taking her noise to the street. *White lady did this. White lady was here. You all see that white lady standing outside my window?*"

His buddy slaps his knee. "Shit," he says. "And the white lady's right here, ringing the goddamned bell!"

The two laugh as if this is the funniest thing in the world.

"So how come you been stalking Feelia?" the first man asks.

Essie sighs and pulls her badge out of her jacket. "Here's how come," she says. "Now which one is her bell?"

It takes Essie a moment to convince Orphelia she's really the detective from the station. The men don't let up.

How come she don't believe you?

Maybe you are the one stalking her.

White lady stalking her, my ass, but here she is.

Finally, the buzzer admits Essie.

Orphelia's place is on the second floor.

"No shit," she says opening the door. "No fucking shit." She's wearing a teal velour tracksuit. The hooded jacket is zipped up over her scar.

She leads Essie inside. The apartment is small, cluttered, and tidy. Framed photos on every surface. Pillows and stuffed animals.

On one wall is a large media center with an old flat-screen and dog-eared books—mostly self-help. Facing it are a set of sliding windows with heavy curtains that are closed. The apartment is lit by the overheads and a halogen.

"This is a trip," Orphelia says. "LAPD paying me a house call because I said pretty-please."

Essie opens her backpack and pulls out the files she'd copied at the station. "Can we have a seat?"

"We can do whatever the fuck we need to now I know you're taking my complaint serious." Orphelia fiddles with her zipper. "But how come you're taking me serious?"

"Let's sit, please," Essie says. "There are a few things I want to discuss with you."

"Like?"

"Please," Essie says, gesturing at the maroon sofa with the file.

"So this shit is not about the white lady stalking me?"

Essie sits on the couch, hoping Orphelia will follow her lead. When that doesn't happen, she opens the file and pulls out the photos of the women who'd been murdered nearly two decades ago. She fans them on the table.

She watches Orphelia cast her eye over the pictures. "Who the fuck are they?"

"Why don't you sit?"

Orphelia folds her arms over her chest. "Why don't you tell me how come you turned up at my place showing me a stack of pictures of dead ladies?"

There will be stages like grief. Denial. Pain. Argument. Acceptance.

If only she would sit.

"Orphelia, these photos were taken from 1996 to 1998." Essie taps one: "This was taken December 1997. About a year before you were attacked."

Orphelia's hand hits her sternum. "Attacked is beaten and bruised. I wasn't fucking *attacked*. Had my throat slit, left for dead in an alley. 'Cept I wasn't dead."

Essie taps another photo: Lecia. "And this, six months before you."

"What do they all have to do with me?"

"Did the police follow up with you?"

Orphelia laughs. "The hell does that mean, *follow up*?"

"Did they ask you more questions? Show you a list of suspects?"

"I'll tell you what they did. Fuck-all is what. Took my statement at the hospital and then ghosted."

"They never came here? Never asked you for information?"

Orphelia laughs again. "Ask me for information? You know what I did back then?"

"I read your sheet."

"What kind of information I was going to give them? As far as the police were concerned I put myself in the way of an occupational hazard. Like getting your throat slit from time to time was part of the job description."

Essie pulls a piece of gum from her pocket and pops it in her mouth.

"You need a cigarette, Detective."

"Never," Essie says.

She wants Orphelia to sit. It seems easier to break the news that way.

She snaps her gum. It's almost like notifying the next of kin.

"Orphelia," she says. "The women in these photos were all victims of a serial killer who operated in South L.A. until eighteen years ago."

"No shit," Orphelia says.

She doesn't get it. Not yet.

"I believe that the same man who killed these women attacked you."

Orphelia's hand flies to her scar.

"It's possible you're the only known survivor."

"Huh," Orphelia says, like someone told her she should consider rearranging her furniture. "So this visit has nothing to do with my own damn complaint."

"You never tried to figure out who attacked you? You never followed up?"

Again, Orphelia's hand flies to her scar. "Figured they'd come to me. And they didn't."

"So you let it drop?"

"Men do all sorts of fucked-up shit out here. Get away with most of it. Anyway, who the fuck's going to listen to me—lady sucking dick for twenty bucks a pop?" She adjusts one of her door-knocker earrings. "I don't do that shit anymore, mind you. So, they catch the guy?"

"No," Essie says. "Not yet."

"So that's why you're here? You want to ask me questions? I'll tell you all about it. I was outside the liquor store. Some guy pulled up in a fucked-up family car—a station wagon or some straight-dude shit. White. I can't remember. Tell you the truth, I don't want to fucking remember. All I know is he wasn't black. Asks me if I wanted to try some of his South African wine. Next thing I know, I'm rolling around in his car. And my head's spinning like a motherfucker. Then there's this pain and for a moment it feels like I'm breathing through my neck." Her hand flies to her scar. "I came to in an alley. First thing, I thought I was blind. Then I realized there's a bag half pulled over my head. Down to my nose."

"A plastic bag?" Essie picks up the file. She scans it quickly. This detail is missing.

"Did you tell the police who interviewed you about the bag?"

"Maybe. Maybe not. Who the fuck knows what I said."

Essie's certain now. Orphelia's one of the victims of the earlier spate of murders. Except no one made the connection. She didn't mention the plastic bag and the detectives didn't bother to ask, or forgot to ask, or thought it was easier not to ask.

Orphelia glances down at the photos. She picks up one. Then another. Then another. "Same motherfucker killed all these women?"

"That's what we think."

"Same as cut my throat?"

"It fits the pattern."

"And he killed how many after me?"

"I think you were the last."

"I was the last nothing. I fucking survived."

"Maybe that's why he stopped."

Orphelia lets out another soft, rolling laugh. "So I did you all a favor. Saved you the trouble of tracking him down."

"That's one way to look at it," Essie says.

"So this is what you came all this way to tell me? I was nearly done by a motherfucking serial killer."

"I thought you deserved to know."

"Deserved shit." Orphelia clears her throat. "Now what I deserve, Detective, is for someone, you perhaps, to take me seriously and get a goddamn restraining order on that lady who's stalking me. See those curtains? You know the last time they were opened? Neither do I."

Essie pulls out a fresh piece of gum. She can feel her mind starting to fly: Morgan Tillett, hummingbirds, Julianna's mother hoping against hope.

"So you're gonna do that for me, Detective, since I've been mistreated by the LAPD and all? You gonna get me a restraining order?"

"If I had a name—" Essie begins.

"If *you* had a name? If I had a name, we wouldn't be having this conversation because I'd have taken care of this problem myself. But seeing as I don't, I've been putting my goddamn faith in you all."

There are ways. Patrol cars. Stakeouts. But no one is going to sign off on these for a nuisance complaint against a ghost.

There's another tactic. PTSD counseling. Therapy. Ways to indicate to Orphelia that grief and fear often manifest in external ways.

Essie takes out her pen and pad. "Now when did this start?"

"Are you a motherfucking goldfish? I told you all this shit earlier today."

Essie flips through her notebook. Orphelia is right. It's all there: white woman, lurking, middle aged (maybe), passing by liquor store, new job. Started just after Orphelia's attack. Then underlined and circled: *PTSD / Paranoia?* She circles these words. Draws a line under them. Adds three exclamation points. The mind is a marvel: suppresses one violence and replaces it with an imagined threat.

Essie clicks her pen. "And the last time you saw her?"

Orphelia gives her a satisfied look. "Day before yesterday."

"Okay," Essie says, gathering up the photos and tucking them back into her file. "I'm going to take a look."

"And if she doesn't happen to be there right now?"

"I'll come back."

"I'm gonna keep my eye on you, Detective," Orphelia says. "I'm going to hold you to your motherfucking word." She leads Essie to the door and holds it open. "You fools owe me. That's what you do. You owe me."

In the doorway, Essie stops. "One thing. You're sure about the plastic bag?"

"I'm motherfucking sure." And with that Orphelia slams the door.

———

"YOU A COP FOR REAL?"

"You the shortest LAPD I ever saw."

"You some kind of kindergarten cop?"

The men outside Orphelia's have been tying it on since Essie went up. Now the afternoon drink has become the evening drunk and their voices are loud and sloppy. Say anything to a lady cop, of course. Seems like an easy target.

"But for real, maybe this is the great white ghost haunting Feelia."

"You haunting Feelia?"

"You her phantom stalker?"

Essie spits her gum into a pile of cups and bottles next to the stairs. She pulls out her badge. "Got this at the ninety-nine-cent store up on Pico. Want it?"

The trouble they'd get in carrying an officer's badge. Still no guarantee it will curb their lip.

"While I've got your attention, maybe you could answer some questions for me."

"LAPD got no height requirement?"

"As a matter of fact they don't," Essie says. "I could be three foot one and you'd still have to come to the station should I arrest you."

"Easy, easy," one of the men says, holding up his hands. "I'm innocent, Officer."

Essie takes a breath. The way she figures it, Orphelia's white stalker is straight-up PTSD. Some sidebar paranoia that consumed her mind after she was attacked. Something that she thinks she can control as opposed to the thing she couldn't. But Essie said she'd check it out. And she's here. So.

"This your regular spot?" she says to the two men.

"Day in day out."

"No doubt."

"How long have you heard Orphelia talking about her stalker?"

"How long is forever?"

"And you've never seen anyone?" Essie asks.

"Seen a lot of people."

"This is a big street."

"Busy street."

"Runs the entire city. North-south."

"I know," Essie says.

"So lots of people. Lots and lots of people."

"What I'm asking," Essie says, "is if you've seen anyone in particular. Let's say a white, middle-aged woman."

"Looking at one right now."

"With my own two eyes."

Essie knows how this would go if Spera were doing the talking. "I'm sure you know what I mean. Have you seen anyone watching this building?"

"Don't pay attention."

"None of my business."

"People do what they want."

She's bled this stone dry.

The sky is purple, fading to black. The cruise is about to pick up.

Essie unlocks her bike. Tunes out whatever comments are hurled at her by the men in their camp chairs. Heard it all before. A thousand times.

Yes, she's sure she's a cop. A detective even. Nope, she's not a child playing dress-up. Nope, she didn't steal her mommy's badge.

She rides a loop—down to Sixty-Sixth, over to St. Andrews, up to Sixty-Fourth. Down Western. Then the same loop but to the east, up on Denker and passing by Orphelia's again.

The men have gone inside. Taken their chairs. Maybe they think they said too much. Or maybe they were just satisfied and moved on to the next thing.

Traffic's picking up. A few people out on foot.

Essie checks her phone. She'll give it thirty minutes. Then head back. Figure out how to solidify the link she's made.

She's at the light on Western and Sixty-Fourth, straddling her bike, one foot on the asphalt. It's simple to imagine. Leave a victim alive. Give up the game. Get scared. Paranoid she'd remember. It's all there, clean and clear.

There's a screech behind her, rubber burning road. A grind of metal. Essie braces for impact. When it doesn't come, she glances over her shoulder and sees a bus has been sideswiped by a small hatchback right in front of Orphelia's house. She hops on the sidewalk, doubling back, riding past the bus to assess the damage.

The driver is out of his car. He's at fault and Essie hopes he won't argue so the bus can get moving. She props her bike on a signpost and walks into the street. She glances at the hatchback and then over its roof toward the carport under the facing building.

And she sees her. A white woman standing there, watching, not gawking at the accident, but staring up at Orphelia's window. Essie takes out her badge. She needs to cross the street. But traffic's too heavy. And in an instant the woman is gone.

9.

———

ESSIE JUMPS ON HER BIKE. SHE BLOWS THROUGH A LIGHT. Oncoming traffic honks. But she doesn't slow.

She's furious at herself. She'd done to Orphelia what Deb and the rest of them had done to her after the accident—mistrusted Orphelia because of something that had happened to her. Like she'd lost her sanity along with who knows how much blood from her neck.

Orphelia had said a white woman was stalking her.

No one believed her.

But they were wrong. Essie had seen the woman. A white woman watching Orphelia. Someone who might have been watching her since she was slashed. Someone who might link the past to the present. Someone who could send this whole thing home to Deb and the rest of RHD.

She arrives home and peers in the living room window. The monitors are still lighting up the den. Mark's awake. The trading day is over but he hasn't called it yet. He's probably on a deep dive into one of the hysterical investment blogs he digests. Gold. Crypto. Next thing they'll be trading air.

Essie puts her key in the lock but hesitates. She takes out her phone.

Back on social media. Back into the profiles of Morgan Tillett's five closest friends—not her best friends, but the ones with whom she shares the most commonality; overlaps of "likes," places visited, and petitions. Two from California have recent check-ins. Not together. But both to Brooklyn. Then she finds another who's visiting Queens from San Diego.

They're congregating.

Coming together.

A protest. An action.

See, there's your answer.

Why is an activist hiding the fact that she's in New York? Because she's staging an action. She'd even hinted at it. What was it she'd said? *From where I'm sitting it looks like the city is about to explode.* Not Los Angeles. Brooklyn. Something big.

Essie puts her phone away. Puts Morgan Tillett out of her mind.

People always complicate things. Essie too. The easy answer was that Orphelia wasn't lying. But Essie had disregarded it.

How many years had Orphelia been making her complaint? Fifteen? And no one listened. No one. Not even Essie. She's no better than the rest of them at Southwest. It turns her stomach.

Because she knows what it is not to be listened to. To be written off as a hysteric. Just today. *It's serial. It's the same guy as before.*

And a brush-off.

No one had believed her at the site of the crash. No one believed that she hadn't been driving. When Deb arrived she'd taken control, taken Essie in hand. *I'm going to make this all right for you. I'm going to fix it for you.*

But there hadn't been anything to fix.

Essie hadn't been driving. Mark had fallen asleep at the wheel.

But Deb wanted to show how blue her blood was, how she was a cop's cop. How she did what it takes. And soon enough she was cleaning up a mess that wasn't there. Soon enough she was swept up into a club of officers who'd gone above and beyond even the law to look after their own.

It was Deb's doing that everyone from the rookies to the top brass thought that Essie, not Mark, had been driving, that when she'd leapt out of the car, running toward the girls tossed in two directions on Sixth and Plymouth, Mark had slid over, taken the position behind the wheel to protect her badge. And that Deb had handled it so no shame had come to the LAPD. Deb. Deb. Deb.

Mark had passed the Breathalyzer.

Deb had urged the cops not to give Essie one. She'd made them look the other way even though there was nothing to see. Deb had coached them into pretending to believe Essie when she said Mark was driving. Saved themselves the headache and imagined they were saving her in the process.

These men, saving her.

But Mark *had* been driving. He'd insisted. Although he was exhausted on their trip from Big Bear. Music up. Windows down. Air on.

He'd been driving. And he'd fallen asleep.

Because of Deb no one believed Essie when she told them the truth. Now all anyone remembers is the cops who covered for something she hadn't done—the cops who made it right so she could keep her badge. That's the story, the answer to the question of what happened that night.

Now it's her turn. She's the one who didn't listen. Didn't believe. Couldn't believe that Orphelia was telling the truth.

Who else hadn't been heard?

How many other women had tried telling their stories, giving clues, tips, answers?

The number must be dizzying. The calls that come in to Southwest. The truths that get jumbled in with the crazies, the loony tunes, the attention seekers. How many give up? Stop calling? Take their problems somewhere else? Or nowhere? Live with them?

Tomorrow, or the day after, the station will be flooded with calls, from everyone who has something to say about the serial killer. Everyone who mistrusts a neighbor, harbors a grudge, has a theory or a feeling.

And in all that noise there could be a single truth. A single fact. Someone who knows something.

Someone who has not been listened to. Someone like Orphelia.

Essie opens her backpack. Pulls out the file. She activates the flashlight on the back of the phone.

She flips through the pages. She casts her light over the notes scrawled in the margins. Looking. Searching.

She's there. Essie's certain. Somewhere in the tips. In the callers. A voice. Someone no one listened to or believed. A person who can tie those old murders to the current ones.

FEELIA 2014

AM I NEW AROUND HERE? THAT'S THE GODDAMN FUNNIEST goddamn question I've ever been asked. And shit—I've been asked some crazy shit.

Am I new around here? Don't make me spit up this drink.

Honey, I've been up and down these streets more times than you'll be able to count. Then multiply that number and I've been around more times than that.

Not even come into this bar once or twice.

What's this shit called? Lupillo's.

Lupillo's. And you got tacos, too. That's a good hustle.

Should have come in earlier. Years back when I used to work these streets. Yeah and that means just what you think it means.

Tell you what. I'm gonna be back. Gonna make this my local. Even though I'm not exactly local. You won't catch me drinking south of the 10. Not in one million fucking years.

But let me tell you some shit. See this? See this scar?

Now don't look away. It's not gonna bite. Shit's fifteen years old.

Got jumped on a job. Well, not exactly on a job. I wasn't exactly working, didn't mean I wasn't trying to hustle a buck. Got in this guy's car figuring it would be the usual.

Usual my ass. Motherfucker slits my throat. Somehow I rolled out of that car and managed not to bleed to death. Came back to life in a hospital.

Don't give me that look. My story's not contagious.

That was one motherfucking wake-up call. One motherfucking wake-up. It got me off the streets. Got me straight. No more tricking. No more easy money.

I work now, which is hard as shit with my record. Felonies are worse than tattoos.

Let me tell you my mantra. Past is past. I know it's not original or anything. But it's the truth. Past is past. 'Cept when it isn't.

You think I think about that night?

Hell no.

I don't.

Shit's just easier that way.

Except check this shit out. Today some lady detective shows up at my place. Tells me the most fucked-up thing in a world of fucked-up things.

Let me ask you something? You think the police did a goddamn thing about the man who cut me? Do you think they found him? Do you think I was even worth a follow-up visit? I'll give you one guess.

So this lady detective turns up at my place. I thought she was there on some other business, but no, she's got this bomb she was fixing to explode in my motherfucking life.

See this scar? No, really take a look at it this time. Don't think of looking away until I tell you what's up.

This shit—this shit right here. I want to see you look at it.

This shit. This motherfucking scar. You know who did that?

Get ready. Hold up. A serial killer is who.

And I'm not fucking with you. I didn't take the bus all the way up to this hood to fuck with you. To tell you lies. A goddamn serial killer.

A serial killer who killed thirteen women way back when he cut me. You know what that makes me: a survivor.

Wait up, wait. There's more to this. Goddamn more. Just get me another drink first.

You think they caught him back then? Hell no.

But you want to hear the most messed-up thing? The worst part? Yeah, there's a worst part.

They knew. LAPD knew. Way back then, they knew. Saw me in the hospital and they knew.

Did they tell me? Did they make mention?

Not a thing. Not a goddamn thing.

Fifteen years someone's known it was a serial killer did this to me. A serial killer they didn't fucking catch.

Fifteen years nobody's bothered to give me the news. Like I'm not worth their while. Like I don't count. Like I don't deserve to know.

Had my throat slit and I don't deserve to know shit.

I don't remember much. But I remember some. Like, for instance, his car. Like that he wasn't black. That's a start. And he had a beard. But don't ask me. I just survived the motherfucker, that's all. Don't bother picking my goddamn brain. Don't bother clueing me in to what happened to me.

Tell you what. I'm a survivor. I survive. Just didn't know what it was I was surviving. And that's damn criminal.

Bad enough some guy made me a victim. Didn't need LAPD piling on, making me theirs, too.

I'm not standing for that shit.

Not standing for it at all.

PART IV

MARELLA

1.

────────

Marella Colwin, *Dead Body #1:* Computer-controlled, two-channel video installation with three 25" monitors stacked on metal shelving showing seven-minute programs. Duration: 8 min., 32 sec. Video, monitor, color & sound. Commissioned by the Campanile Fund at San Diego State as part of the Artist Scholarship Endowment Fund. Collection of the artist.

DEAD BODY #1 is a story of decomposition, how life turns into its opposite. The top monitor is a study in vitality, showing women swimming in the water off La Libertad, El Salvador. In the middle is a time lapse of refuse collecting next to a jetty on the same beach. Colwin is a fatalist, turning the water not into a life force but a place of decay. The sea is usually a place of regeneration and movement, but here it is a trap, something that drains life instead of giving it. At the bottom is a re-creation of decay, as a woman's naked body is showered in blue paint, eroding her skin and her physicality, destroying her beauty and her place in the world.

Marella Colwin, *Dead Body #2:* Video, monitor, color & sound. Duration: 17 min., 36 sec. Collection of the artist.

Dead Body #2 presents a crisis of solidity. A woman runs down a dark street. She stumbles. She continues. As she runs, she is taken back to the elemental. She loses her clothes. She is animal, wild and trying to escape. How long before she collapses? How long before her body gives in? She comes apart in pieces. Her body returning to the earth. Her journey begins again.

Marella Colwin, *Dead Body #3:* Three-channel video installation with three projectors. Projection cycle: 5 mins. Video, monitors, color, found objects. Collection of the artist.

Dead Body #3 is a cycle of femininity and fragility, as well as a study of power and subjugation. The three monitors project a loop of found photographs of women on the edge of a crisis that is never reached. In their own worlds these women project an aura of confidence. Outside, the balance is challenged and their power is stolen by the place where they seek to establish it. But the cycle continues, the dominant and the vulnerable switching places over and over again.

IT'S A SMALL SHOW. Three pieces in a gallery on Washington. But they are strong and there's already been a preview in the *L.A. Times* and in a few free weeklies plus the usual blogs. Anyway, it's her first solo, which is not bad two years out of art school.

But it could be stronger, always. That's the thing. It needs to be more of a gut punch. Marella wants people walking away horrified. She wants them to take home a terror they can't escape.

She wants them to feel it—that sensation of being followed down the street, being watched. Except worse. Not just followed, caught. It's too easy to walk away from art.

Marella checks the connections and the circuits. She stares at the faces flashing back at her on the monitors of her third piece.

This one had been hastily assembled. Edited and arranged in forty-eight hours with little sleep. It also poses a problem. The photos are not Marella's. She discovered them on a cell phone that she found on the street outside her house. The phone didn't have a code. It was just there, an open book.

By the time she finished looking through the photos she knew what she was going to do. Download them, make them into her art. The photos were rawer than anything she'd captured. Dirty and honest, accessible and threatening in a way she can only mimic with her performance pieces and video installations. These photos are a truth far beyond the reaches of Marella's creativity. As for her work—well, she can only tell stories and not even her own. Those women, the powerful mess of them. The confidence fading to vacancy. The power dissolving into despair. The challenge they pose to the viewer, the confrontation and the temptation. The strength and desperation. Now that's art.

Marella also knew whose camera she'd found, who had taken the photos. Julianna. And she knew that Julianna was dead. Murdered.

It was on the news last night. Every station had the story. A serial killer in South L.A. Julianna had been one of his victims.

Marella had watched the press conference. Four dead women in South L.A. found over the last eight months. She tuned out most of what they were saying. She needed to keep it at a distance or else she couldn't do what she wanted to do.

She recognized two of the faces on the television: Julianna Vargas and Katherine Sims.

But serial killer or not, she needed those pictures on Julianna's phone. They give her the edge she craves. They animate something she finds impossible to express in her own installations. The violence of the everyday—the violence down the street that seeps in through her windows. The casual terror. The anger. And the power over these things, albeit fleeting.

And here it is, bubbling inside her even in the quiet of the gallery with only the hum of her thrifted monitors and the gentle clicking of a geriatric projector. Her mind flashes to black. Her fist balls. She stops herself before she drives it into the wall. Instead she pounds her thigh—deep into the ridge of bone below flesh. A satisfying shock that radiates through the nerves down to her ankles.

Marella exhales. The dark lifts.

She's relieved she didn't damage the walls. The show opens tomorrow.

IT'S NIGHTTIME and she can still smell the smoke from last week's fires. But now there's another smell in the air. Mold. Rot. The heaviness of coming rain.

The rain will stop the city in its tracks. Cars will skid to a halt, creating more accidents than if they'd simply kept going. People will panic. The news will be dominated by the stuff falling from the sky—an exaggerated apocalypse. The dust in the Inland Empire will rise. The alluvial fan will flood. Mud will slide.

Marella checks the zip on her backpack, making sure her computer is protected. She fumbles around, adjusting the Velcro on the protective sleeve. Her hand hits something smooth. Not her phone. Julianna's.

Her hand recoils as if a violent death is contagious. She needs to get rid of the phone. She got what she wanted from it.

The rain hasn't started, which is good because Marella's on foot. The gallery isn't far from the street where she grew up and where she's been sleeping when she can stand it.

Mostly she crashes around town. Other artists' lofts. The family homes of classmates from SDSU. Even in galleries from time to time.

A transient, her mother calls her when she's angry. Marella likes the sound of that. But not the anger.

Her parents would be horrified to know she's walking around

here even if it's less than a mile from home. When she was small, Marella's parents moved from one war-torn country to the next—Haiti, Honduras, El Salvador—but Los Angeles was the only place where they seemed afraid. They've kept her, as much as possible, in a kind of isolation from the neighborhood. Two years of junior high up in Ojai with her aunt. Then boarding school outside Santa Barbara, a scholarship student. Summers in YMCA camps by the ocean. Never played on her own block. Didn't ride her bike. Didn't know her neighbors. No backyard birthdays. The only time the outside ever came in was her father's weekly dice game. And she was never allowed to be around for it. They didn't move because they couldn't afford to. They owned the house. And the house was nice.

Nearly seventeen years in Jefferson Park and Marella feels like a stranger. Crazy to be afraid of your own backyard.

You try to brush aside your parents' insanity and see the world through your fresh, wise eyes because you're hip to a new way of being and you know what's up. But the fear slips in. She didn't have sex until she was twenty-two and even the mild violence of the experience left her reeling.

There are several ways to get home from the gallery and all of them involve crossing the 10 on one of the bridges that keep South L.A. connected to the north. There's Western, wide and grimy, busy with buses and homeless making camp next to the on-ramps. There's Arlington, narrower and usually clogged with traffic. There's Gramercy, the quietest crossing that ends in the elegant streets of Kinney Heights. And then there are the little-trafficked pedestrian bridges, caged off with fences overgrown with vines, perfect hideaways for all sorts of illegal behavior. These are out of the question.

Marella chooses Gramercy because it's the closest and the most direct. But it's a smaller street, which means fewer eyes on her, less oversight.

It's eight P.M. And the freeway is going slow beneath her. It's dark on the overpass. The lights of Washington Boulevard recede to the north. Marella won't pass another store or busy intersection before she reaches home. It's all residential here, people minding their own business and hoping you'll mind yours.

She's midway across when she hears someone behind her walking fast.

It's easy to stand naked in a room full of strangers. Easy to cover herself in blue paint, douse herself with water. There's no question of sex or desire. No wanting or needing. No giving. She strips that part away but makes herself visible. By standing there for everyone to see, she isn't what they want. Sex is something people need from you, want to take from you, a violent exchange.

She steps into the street, waits for a passing car, then crosses to the east side of the bridge.

The person behind her does the same.

HERE ARE THE WAYS a body can come apart.

It can drown or be drowned and turn the color of a deep-sea creature that has never seen the light of day. It can get trapped between the dirty, barnacled rocks and bang on them for a day or more until someone takes it away. By then it will barely seem a body at all, but rather an obscene organism, a swollen alien form.

This is another way. A body can be ripped across the throat, a gash like a crescent moon. Its head can be secured in a plastic bag. It can be tossed in an alley, its arms and legs landing at angles impossible in life. It can be nibbled and gnawed by the feral creatures that prowl South L.A., cats and rats and worse.

It can fly off a scooter on Western, get trapped under a van, and be dragged for half a block. It can be lifted from under the chassis, trailing a sticky slick of blood that might initially be mistaken for hair.

These are the ways Marella has seen close up.

Of course, there are other ways too—collisions, electrocutions, falls. Unspeakable acts of violence, all of which Marella's heard about, read about, been warned about but not seen.

Marella can hear the footsteps behind her drawing close.

The first dead body she saw leaps to mind—a woman bobbing in the water and scraping against the rocks behind her family's former home in La Libertad, El Salvador.

The woman in the water was a *puta*. She worked the far side of the jetty where the prostitutes' pimps robbed tourists during the slow hours. The body had washed up into the small rocky outcrop overnight. Marella had spied her from her bedroom window. She thought the thing bobbing in the water was a dolphin, so she'd run to the beach.

By then a crowd had gathered, watching the fish-belly-pale woman trapped in the outcrop facedown dragged back and forth with the waves. She was wearing an electric-blue miniskirt and neon halter.

This is how the world pays you back, Anneke explained when Marella had stopped crying.

It's the traffic, Marella realizes, that is dragging her back to that moment. It sounds like the ocean.

Two more hookers died that year. But Marella didn't see them. They stationed a policeman near the beach. She overheard two men saying that was bad for business. But she didn't see any business on the beach besides the guys who sold mango and coconut.

Then Marella and her family moved to Los Angeles. Her father found a different job at a different school teaching ESL to Spanish speakers. Anneke quit her NGO and began working for a nursing home in Malibu.

WHAT IS IT going to feel like when this man catches her? Will he drag her to the shadowed area just before the public school where the carob trees have left their dark, sticky stains on the sidewalk? No one walks there because of the mess so no one will see her. What will happen? Will he toss her to the side when he's done? Leave her and kill her or roll her down the trash-strewn slope that leads to the 10?

There's a wail from below.

Marella wheels around and is face-to-face with a middle-aged Latina woman. She screams, her face inches from the stranger's.

"The fuck is wrong with you?" the woman says, hurrying past, leaving Marella staring at the semitruck, chugging east, still laying on the horn.

2.

———————

SHE IS OUT OF BREATH WHEN SHE REACHES TWENTY-NINTH Place. She passes her house, where the curtains are drawn with only a thin seam of light visible at the edges. She pulls the phone out of her backpack and opens the gate to the neighbors' house. The hinges scream, startling her.

So she knocks, her fist rattling the iron riot gate.

Julianna's mother opens the door. Marella doesn't know her name. She can see past her to flowers and wreaths, casserole dishes and trays of cookies. Marella has brought no tribute, no condolence gift.

"Yes?"

"I live next door," Marella says.

"I know."

Marella holds out the phone.

"What's this?"

"A phone. Maybe your daughter's. I found it."

Marella's mother takes the phone, flips it around in her hands. "Hector." She turns back into the house. "Hector!"

A young man emerges. He's heavyset. His eyes are submerged in purple circles.

"Hector, does this look like your sister's phone?"

Hector stares at his mother as if she's speaking another language.

"This phone? Is it Julianna's?"

"How come you think it's Julianna's?" the woman asks Marella.

Hector won't take the phone from his mother. "Just click the button, Mami. Probably a picture of her on the screen."

His mother stares at the phone in her hand as if it's an object she's never seen before. "What button? How?"

"Mami, the button. There." Hector points at the top of the phone that his mother is holding upside down. But she just looks at her hand. "Come inside," he says, pushing the door wider so Marella can step through.

The house smells like dead flowers and stale food. On the mantel is a row of photos of Julianna in ornate frames.

"What is this?" Julianna's mother says, holding up the phone.

"It's Julianna's phone," Hector says.

"How did I get it?"

"The girl next door," Hector says.

"How'd she get it?"

For the first time Hector looks straight at Marella. "How come you have my sister's phone?"

"I found it. Between our houses."

"When?"

"A couple of days ago."

"A couple of days? You had it for a couple of days?" He says it like Marella had been hiding his sister, not her phone.

Excuses and lies flood her head. All of them sound false.

"Sorry," Marella says. "I only figured it out from the photos." Even mentioning the photos fills her with guilt. "I didn't know her well."

"Photos." Marella and Hector turn at the sound of his mother's voice. "Julianna loved her photos." Her eyes go from the phone to the table. "There's so much food. You should take some. We can't eat all this food."

"I'm okay," Marella says.

Julianna's mother finally finds the home button on the phone and wakes it up. Julianna's face bursts from the screen. "There she is. There's my girl. How many years you lived next door and you didn't know her?"

Marella's throat catches. But the mother doesn't wait for her reply. "Probably twenty. Twenty years and you missed knowing my baby. She was too wild for this world. This place, it bored her. She was like a wildfire. We come from El Salvador. But Julianna was born here. A good thing to be born in America. To be an American. My American daughter. A *gringa*. That's what my sister back home calls her."

The smile on Marella's face is getting tight as she listens.

"Everything was too small for Julianna. This house, school, her friends. She needed more. Like when my parents' neighbors would burn their sugarcane fields in the spring. That fire was hungry. It wouldn't stay put. It needed our land. Ate our fields. That was Julianna. She needed more than anyone could give. And she tried to take it. That was who she was. Beautiful. Destructive. A bomb."

Hector puts a hand on his mother's arm, but she shakes him off.

"So many things I feared for her. Boys. Drugs. Cars. Gangs. Police. She brought it all to me, dragged all that through the front door. I see girls like her on the streets, on the buses, going in and out of places, girls with tattoos and tight clothes and makeup and hair. Drunk girls and smoking girls and girls being escorted by men old enough to be their papis. And I think, thank God that's not my girl. But it is. That's my baby covered in tattoos. That's my baby chain-smoking. That's my baby smelling of marijuana. That's my baby smelling of sex and worse." Her voice catches. "You know what the worst smell on earth is? Worse than a body burning up in a sugarcane field? The smell of strange men on your baby. But I smelled that. And I saw the marks on her—the ones she did. The ones others did. I saw her red eyes and her bleeding lips. She couldn't hide that from me. She didn't try. And how many times did I have to listen as she tried talking to me, pretending like she was just fine? But she wasn't making any sense. Just talking and talking and talking like she could talk her way out of all the things she'd put in her body. Like if she kept talking they would go away.

"And then one day your baby doesn't look like your baby. She's someone else. She's got someone else's hair. She's got writing on her. She smells like someone else. She talks like someone else. She looks like one of those girls on TV. The ones who get arrested. Or worse, like one of those girls in bad magazines or bad movies. And you know what you want to do? Do you?"

Marella isn't sure if she's supposed to reply.

"You want to give up and say *That's not my baby. That's some other messed-up chica who came and stole my baby—possessed her— and I don't have to care about her because I don't recognize her.* And you don't want to recognize her. You won't want to recognize her. You'll try not to recognize her. You'll try and try. But it's not going to work. Because she's still your baby, even with all the things she's done to herself. Every one of them, no matter how bad."

Hector coughs quietly, catching Marella's eye. With one hand, he gestures toward the door. Julianna's mother continues, oblivious.

"There are bad girls. You see them everywhere. Bad, bad, bad girls. And you wonder about their mothers. You wonder what they did wrong. How they messed up. Maybe they didn't pray. Maybe they ignored God. Maybe they accepted the devil. Maybe they drank or smoked or took drugs."

Marella takes a step back. "Maybe they did crimes. Maybe they were thieves. Or murderers. Maybe they had abortions. Maybe they had many men. Because it has to be their fault. The mothers of these bad, bad, bad girls. But it's not. I pray. I take care of my husband even when I'd rather kill him. I take care of my son. And I take care of Julianna. No matter. I do what's right. And still people look at me like it's my fault she was like wildfire. My fault she drew all over herself, let men have her body. Like it's my fault my baby died. All this food? You know why there's all this food? Because people don't know what to say about my baby. So they bring this food. They don't know what to say because they think it's my fault. They think—"

The metal gate bangs into place behind Marella. She's out on the porch. Then down the three steps to the street. Back on the bumpy sidewalk. She gasps for air like someone has just taken his hand from her throat.

3.

———

MARELLA'S HOUSE. DINNERTIME. THE RAIN HASN'T STARTED.
But it's coming. You can tell by the way the city seems to be holding its breath—how the trees stand in suspended animation,
bracing.

The house, too, seems mired in time and fog. Roger is on
the couch. He's staring at the fireplace, which has never worked.
The way he's looking at it you'd think it was filled with leaping
flames. Marella knows he's in one of his fugues, black places that
make Anneke's moods even darker.

Anneke's in the kitchen making beef curry. Marella knows
her mother's anger will find its way into the wild and aggressive
flavors of her stew.

It's been two days since she came here, two days since she
found Julianna's phone on the pavement between their houses.
After that it's been a flurry of work to get her new piece ready for
the opening.

Marella squeezes her father on his shoulder. He turns and
looks straight through her. He's wearing headphones plugged
into a first-generation iPod. She can hear the monotone of one
of his audiobooks. War histories. Thousands of pages. Hundreds

of hours. Details, data, stats, death tolls, longitudes and latitudes. Over and over again for days on end until he emerges from his funk as if he'd never been away.

Marella goes back to the kitchen. She places her hand on her mother's arm. Anneke recoils.

"How long has it been this time?" Marella asks. She inclines her head in the direction of her father on the couch. "How long has he been listening?" There have been times when he's listened for three weeks straight, only taking off his headphones to shower or to teach his ESL classes.

"Where have you been?" Anneke asks. "Don't tell me. I don't want to know."

Marella's house is one of the few two-story Craftsman homes in Jefferson Park. Her room is upstairs. From her bedroom window she can see into the house next door.

Her neighbors' lights are on. All the shades are drawn except for the ones in Julianna's brother's room.

Hector is sitting on the edge of his bed, his hands between his knees, his head down. There's a girl next to him, patting his back until he swats her away. She scoots back on the bed to give him some space. His shoulders rise and fall.

A light behind the curtain in the living room turns it into a shadowbox. Marella can see the silhouettes of Julianna's parents. She's occasionally eavesdropped on their raised voices, their the-atrical anger. She's heard the crashes, the door slamming, the noise that reaches into her house. The bilingual curses and ac-cusations. They are unashamed of their rage. It sparks, explodes, and fades. They run it out. Burn it off. Then they watch TV or do whatever else they were planning on doing.

Do you know what's worse? The subtle violence. The hidden anger in her house.

Anneke always kept her voice low as she put her daughter to

sleep, hissing about what a bad girl she was, listing the sins of her daughter's day—the accidents, the things dropped, put on inside-out, or forgotten. Recounting the times Marella took too long to respond, the times she spoke too quietly to be heard. A litany of evidence that suggested Marella was willfully disobedient and had set herself on a path to reform school or worse.

If Marella took too long to settle into sleep, if she thrashed or kicked to make herself more comfortable in her bedding, Anneke would deliver a quick pinch or a slap on the legs: *bad girl, horrible child, disobedient.* She never raised her voice, never sounded angry. She simply slipped these rebukes into the bedtime routine between books and songs.

She loves you, Roger told Marella. *She's challenged by how much she loves you. It overwhelms her. She worries about how you will make your way in the world.*

Marella wished her mother would scream like the people next door. She wished she'd allow the world to witness her anger so that she didn't make Marella feel the shame of it.

It's the world that worries her, Roger told his daughter. *Not you.*

The figures behind the living room curtain next door are putting on a pantomime. Julianna's mother is raising her arms above her head. Her father is standing still, a wall absorbing his wife's grief or anger.

When Marella got too old for Anneke to pinch or hit, her mother changed course. She'd drag Marella to one of the bedroom windows that looked down at Julianna's house. *You want this to happen to you? You want to turn out like her?*

She liked to time these lessons to a moment when Julianna, only a year older than Marella, could be seen climbing into a fast car driven by an older man, adjusting her crop top and yanking down her miniskirt.

The world destroys girls like that.

ANNEKE DOESN'T BANG THE PLATES and bowls on the table when she serves dinner. Everything is polite. No mention is made of the fact that Roger is at the table still wearing headphones.

The Battle of the Bulge. December 1944. Antwerp. Surprise. Bastogne. 410,000 men. 1,400 tanks. 1,600 something else. 1,000 something else.

Bits of information reach Marella's ears. Her father's eyes are fixed. He's looking at the wall. He doesn't see it. Marella taps his arm to draw his attention to the food. Roger blinks, glances down, and begins to eat.

Marella supposes it could be worse. Roger's black moods don't involve booze, drugs, or long absences. They aren't violent or aggressive. Instead, he's just lost in the world of his war histories, stories he must know by heart. Marella wonders if he's actually hearing them at all.

Roger's black moods make Anneke angrier. Which is why Marella touches her father's arm again, suggesting he take another bite of curry, keep up the pretense of a regular family meal.

She can see her mother's jaw tense.

"Leave him alone. Don't touch him."

Marella withdraws her hand.

"If he doesn't eat, he won't starve." Anneke takes a deep breath. "Barbara and Glenda both read about your show in the paper. They were impressed."

Anneke gets most of her news second- or thirdhand from the women in the nursing home in Malibu where she works as an aide and where newspapers, the local news, and board games pass the time.

"They say it's about the body." There's a tightness around Anneke's mouth as she speaks.

"It's about women," Marella says.

"I hope it's positive," Anneke says.

"You mean tasteful."

"There are already so many ugly things in this world."

"I've heard," Marella says.

"The women at the home have been painting flowers. We have a new still life class."

"I don't paint flowers, Mom."

"I've heard," Anneke replies, giving Marella a wan smile.

Marella learned to not talk about her mother to her friends.

Your mom's a bitch.

Your mom's some kind of control freak.

Your mom's a fucking nightmare.

But they didn't understand. It was Anneke who helped Marella get into good schools, who would have figured out how to pay for an out-of-state college, too, if Marella had wanted to attend one. It was Anneke who found the summer programs and gave up her weekends to take Marella on adventures far away from Los Angeles. It was Anneke who didn't blink when Marella declared she was going to study art and then stay for an MFA.

"You never even drew flowers as a kid," Anneke says. "Always monsters and mazes."

Marella takes a bite of curry. The chilies burn her tongue. She holds it in her mouth, intensifying the flavor and the pain.

"Too hot," Anneke says.

Marella's mouth is on fire and she can't reply.

The silence that follows is shattered by the front door slamming at Julianna's house, then the loud rattle as the rusted gate is flung open and bangs back.

"I saw her that day," Marella says.

"Saw who?"

"Julianna."

Anneke stops her fork at her lips.

"Did you take them something?"

"Who?" Anneke says.

"Julianna's parents."

"Take them what?"

"A casserole. Some cookies?"

"Why?"

"It's a gesture, Mom. It's what you're supposed to do."

"Cookies aren't going to help them."

As a kid, Marella remembers her mind growing blank, then black. She's not sure what set it off—what flipped the switch. Suddenly everything was wrong. That was the worst part, not knowing why.

Imagine you were a dog and someone insisted on combing your hair the wrong way. Or all your clothes were put on backward, your shoes on the wrong feet. Or there was a high-pitched frequency you couldn't locate. Something wrong, very wrong.

So she reacted. She threw things, hit things—her toys, her stuffed animals, even her parents in a frantic attempt to bring the world back into line.

It didn't happen in public. Only at home.

It was her father who reacted, not Anneke. The only things that penetrated Marella's fugue were the white high-beams of Roger's panicked eyes and his insistent voice telling her to calm down. Begging her.

But she couldn't. It was impossible. The hole was too deep. She was sinking. Her father was standing over her, looming out of reach. He was pleading for her to do the thing she couldn't do. Stop.

Then he would take her to her room for punishment. He'd sit against the door and watch as she tossed her stuffed animals, barring her escape. He was never violent, but the look in his eyes, the desperate need for her to calm down both scared her and made her keep going.

From the hall she could hear her mother crying, begging to be let in to comfort Marella, insisting that she could make it right and make it stop.

Roger never let her in. And Marella raged on, always keeping an eye on her father to figure out what he wanted from her and why. This is how she drew him out and snapped him back to reality, smashing that dumb, placid exterior to make him present.

Just like when she was a child, just like earlier that evening in the gallery, she feels the internal shift, the lights dimming, her eyes losing focus. The next few moments will be out of her control.

She reaches across the table and yanks the headphones from Roger's ears, tossing them and the geriatric iPod across the room.

It's not Roger who reacts but Anneke, standing up and smashing her soup bowl to the floor.

"Leave him alone. Leave him alone. Leave—"

Marella is outside when her mind clears. There's curry on her clothes. She stares inside at her mother, who's cleaning the crockery, and her father, who's listening to his war stories again.

4.

"HARDER." MARELLA IS DOUBLED OVER, PANTING, SWEAT dripping down her forehead. "Harder."

"Enough, Colwin, step out."

A martial arts gym on Jefferson that specializes in everything from jujitsu to boxing. You can find them all over Los Angeles but they are particularly common in South L.A. Simple storefronts with a mat on the floor and martial arts equipment. Daytime, kids learn tae kwon do, karate, judo, and self-discipline. The adults come at night.

And some, like the one where Marella is struggling to catch her breath, run illegal free fights after close. It's Ladies' Night.

One-minute rounds.

Round robin.

Winner stays on.

You pay to play.

Marella paid thirty bucks. And here she is, losing.

"Harder," she says once more.

Her opponent is Liz Acevedo, a former pro boxer from Long Beach. She's lean, streamlined. Like a string bean with muscles. Her face is an oval, her long black hair pulled back into a glossy tail. Her eyes are cold like stones in a river. There's nothing hulky or brutish about Acevedo. She's smooth like she's carved from obsidian. She looks like gloves can't touch her and if they somehow did she'd bruise golden.

She's a killer. She always wins.

"Step out, Colwin," Acevedo says. This is Acevedo's show. She runs Ladies' Night. And she dominates it.

There are ten seconds left on the buzzer, but Acevedo has called the round for mercy. Marella is a novice. She shouldn't even be in the mix. She's only been boxing for a year and mostly against the bag. But she paid and she's here.

Before Marella can object again, the buzzer rings.

There are five women at Ladies' Night. They rarely talk between rounds, they just watch the action in the makeshift ring, pumping themselves up for their next go.

Marella's only been up once, straightaway against Acevedo, who immediately pinned her to the ropes with a few light jabs to the stomach, nothing painful, before calling time. Bouncing in place to keep her muscles loose, Marella can feel the spots where her opponent's gloves collided with her abs. But there's no satisfaction. There wasn't enough impact. Acevedo held back, kid-gloved her, which only reminded Marella of her own frailty—she remains breakable. And this infuriates her.

She craves the brutality of the attack because when it comes it will be a release. The wait will be over. But in the ring she can control it—decide when it will happen. The pain will be on her own terms.

But Acevedo didn't let her have it. And now Marella's all wound up inside, filled with an unsettling energy that only a hard punch to the gut can release.

She keeps bouncing. She's wearing spandex shorts and a bra top. She's the worst, the rookie, the *PowderPuff*, the one the rest indulge with patty-cake punches and rolled eyes. She's their breather, their time-out, their guaranteed victory.

Tonight the gym is all talk about the serial killer, making them fight faster and more furiously.

Kill that motherfucker before he laid a hand on me.

It's not enough to cut them. Got to suffocate them too.

I knew one of them—the Kathy one. Kathy goddamn Sims. Ran with her back before I found the discipline.

Marella keeps her eyes on the ring as she stays warm. Acevedo is up against a woman she knows only as Casper. Casper is black and built like a former professional athlete—bulky muscles and compact power. She punches hard and precise, but her heft curbs her movement and she has trouble dodging the swift blows Acevedo's whipping at her head. The fight has gone out of her by the time the buzzer sounds.

The room smells of the fight—sweat and spring fresh deodorant and a metallic odor Marella imagines is blood although no one is bleeding. There's music blasting—power rock, angry thrasher stuff that matches the adrenaline in the small gym.

Acevedo's making short work of the rest of the women tonight. She's on a mission and it shows. Normally the women don't talk when they're waiting but tonight's different.

Fuck's up with the bitch?

Somebody's motherfucking pissed. Motherfucking hormonal.

Somebody dump Acevedo's ass?

She on the rag?

They talk different in the gym, bringing in the language of the things they fight against in the real world. Giving voice to the voices they want to beat the shit out of every day.

I'm-a take that bitch down.

I'm gonna take her out.

She don't own this goddamn ring.

But Acevedo does. Every inch of it. The ring is hers to do with as she pleases. The other women are just toys, Weebles who wobble who keep coming back for more.

They are gasping, trying to recover between rounds, trying to summon the willpower for another bout. Two of them throw in the towel.

Then it's Marella's turn again.

You're up, rookie.

Time for the PowderPuff Girl.

You gonna take her? Watch this, PowderPuff's gonna take her.

Marella ducks into the ring. She tightens the Velcro on her gloves, backhands her hair off her forehead. She raises her hands over her face, peering out at Acevedo from behind the padding. Acevedo looks bored, like *letsgetthisoverwith* and *givemearealchallenge.*

The bell dings.

Suddenly all Marella can hear is the music blasting—the grinding guitars and pounding drums, the death metal shriek. She sees Julianna's face and Kathy's face staring at her from the television news reports she saw earlier today.

Whatyouwaitingfor, PowderPuff?

She keeps one glove over her face as she learned in the few kickboxing classes she took, then jabs lamely with her other hand. The punch falls far short of Acevedo, who's dancing around, running out the clock as if it's too much trouble even to punch Marella.

Marella steps into Acevedo's strike zone. She tries a quick combo—jab, cross. Both miss. She gets a soft punch to the gut for her troubles.

Thatallyougot, rookie?

Grandma hits harder than you.

Normally the women on the sidelines are quiet. But Acevedo's ferocity has them fired up. Since they can't beat her, they settle for verbally abusing Marella.

Marella tries another combo. Hook, hook, cross. The cross

grazes Acevedo's forearm. She looks up, surprised, a little annoyed. She raises her eyebrows, a dark gleam in her stony stare. She pulls back for a cross. There's nothing Marella can do to escape it. She braces for impact, turning her head away from the trajectory of the blow. The punch lands, soft on Marella's jaw, like nothing, like a playful cuff on the chin, like she's being toyed with.

"Fuck that," she says. "Fuck that pussy shit."

Acevedo shrugs.

Marella puts her gloves up and steps to her opponent. She launches into a senseless volley of reckless punches that go nowhere. Acevedo deflects them all, then sends Marella off balance with a mild blow to the shoulder.

"Harder, bitch," Marella says.

PowderPuff wants it hard.

PowderPuff not getting any dick.

PowderPuff needs a beating.

If they only knew. Each of Acevedo's lame blows makes Marella crave the real thing even more. Each one is a tease, a taunt. Each one is torture.

"I said, harder, bitch," Marella spits.

"I heard you," Acevedo says. She's barely out of breath, barely working. Cool and even-keeled.

Marella charges with another ill-conceived assault. Acevedo holds up her gloves, then pushes Marella away, sending her tumbling.

She bounces once then lies still. The buzzer goes.

She's fired up inside with a rage that tastes hot, salty, and bitter like you want to spit it out but also savor it. "I told you to hit harder," she shouts.

"Saving my strength," Acevedo says, taking off her gloves and headgear to fix her ponytail.

There's something in the air—a loose wire spinning freely, a horrible current, a reaction to the violence that's haunting and hunting on their streets. The women are wild. Acevedo's wilder. And Marella's mind is spinning into black.

She springs to her feet. In one swift motion, she pulls back and lands a blow on Acevedo's temple. A sucker punch that makes her stutter-step. It's satisfying to connect, to feel flesh and bone and the solidity of Acevedo's skull through her glove, to sense her brain shudder and shake even a little. But it still doesn't give Marella the release she craves.

There's a moment of perfect stillness when Acevedo is frozen, staring at Marella with her dead black eyes, and the women on the sidelines are standing openmouthed, their last words hanging on their lips.

And then everything explodes. A brilliant firework crack to the cheek. A barehanded punch that breaks the skin.

Marella staggers back. She can feel everything flying from her chest—all the pressure and worry, the anxiety and unease. Because it's happened, the assault, the attack, and she's still here. She's still Marella, falling backward, tasting the blood that's trickling from her busted cheek into her mouth. And she's laughing, laughing, laughing.

5.

———

MARELLA'S OUT ON THE STREET, PUNCH-DRUNK AND STAG-gering on Jefferson. Her cheek is bleeding. It's throbbing. It has its own heartbeat. Her mouth tastes of warm metal. She licks her lips.

She puts her fingers to her cheek, feeling the raised bump and the gash. It's not big, maybe an inch. Amazing how much can be released through something so small—how much anger and tension and anxiety can escape.

Marella looks up at the smudged sky. She senses the rain before it starts. Another pause, as if Los Angeles is holding its breath, preparing itself. And then comes the deluge—a waterfall that pours from the sky.

She tilts her head, letting the water wash away the blood and sweat from her face. It runs into her eyes, fills her mouth, soaks her through.

The cars on Jefferson and Western all slow at once as if choreographed. Their lights slither and slide in the pools of water slicking up the asphalt.

The rain's coming in sheets.

Los Angeles is a blur of bright lights wobbling behind the

falling water. Marella feels as if she is squinting, but her eyes are wide open.

The gutters are filling. The sewers are rushing. The trash that never gets picked up is swirling, flowing. A river of soda cups, Styrofoam containers, wrappers running along the curb.

Marella is soaked. The rain and sweat chill her. Her wet clothes are like glue.

She can't go home. The minute she steps through the door the release will be undone. Her bruised, bleeding cheek will be a problem instead of a solution.

She takes Western north across the 10. Beneath her the traffic is arrested as if the rain has glued it in place. The taillights heading east are a solid red glow. West, it's white lights. She passes a twenty-four-hour taco place. It's freestanding with an enclosed seating area and a large parking lot. There are hot pink and green cartoon illustrations of tacos and burritos on the windows. The scratched glass, the graffiti, the battered plastic tables tell Marella it's been there for decades. But she's never seen it before.

She slows as she passes. There's a machine filled with stuffed toys that you can fish out with a crane if you're lucky and an old TV with a fuzzy picture. There's a woman eating alone. Raindrops are suspended on her voluminous black hair. Her large gold earrings sway as she forks a bite of quesadilla into her mouth.

Marella has never been allowed in places like this. She's not hungry but she steps inside and looks out at the cars on Western sliding past the rain-streaked glass.

Now she thinks she's seen this place before. She's sure of it. She takes a seat.

A woman leans through the window where customers order. "No sitting without eating."

Marella holds up her hand as if to say, *I'm only going to be a minute.*

"Lady, you can't sit here without eating. What if every girl on Western came inside just because it's raining?"

Marella glances at the solitary customer. And then she realizes why she knows this place. Julianna's photos. Two of them, maybe more, were taken here. Both are of a woman she now recognizes as Katherine Sims from the news reports, with her short, dyed blond curls, laughing like something was killing her.

The woman behind the counter has wedged her torso out. "Lady, don't make me come out there."

But Marella is already on her feet and out the door.

She turns left on Washington, heading for the gallery. There's a bathroom with a small shower in the back where she can get clean, and there's a sleeping bag that has made do more often than she'd like to admit.

The rain is falling so hard that it can't do anything but rush away in torrents, creating havoc without bringing relief to the parched earth.

Marella shakes her hair, jumps up and down a few times before unlocking the gallery. She strips at the door and leaves her shoes. Then without turning on the lights she makes a dash for the back. The water in the little shower warms her. She dries herself with one of the small towels and pulls on a clean set of clothes from the laundry bag stashed in the office.

She unrolls the sleeping bag but instead of camping in the back, she brings it out front. She finds the remote that controls the projectors for *Dead Body #3* and turns them on. It takes a moment for the images to emerge. She orchestrated them to rotate out of sync with one another, creating a sense of disorder but also allowing the eye to drift from one screen to the next without feeling rushed.

Click.

On the left—a close-up of a bruised and battered eyebrow. The eye beneath it makeup streaked, pupils wide.

In the middle—five women vying for space in front of a mirror, backs to the camera, dressed in thongs, in miniskirts, boy shorts, and nothing at all. Their faces defiant in the reflection, challenging themselves with their beauty, arming themselves with kohl and gloss.

On the right—a woman eating a sandwich at a bar. Behind her the pole of a strip club. A stolen moment between times.

Click.

In the middle—a woman with wild yellow curls just turning away from the camera, her hair flying, a tattoo of cat claws visible on her breast, her face relaxed, neither mugging nor posing.

On the right—three women shot from behind, walking down Western wearing micro shorts, mini shirts, breakneck heels, arms looped together like the street is their yellow brick road.

On the left—a dressing room, makeup dumped on the floor like an explosion of Halloween candy and a woman asleep clutching a pink tube of mascara, her face serene, her lashes caked black, her lips outlined in dark pencil.

Click.

On the right—a shot from over the shoulder of two women sitting together peering at a cell phone while another woman is leaning toward the camera, her breasts pressed into an M, her mouth puckered into an O.

On the left—Katherine Sims standing on a street corner, cropped puffer jacket, jeans that are more rip than jeans, head tilted up, eyes closed, steaming cup of coffee hiding half her face, a donut in the other hand, ignoring the car that's pulled up beside her.

In the center—a coffee table and a tray with a couple of CD cases with lines of white powder, an ashtray with lipsticked butts, a hand tapping a cigarette, a hand replacing a drink, a hand removing a paperback: *Breaking Dawn.*

Click.

In the center—Katherine Sims again at a table at a fast-food Mexican place, head thrown back, mouth open wide, a laugh like an explosion. A man behind her, staring at her like she's candy.

On the left—two women on a couch, half dressed or barely dressed, turned away from each other, each staring at a phone in her palm.

On the right—Julianna reflected in the window of an upscale coffeeshop, hair big and loose, jeans tight, halter top tighter. Inside at the counter a man in a flannel shirt, sleeves rolled, handlebar mustache, porkpie hat, making coffee.

Click.

On the left—the woman with the tattooed claws on her breast in bed, *Breaking Dawn* in one hand, a cigarette in the other, an alarm clock on the nightstand: 4:34 A.M.

In the center—the beach, a sheet spread on the sand, bodies spread on the sheet, the women from the previous pictures wearing bikinis that somehow seem innocent and modest.

On the right—Julianna crouched down on Western, fronting, throwing up some kind of sign with her fingers, above her a banner for the Larry Sultan show at LACMA, her expression like she owns the street, the city, like she owns Larry Sultan.

6.

———

THE GALLERY IS FULL. PEOPLE CAME. THE RIGHT PEOPLE.
Marella is talking to everyone at once—one conversation spilling
into another as she's pulled this way and that. There are rainy
footprints on the floor, umbrellas and puddles near the door.
Everyone talking about the downpour—an end-times deluge.

There are a few gallerists from the bigger outfits, a critic from
the *L.A. Times*, and another from one of the big online sites. There
are the usual cheese platters and crudités and a table with pass-
able wine.

She's dressed in black jeans, a tight black tank top, and a black
kimono jacket.

Marella listens to herself overexplain her work. Because the
work can't stand on its own—that's the problem. It needs a voice
to give it resonance. And even then it sounds flat.

She worried that the show would be upstaged by the news.
First the serial killer who's prowling these streets. Then the action
on the Brooklyn Bridge.

Now, that's art. Real performance art. Marella can't deny it.

A band of protesters led by Morgan Tillett, a Los Angeles activist with Power Through Protest, climbed one of the towers of the

Brooklyn Bridge last night. Her group made camp. Unfurled banners. Staged their protest against the killing of Jermaine Holloway. Jermaine's mother, Idira, was with them. She had a bullhorn and made a speech that was projected into the night and echoed off the bridge, down the river, over to the city. They had speakers and amps. They had strobe lights and smoke machines. They staged an entire hip-hop concert on the blustery top of the bridge, their backs to the New York skyline. They blasted the city—the world—with their songs of outrage. They took over.

Then Idira read a letter she'd received from a woman in California who told her never to stop fighting. The group on the bridge ended their performance with a song called "Violence All Around." As they sang, the chant went up through the city: *Violence All Around.* It rang down avenues. From office buildings. From people they'd planted on ferries and tour boats. On the subways. They paid pedicabs to take the chant to the streets, riding it up and down the Bowery, Central Park, Times Square.

They arrested the city, held it captive for thirty minutes.

Violence All Around.

The iPhone videos went viral. The news cameras legitimized it. You couldn't look away.

It was impossible to escape. It was in you and on top of you. It was everywhere.

The show went on with Morgan Tillett and Idira Holloway at its center—rock stars, icons. Women who will be remembered.

Marella takes a glass of wine. This one—her second—gives her courage. Maybe the work isn't as bad as she thinks. Maybe it's next level, the next thing. Maybe it's going to launch her.

Marella's college friends are here. Friends from the art scene. Up-and-coming artists. Established ones. A huge turnout for a small space especially considering the rain battering the windows.

The young, celebrated muralist from Skid Row is there—the one who painted Idira Holloway being reborn from her deceased son's head. So is an acquaintance who is doing an installation in the courtyard of MOCA downtown—a woman who has by all accounts "made it." Marella watches her watch *Dead Body #3*. Her eyes are expressionless as the images of Julianna's life reflect on the lenses of her saucer-sized glasses. The photos bounce off her like she's a force field. She turns away, laughs at something a man with asymmetrical hair has just said.

How can she be laughing? Marella downs her wine.

She's pulled aside by a writer for a feminist blog and asked a dozen questions about the female body and its objectification.

Does her work celebrate *woman-as-object*?

Does it liberate?

Does it simply address the harsh realities?

Is she trying to subvert conventions of beauty?

She braces herself for the tough question—where did the photos in *Dead Body #3* come from? But no one asks.

She has another glass of wine.

There's another critic, one she doesn't recognize. A short woman with choppy blond bangs and a suit like a bank manager's. Either Marella didn't catch where she said she was from or the woman didn't mention it. But she has her notebook out and unlike the other people in the gallery who are glancing at the work, this woman seems really into it. She clicks her pen.

"Can I ask you a few questions about all this?" she says with a gesture at the projectors and monitors.

"Of course," Marella replies.

Click, click. Then she taps the pen on her heavy notepad.

"I'm wondering about your materials."

"It's mostly projectors, computers, monitors. I try to use ones that are more reflective of a time period or that create a discourse between medium and message. Ones that produce a gritty, more granular quality."

"And what time period is that?"

Marella does the math. "Midnineties."

"Why those years?"

Marella waits for the woman to look up, then holds her stare. "They were formative for me in terms of development—my own. I came into my awareness of myself as a woman."

"Oh yeah." The woman's scribbling again. She doesn't sound the least bit interested in Marella's response. "So these monitors and whatever, they are the *found objects.*"

"Excuse me?"

The woman glances over toward *Dead Body #3*. "It says that the final piece involves *found objects.*"

Here it is, the question Marella's dreading.

"Oh," Marella says. "Sure. I found one of the monitors on the street." Not exactly a full-on lie. She'd found it in a storage unit behind a friend's studio that opened onto an alley. "I like to make use of discarded technology. I think, more than simply summoning a link to the past, it conjures the past itself."

The woman doesn't write this down. But she waits, pen poised on her pad. She taps the tip once, expecting more.

"And some of the pictures—I found them."

The woman purses her lips, a small gesture of agreement.

"Or rather I sourced them from the internet."

"Sourced?"

Marella looks over her shoulder. She wants this interview to end. "It's called bricolage," she says. "Borrowing from other sources, compiling and collecting to tell your own story."

Now the woman gestures at *Dead Body #3*. "And this is your own story?"

"It's everybody's story," Marella says. "Don't you think?"

"I don't know," the woman replies. "One more question. What's the inspiration behind your work?"

Marella takes a deep breath. This is what she's prepared for. The spiel slips out. "I have always been interested in the destruction of the female body. Or perhaps in how the world is out to destroy it. It is, I'd guess, more than anything else the target of more violence, physical, psychological, emotional, let's say, than anything else in the world."

The woman cocks her head to the side. "But why?"

Marella raises her eyebrows in what she hopes is a *do-I-have-to-tell-you* expression. The truth is she doesn't exactly know why and her work isn't bringing her any closer to understanding. "Why do men and other women want to punish women?" She takes a deep breath, trying to compose a response. "Well, first of all, there is the physical power dynamic, you know—a question of size."

The woman stops writing, but doesn't look up. She holds out a hand to stop Marella. "I mean why does this interest you?"

"Oh."

"How did you become interested in such extreme violence?"

Extreme violence. Marella has to stifle a smile. Because that's what this is and it's finally been seen. It's not art or performance art or the re-creation of an emotion or event. It's violence itself.

"It's inevitable in the world we live in, isn't it?"

"Is it?"

The woman is challenging her, making her uncomfortable. She's barely met Marella's eye.

"I mean, look around, the images on TV and on the news," Marella says.

"So you got interested in all this because of something you saw on the news." She clicks her pen, scribbles something.

Marella's hand lashes out, almost pulling pen from paper. "No," she says. This is her work, her life. She didn't crib it from one of those sensational newsmagazines or get inspired after watching too much *Law & Order SVU*. Her work doesn't derive from hearsay or secondhand information. It's not a story she's invented. It's real.

The woman looks up, startled by the force of Marella's gesture. "It's more than that," Marella says. "It happened."

The woman takes a deep breath, as if at last Marella's said something interesting. Before Marella can elaborate, and she's not sure exactly what she would say if she did, she finds that she and the woman are standing in the center of people. Someone is clapping for silence. The woman steps back, leaving Marella to her audience.

Marella stands in the middle of the gallery with everyone surrounding her. She takes a gulp of the drink she's holding. They are waiting.

She had a speech planned about the intersectionality of bodies and objects, life and decay. About the line between subject and subjugation. But the conversation with the brusque woman drove it out of her mind.

"When I was eight years old I saw a dead woman floating in the sea behind my house outside San Salvador. She was bloated and blue. She looked like a sea creature. She'd been murdered, then tossed in the water. Whoever killed her started the job and the sea finished it. The world is out to destroy our bodies and all we have is our bodies to protect us."

In the crowd she tracks the woman she'd just been speaking with. She sees her near the front, still jotting in her notepad.

"It's hard to sleep at night when you start thinking about all the things that can happen. About how easy it is to rip your flesh open. It's crazy that we make it through any day intact. Life is measured in millimeters. A car just missing you. And what about time and timing? What about meeting a stranger on an empty street? What if he's distracted? Doesn't see you or doesn't see what he wants to see in you? What if he lets you go because he isn't quite in the mood yet? What if he grabs the next woman who passes instead? How many encounters have you had like that? Hundreds? Thousands?"

The guests arrayed in front of her are shifting from foot to foot. She can see them fighting the urge to look away, to check their phones, chat among themselves. She can sense their need for her to wrap it up. She's made them uncomfortable, which is more than her art did. Because how could they look at what she created and keep eating and drinking and laughing and talking? All that tells her is that the work still isn't strong enough. It's not Darren Almond's bus stop to Auschwitz or the sculpture of the manacled semi-naked family outside the National Memorial for Peace and Justice in Montgomery. It's not the pope on his knees taking it doggy style. It's not Hitler as a schoolboy. It doesn't shock people into silence, summon terrors that they haven't experienced. Make them feel something that they haven't felt.

Marella feels the black wave coming for her. If she isn't careful, she's going to snap the plastic cup she's holding and spill her drink. She winces to fight back the black. The cut on her cheek smarts. She can feel the quick throb of the bruise. It grounds her. Steady.

"And then the women who get murdered around here. You've seen the news, right?"

She waits.

"Or do you think it has nothing to do with you? Maybe you give yourself that luxury. That must be nice. For me it's different. First of all, this girl who used to babysit next door. And my next-door neighbor too."

She's running on too long but she can't stop herself.

"The places that you think are familiar aren't. Your home isn't your home. My art isn't art. I'm trying but I'm not getting anywhere. It's hard to convey the violence. Because the violence is too violent. To do it right would hurt. It would hurt you. I want it to hurt you."

Marella staggers a little. Then she lifts her glass like she's making a toast. And everyone around her claps tentatively.

"Anyway—" Marella says. But she doesn't have to say any more. The party has closed around her.

Someone leads her to the back of the gallery and sits her down. She's given a bottle of water, which washes away the sour taste of the wine. She props her head on her hands and stares through the door of the small office at the party. The majority of the guests are gathered around the monitors showing Julianna's photos. Some have their cell phones out, taking pictures or making videos. A few are even taking notes.

There are a few women from Jefferson Park—middle-aged, black. Community minded. They stick out. But they are the ones who give the work the right kind of look. Their gazes don't pass over it. They drink it in as if they know.

7.

———

THERE ARE A FEW HANGERS-ON AND A FEW LATE ARRIVALS,
but the gallery has mostly emptied out. Cups litter the floor, the
window ledge, even near *Dead Body #1*. Marella can feel the hang-
over she's going to have tomorrow.

Whenever the door to the gallery opens, she looks to see if her
parents decided to support her. But it's just people leaving.

A few stragglers stop by to say goodbye. A local woman peppers
her with questions about how she became an artist and whether
she could perhaps talk to the woman's daughter who wants to get
into comic book illustration but needs some guidance. Marella
gives the woman her email just to be rid of her.

Tomorrow there's a studio visit from two potential patrons,
TV writers who are getting into collecting. And that's it. The show
will stay up for a month. But Marella's part is done.

The door opens. It's the small woman with the choppy bangs.
Before Marella can stand up, the woman has crossed the gallery
and is in the small office.

"Was there something else you wanted to know?" Marella asks.

The woman is holding out a card. *Esmerelda Perry, LAPD Detective.*

"Detective?"

"Mind if I sit?" Detective Perry asks, pulling out the chair opposite the desk.

"Be my guest," Marella says.

Detective Perry is chewing gum as if she wants to destroy it.

"You're into art, Detective?"

The detective has her pad open. She snaps her gum. "You grew up in Los Angeles."

"It's all on my bio," Marella says, handing her the press materials from the show.

"It says you grew up in Los Angeles, but you went to middle school in Ojai."

Marella raises her eyebrows. "That's not in my bio."

"So Ojai or L.A.?"

"I lived with my aunt for a few years. Better schools."

Detective Perry looks up. "What happened to your cheek?"

Marella's hand flies to the bruise. "Boxing."

"And after Ojai you went to boarding school."

"In Los Olivos. And then to college and grad school in San Diego."

"And when did you come back to Los Angeles?"

"I'm sorry, Detective, what's going on here?"

"How often do you box?"

Marella shakes her head, startled by the directional shift. "Once a week. Maybe twice."

"Are you good?"

"I suck."

"Why do you do it? Self-defense?"

To control the violence. To experience it on my own terms. That's the real answer, but what Marella says is "Kinda."

Detective Perry places her notebook on the desk. "So what I'm trying to do is establish a timeline here. You were gone from Los Angeles from 1998 to 2013?"

"Pretty much," Marella says.

Click. Snap. Click. Snap. Between her gum and pen, Detective Perry is a full-on rhythm section.

"Listen, Marella, I don't know much about art, but I'm really wondering about this business of found objects."

"It's from the French practice of *objets trouvés*—turning things that are not normally art into art. Basically, it's the art of recontextualization."

Detective Perry pulls out her phone and starts tapping on the screen. "So how long have you been boxing?"

"Excuse me?"

"Boxing?"

Tap. Tap. Tap.

"About a year and a half."

"So just after you got back to L.A.?"

"I guess. What—?" But Detective Perry beats her to the next question.

"Where do you live, Marella?"

"At home, mostly."

"So you live somewhere else, too?"

The headache is settling in. Her skull feels as if it's shrinking, compressing around her brain. "Would you like living at home at twenty-five? I move around."

Detective Perry glances up from her phone. "You know that you are showing photos of dead women in your show—murdered women."

Marella opens her mouth.

"Is that what you consider a *found object*?"

"Do I need to credit the photographer or something?"

The detective is back on her phone, tapping away like a teenager on Instagram. "You're twenty-five. You're good on the internet and social media. I'm sure you know how to do a reverse image search." She's tapping away again. The sound of her finger on the phone's glass is twanging Marella's nerves. "Everyone imagines that pictures are two-dimensional. But not on social media. Not today, with everyone having a camera and documenting everything at once. Think of it this way—if you see a photo looking in one direction, there's most likely a photo of someone looking in the other at the same moment. You just need to find it." Detective Perry turns the phone around and hands it to Marella.

It's a Facebook photo. Marella recognizes the setting instantly. The same apartment where many of Julianna's photos were taken. She recognizes the scene, too—the table strewn with the same late-night detritus that appears in one of her loops—the drugs, cigarettes, booze, *Twilight* paperback. Except in this photo the angle is reversed, the foreground turned into the background, and behind the table is Julianna holding a phone, capturing the mess in front of her.

Marella scrolls through the pictures. She sees the account belongs to a woman named Coco, who appears in many of Julianna's photos. The photos are messy, lazy, with none of the clarity of Julianna's shots.

"How'd you get the phone?" Detective Perry asks.

Marella imagines this is how murderers feel when they are finally caught. Relief. Release. "I found it."

"Where?"

"On the street."

"Exactly where on the street?"

"She lives next door."

"Lived."

"So between our houses. On the little scrap of grass around a tree near the curb."

"It didn't occur to you that you might have been in possession of evidence?"

"I didn't know she was dead when I found the phone."

"So you found it the night she died?"

"I guess."

"Do you understand the concept of evidence? A woman is murdered and you find her phone on the street. Her parents had the sense to call me right away." Detective Perry closes her notebook and puts away her phone. "I suppose you think that now Julianna gets to live forever in your work."

"I hadn't really thought about it," Marella admits.

The detective spits her gum into a wastebasket and unwraps another stick. "It's real, you understand. The women in those photos really died. They were really murdered. The person who killed them hasn't been found." She stands up and heads for the door. Halfway across the gallery, she turns back. "Why are you interested in these sorts of images?"

"I think I already answered that," Marella says.

"You tried to answer, but you didn't. Don't worry," the detective says. "One day you'll figure it out." She continues to the door. As she opens it, she stops once more, the door ajar, the rain blowing in. "Marella." She lets the name hang there for a moment, lashed by the storm. "Marella, do you have any idea who killed Julianna?"

The question travels across the gallery, a bullet slowed down by a special effect so that Marella has time to observe it collide with her chest, take her breath away. "I—I . . ." Why would she? Why would she have any idea who killed her neighbor?

"Or maybe the others," Detective Perry says. "Maybe you know who killed Katherine Sims or Jazmin Freemont."

"Why—?" Marella begins.

"I just thought I'd ask." The detective pulls out her notebook again, then quickly crosses back to the office. "One more thing." She's holding out a phone number scrawled on the lined paper. "Do you recognize this number?"

"That's my parents' landline from when I was little."

"That's what I thought." And without waiting for a response, Detective Perry exits to the rainy street.

8.

————

THE RAIN POUNDS THE WINDOWS AS IF IT INTENDS TO BREAK them. The gallery is dark. The only light comes from the glow of the monitors and the streaky headlights from cars rushing down Washington. Tomorrow Marella will add Julianna's name to the tag on *Dead Girl #3*. "In collaboration with Julianna Vargas."

She turns out the lights. She doesn't want to be visible alone in the gallery.

The street is dark—the windows streaked with rain. She can barely see out.

She finds a bottle of wine and tips it into a discarded cup. She's not sure she wants to go home. It's probably best to let her parents' absence go unremarked.

Detective Perry's question hovers in the gallery.

The monitors whir and click. The videos run on their loops. Julianna's life slides past.

Do you have any idea who killed Julianna?

The question opens a door. Summons a fear. Does precisely what Marella hoped her art would do. It upends her sense of safety in a place that is her own.

She glances around the gallery, checking the corners. She lets her eyes drift to the street. But she can see nothing beyond the window. She feels alone and on display.

Something shifts along the floor. Marella's heart catches. But it's only headlights from an idling car that have reconfigured the shadows inside the gallery.

She wants to turn off her installations. But that will leave her in the dark.

Fear is fickle. Last night alone with her work Marella felt nothing but courage and pride. The images were powerful, made her feel powerful and in control. But now she sees dead women. She sees their desperation. She sees they were doomed.

And what's worse, she's turned herself into a victim, filmed herself being chased down the streets, cornered. She thought that by turning her fear into art she'd master it and get the jump on it.

But she's not in control. Not now and not when she was making and creating.

It's an illusion, a feint. Just like in boxing. For an hour in the gym she can pretend she's got the upper hand on the impending violence, that by submitting to it on her own terms, she controls it. But the high only lasts until she has to step out onto the street.

She lets her eyes linger on *Dead Body #2*—the loop that shows her being chased through the streets from her pursuer's perspective as she sheds clothes, gets bruised and bloodied, her self scraped away until she collapses. Then she turns to *Dead Body #3*. The image on the left is Julianna's face underneath the Larry Sultan banner.

It's one of the last pictures on the phone and one of the few that actually shows Julianna.

It was the one that first caught Marella's eye—the one that told her Julianna's images were intentional, not accidental. That she was a photographer, an artist. That she was a storyteller, a memoirist.

This was the image that inspired Marella to do what she did.

But now in the disorienting wake of the detective's question she sees something else in the picture. A woman on a death march. A countdown clock.

How long had Julianna lived after this photo? Marella could check the file on her computer. But she doesn't want to know.

She looks at Julianna's defiant stare and sees her mistake. She doesn't own the streets. It's the other way around.

Click. The picture vanishes, replaced by another. A white sheet on a bed. A woman sleeping facedown. On her right, a box of half-eaten Winchell's donuts. On her left, a tipped-over coffee cup, draining pale brown liquid onto the covers.

The woman's legs are bare. She's wearing a short robe. Underneath it a sliver of a teal lace thong is visible.

This sliver of lace—this suggestion—that's what turns the watcher into a voyeur and makes her feel as if she's seeing something she shouldn't. It tempts the eye higher, makes it crave more, makes it confront its carnality.

Marella stares. She can't help herself. Her eyes travel from the depression between the sleeping woman's legs up to the hem of her robe where the lace is a bright light in the shadow. Her gaze lingers, prying, frustrated at the limited reach of the photograph.

And then, as she's staring at this woman's body, wanting to see more than she should, a man's face appears. It materializes on the screen, perfectly framed in the center of the photo. His eyes are hidden in the dark spill of coffee, but he's there. He's gazing out from the picture—an apparition, staring directly at Marella.

She screams and turns from the monitor. Her heart is galloping.

Now, through the dark onslaught of rain, she can see her mistake. The man isn't staring out from the monitor, he's staring into the gallery from the street, his face captured and reflected in the glowing screen in front of Marella.

She doesn't want to, but she shades her eyes and squints out into the dark street. There's no one there. She turns back to the monitor, which is now showing a picture of a woman removing her makeup in a cracked mirror. All she sees is the photo.

She checks the window once more but sees no one.

The door to the gallery rattles. Someone is knocking and pulling on the handles.

"*Marella!*"

She is startled by her name.

"*Marella!*"

For a moment she thinks she's imagining it.

She takes a deep breath and shades her eyes so she can see beyond the glass.

Roger. Her father. Standing in the rain, his bushy, graying hair plastered to his head, his beard dripping. "Marella, are you going to open the door?"

For a moment she is too stunned by this apparition of her father to move. A day ago he'd been in one of his fugues, barely capable of eating, unable to acknowledge Marella or her mother. And now, here he is back in the world and calling her name.

Marella fumbles with the deadbolt.

Roger enters with a gust of wind and rain.

"I missed it," he says. "I lost track of time."

"That's okay. You're here."

Marella tells him to wait. Then she fetches a towel from the back and watches as her father shakes the rain from his hair and shoulders and brushes it from his beard. She flips on the overhead and the room comes to life. The colors on the monitors recede.

Roger looks up from the towel. His eyes are animated.

"So," Roger says. "This is it. This is what you do."

When was the last time Marella had been alone with her father? She can't remember. Anneke was always there.

Roger hands her the towel and glances at the installations.

"Mom didn't want to come?"

He's peering across the room. "So that's it?"

"Where's Mom?" Marella asks again.

"Tell me about all this. You made this?"

"Mom didn't want to come?"

"I don't know," Roger says. "I just left."

"It's better if you look at it up close," Marella says. "From over here it's just a bunch of monitors and screens."

Her father doesn't reply. It's almost as if he doesn't hear her. He moves away from the entrance toward the installations. He starts with *Dead Body #1*. He stands in front of three stacked monitors. Marella wonders if he recognizes the beach behind their old house in El Salvador.

She'd paid for the trip from a grant she'd received at SDSU that funded works of art in Central America. She never told her parents about returning to La Libertad.

She expects him to spend a few polite minutes in front of each of her works and move on. But Roger is watching. He's seeing. For a full five minutes he doesn't move from *Dead Body #1*, his eyes absorbing the videos on each monitor in turn, giving them their due. He's patient. He has the eye of a collector, a critic.

"You like it?" Marella didn't mean to ask such a needy question. She knows it's not what you ask about art, ever. It's not a meal you've prepared, a scarf you've knitted. It's not meant to please.

Roger doesn't answer. He just keeps his eyes on the monitors.

"Dad?"

Marella is tempted to shake him.

"Dad?"

"Who's that?"

Marella follows his gaze to the bottom monitor.

"Who's that in the video?"

"On the bottom?" She can't believe she even has to answer this question because it should be so obvious, especially to her father of all people. "It's me."

"What's you?"

"On the screen, that's me."

He doesn't take his eyes from the monitor. "You."

"You remember the dead woman in the water in El Salvador?"

Roger turns from the monitor. "But that wasn't you. That wasn't you at all. She was just some whore who came too close."

Whore. Marella's never heard this kind of language from her father. Sex worker. Prostitute. But never whore. "Too close to what?"

Roger doesn't answer. "Now the world has seen you naked," he says. "I don't like that."

It's not exactly *the world*. But Marella doesn't correct him.

She wouldn't have made this piece if she had a problem with people seeing her naked, her parents, friends, anyone else. Her art desexualizes her, takes away the thing that makes her vulnerable. It's barely her body or a body at all on the screen. It's an erosion doused in blue paint—a reversal of the piece she'd performed at the fund-raiser for the derelict mansion. It's not a celebration, an invitation, or a taunt. It's the opposite. It's the aftermath.

It's supposed to revile, repulse, repel the suggestion of decay and violation. But that's not how her father is looking at it. His eyes are hungry—each ladle of blue paint that covers Marella is a disappointment.

"Your body doesn't belong to others," Roger says.

"You sound like Mom."

Marella steps behind the monitors to get a better view of Roger's face.

He's staring at the video the same way she'd been looking at the photo of the woman lying facedown on her bed, the flash of teal lace inviting the eye to want more. The teal thong excavating a dirty desire.

He's not watching the loop the way you are supposed to look at art—appraising, critical, considering—but the way you look at something when you are alone, when you permit yourself the impure thoughts of lust and disgust.

"Dad? Daddy?"

Car tires skid, shriek, and slosh. There's a squeal of brakes.

"Dad."

Roger looks up. It takes a moment for his eyes to adjust to the world away from the monitor, to dial Marella in.

"Interesting," he says.

His voice is distant, like the echo of a voice. The wind and rain batter the windows. The world outside the gallery seems far away. There is only the gallery, the installations, Marella, and her father.

He's looking at her strangely. Marella backs closer to the wall behind the monitors, hoping Roger will move on to the next piece. There's a twang in her nerves, a premonition that anticipates impact.

His eyes are roving over her body. She's not sure whether he's trying to reconcile the woman on the screen with the daughter in front of him or if it's something else.

"Dad?"

Marella folds her arms over her chest, rounds her shoulders, caves inward.

A dark look clouds Roger's face as she tries to shrink away.

"Dad, what are you looking at?"

"You," he says. "I'm looking at you."

Marella squirms against the wall, driven there by her father's stare. "Don't," she says. "Don't. Not like that. The work's not sexual," she adds. "It's challenging. That's the point."

He's still staring.

"Dad!" Marella shouts, stepping away from the wall, placing her hands on her hips and frowning like a petulant teenager. "Stop!"

Roger blinks, takes a breath. "Sorry," he says. "I guess your work is transporting."

"Okay," Marella says. "That's good."

Finally, Roger moves on to *Dead Body #2*.

She watches him watch the video.

"That's me too, Dad," Marella says. "It's not real, you know. It's staged. But not like a movie. It's supposed to *be* something. Like, be it, not re-create it or represent it." She's blabbering, filling the silence of the gallery with her chatter. Talking over and around and through the disquieting look in Roger's eyes, the gaze that tells her that there's more that he wants from the images on the screen, that she's awakened something in him.

"What are you running from?" Roger asks.

"You know, like, it's an abstract concept but also a real one. Violence is all around us. Sexual. Physical. I am embodying that. I'm re-creating the everyday fear that goes hand in hand for women— the lack of safety. We are prey."

"Prey?" Roger says. "I hadn't thought of it like that."

"What I'm trying to do here is to master the fear. I want to control it."

"But you've become the prey," Roger says.

"I guess."

"So you can't control it. Ever. Look." He points at the screen. "You've lost. Whoever is chasing you has won. He always wins." He sounds almost triumphant.

"Well, it's not about him," Marella says.

"I like it," he says.

Marella wants to tell him that he's not supposed to *like* it. It's supposed to disturb him.

"Good," she says. "Thanks."

The smile on her face feels forced.

He's on to the third piece—*Dead Body #3*.

The wind hammers harder. The lights flicker, the monitors flash. Then everything is restored to normal.

Roger takes a step back so he can see all the monitors at once.

He takes his time, his eyes lingering on one through several revolutions before moving on to the next. Marella marks time. Cars swish by. She can hear the buzz of the overhead lights.

"Dad? Dad?"

A volley of rain assaults the window.

"Dad?"

"How do you know these women?" he says.

"I mean Julianna lived next door so—"

"Julianna," he says. "But you don't know her."

"We've met."

"But you don't know her. I know you don't. You don't know any of them. You don't know Katherine."

"How do you know her name?" Marella asks.

"This isn't your world. This is a dark, dark place. A very dark place."

"That's not the point," Marella says. "You can find beauty anywhere. Or at least power. Or at least the suggestion of one of those."

Roger's not listening. He's staring at the monitors like there is nothing else in the entire world. She wants to slap him out of his reverie. She dips into the office and finds a bottle of water that she hands to him. She watches him open it and drink as if in a trance.

"These women," he says. "Look at these women."

Marella jumps at the sound of her phone ringing in her pocket. She takes a deep breath, then another, trying to summon a calm tone before answering. She looks at the screen. Her mother.

"A family reunion," she says, holding the phone to her ear.

"Marella?" Her mother's voice sounds tight.

"At least one of my parents remembered my show."

"Your father? He's there?"

There's an edge in Anneke's voice Marella doesn't like. "Mom?"

"I'm coming to get him."

"He's fine, Mom."

"Marella, I'm coming to get him."

"Just let him be. Let him enjoy my work."

But Anneke has already disconnected.

Marella puts her phone away. If Roger was aware of the conversation, he doesn't indicate it.

"These women," Roger says for the third time. "They don't belong here."

"It's an art show."

"But they don't belong. They shouldn't be here. Not here. Not with you."

"What do you mean?"

"Where did you get these photographs?"

"It's a collaboration."

"But where did you get them?"

Marella sighs. "I found Julianna's phone."

Roger looks away from the monitors for the first time. Suddenly he's all business, his voice precise, on point. "Tell me exactly where you found it."

"Right outside our house by the tree on the sidewalk."

"Do you have it?"

Marella's stomach begins to flutter. Her fingers tingle. "I gave it back."

"Marella, what have you done?"

Roger looks down the row of screens. He squats down, looks at each one in turn. He reaches toward the middle screen, presses his fingers to the glass. Leaves them there. Marella watches the images rotate, reflecting on his face as they do. "These women don't belong here. They don't belong anywhere."

Marella realizes she's been holding her breath. Realizes she has been holding it not just now but for years. Waiting. Waiting. Waiting.

And the violence, it's not elsewhere, it's not upstairs with her mother or out on the streets. It's here.

And she's not ready.

FEELIA 2014

YEAH, IT'S ME. I'M BACK. SO WHAT. I GOT BUSINESS HERE. Lemme talk to a detective. This isn't some made-up shit. This shit's important. I have evidence. I need someone to take my motherfucking statement.

No? You're gonna tell me no?

Take a look at this motherfucker. This motherfucking scar— you know what that is. That's you not doing your job.

You want me to go into that now? You want me to make a scene? Got my throat slit and left for dead and LAPD did fuck-all.

But listen up. I'm not gonna haul that dirty laundry out right now. I'm going to turn the tables. I'm going to do you a favor. I'm going to help you out. That's right, you heard. I'm going to help you out.

What's that? You think I can't be of any assistance. Well, excuse me, Mr. Desk Sergeant. Excuse-fucking-me.

I think someone is going to want to hear what I got to say about the man who tried to kill me. Because I remember something. Got my memory jogged.

You want to know what it is before you call someone? You a fucking gatekeeper?

Fine. Lemme tell you.

The guy who cut me, he was drinking this wine. Said it was South African. That shit made me laugh, because no way there's wine in South Africa unless they got giraffes making it. But then he told me to stop laughing. He told me his wife was from South Africa.

How come you're looking at me like that?

That's what I remember. That's what I just remembered.

So you gonna call someone, take my statement.

Listen, you all got a serial killer running loose around here. So who are you to decide what's worth repeating up the chain? You want that on your conscience?

Thank you.

Thank you for doing your job.

Thank you for picking up that phone.

Now hold up. Who's that you're calling?

Homicide?

Fuck Homicide.

I know this is attempted murder. But the detective I want to see is in Vice. Detective Perry. Get me Detective Perry.

How come?

Last time I was here you were more than happy to show me to her desk. Now it's all, *how come?*

Let me tell you *how come.* Lady's the only one who ever listened to me. That's the truth. So she's the one I'm bringing this to.

Call her.

I'm waiting.

PART V

ANNEKE

1.

———

THE GROUND IS SWAMPY. THE RAIN HAS RAISED THE MUD above the grass. This is not a nice corner of Rosedale Cemetery. Too close to Washington and Catalina—a filthy side street with dirty houses and human waste from the residents of the campers that are never moved or ticketed. Anneke supposes people don't consider everything when they choose their child's grave. She can see how you might overlook certain details. But still the Vargas family should have been more thoughtful. It just goes to show— there's a pattern. Careless in one respect, careless in another. Bad things happen for a reason.

Dorian had picked better, up on a hill with a view. Shady in the summer. Green in the late winter and spring.

Down here is a different story, a muddy, sodden mess of wet earth and debris that's run downhill.

At least Julianna's parents chose Rosedale. At least they didn't skimp for something farther south.

Not that Rosedale is as clean or respected as it was even two decades ago. There was a notice at last week's neighborhood council meeting about a woman who scattered her daughter's ashes in the cemetery and then claimed one of the most stately graves as her own. She'd even vandalized the chiseled name with spray paint.

The last time Anneke was at a funeral here was Lecia Williams's fifteen years ago. A sad, small affair—just the mother, an elderly black couple, and a few school friends of Lecia's. There were a couple of bouquets, nothing like the garish wreaths and floral crosses propped up on easels at Julianna's gravesite.

Today's event is tasteless and immoderate—a gaudy display of grief and religion.

Look at Julianna's friends in their miniskirts, tight dresses, thigh-high boots, and halter tops, their artificial hair and fake jewels. They show too much cleavage and their faces are streaked with runny black makeup. Their laments are vulgar, peppered with coarse words and outsize grief.

Anneke keeps herself apart from the crowd under one of the few trees in this section of the cemetery. The low winter sun is a healthy yellow orb, neither dangerously hot nor painfully bright. The rain stopped last night and the sky is clear.

People think that rain is a cleanser, that it washes away the dirt and grime. They think it's baptismal. Anneke knows better. Especially in the places she's lived—El Salvador, Central America, India, Thailand, where mud is a disease. Just look around the cemetery at the dirt and funk lifted by the storm—the city's underbelly bared. The rain hasn't scrubbed anything away. It hasn't washed or cleansed. What it's done is reveal the nature of things, the grime below the surface, the violence glossed over.

The pastor is alternating between Spanish and English. Julianna's mother, Alva, is being supported by her husband and her son. Armando doesn't strike Anneke as much of a crier. He's a snake, that man. From her second-story window she's watched him cheat at dice over the years. He uses a controlled throw, predetermining his outcome—using one die to stop and trap the other. A cheap but skillful trick she's never reported to Roger or the rest of them. Let them lose their money if they're too dumb to figure it out.

She's also heard their fights—the way Armando bellows at Alva, his coarse anger just like someone on a bad TV show. He should have more respect, not just for his wife but for the neighbors. It's selfish. Improper. That's what walls are for, to keep everything inside. You pull the curtains. You keep quiet. You maintain order.

Anneke feels sorry for them, the way they lost track of their daughter. She's not saying it was all their fault. But there are steps that could have been taken, steps she's tried to take on their behalf. Thankless is what she'd call them.

That's what people don't understand. All her work to remove prostitutes from Jefferson Park—the plans she's unveiled at the neighborhood council for photo-shaming, online exposure, and citizen patrols—isn't simply to make the neighborhood more genteel. Her efforts are not to raise her home value. She does it to save the women, make them feel unwelcome and move on. Because look around—this is no place for someone to be working the streets.

Anneke folds her arms over her chest and purses her lips. She can feel the twitch coming in her right eye. She tightens her lips to try to still the tremor, pinching them so tight her teeth grind against one another.

Dorian, dressed in an old black dress now blue with age, is standing off to the right of the family. You would think that one time would have been enough for her to go through this. But here she is again like she's inviting the pain.

Her daughter—now that was a shame. She wasn't like the others. Even Anneke knew that. But it doesn't matter how you lived, only how you died.

If only Dorian knew what she was doing by feeding those women, grounding them here and making them comfortable.

Anneke tried to show her. But no one pays attention. No one listens to her.

A decade and a half of working at NGOs around the world taught her that. Fifteen years of explaining hygiene and hazards to mothers who looked at her with blank faces like there was no way a prim white lady could understand how their bodies work or the work they did with their bodies.

Roger taught school in those impoverished communities. That was a better job. Anneke didn't have the patience for schoolchildren.

By now she no longer has the patience for any of it. Which is why she moved into elder care when they settled in Los Angeles—a city that often seems little better than their third-world communities. At least there's nothing she needs to teach her wards in their sanitized home in the cliffs of Malibu. There's nothing left for them to learn. All they need is to pass their days in peace—a card game, a craft, a digest of bland midday television.

It's a relief not to care whether or not someone listens to her, whether anyone follows her directions. There is only so often you can tell people about the diseases in a droplet of water, in a puddle of mud, a pinprick of blood. There are only so many times your warnings can go unheeded before you grow angry, filled with the sour venom of disregard.

The women in Malibu are always happy to see Anneke. They already know that the world provides no spectacular surprises and that they are not invincible or immune. They are done, coasting to their inevitable close.

She puts a hand to her eye to stop the twitch. Her skin feels hot, as if it, too, were angry.

They are singing a hymn now, first in Spanish then in English. The congregation has come together—the family, those women, and even Dorian. They are clasping hands, singing to the Lord that Julianna be preserved.

There is no Lord. Anneke could tell them that. Her father was a missionary, her mother an international Red Cross nurse. They met outside Johannesburg. Soon the family was moving from country to country as one preached and the other tried to heal, and not once—not in any of the slums, not in the famine areas, not in any of the war-ravaged cities or the refugee camps—had she detected an iota of God's grandeur or grace. All she saw was chaos and desperation.

Which is why you need to tend your own house, keep it neat, make rules, instill traditions, anything and everything to keep the chaos out and the evil at bay.

But her father saw things differently, putting his trust in God, pronouncing his benediction, commanding his wards to believe as if that was all it would take.

May God preserve you in his light.
May God preserve your family in your heart.
May the beauty of God be reflected in your eyes.
May the kindness of God be reflected in your words,
and the knowledge of God flow from your heart,
that all might see his grandeur all around you
and in seeing, believe.

Every day these words. Sometimes hourly, sometimes more. And never once did Anneke see God's grandeur. Never once did these words elevate or ameliorate. They didn't fix anything, and as far as she could tell, they didn't keep anyone safe.

Babies died.

Mothers died.

Men were murdered.

Men murdered.

But still:

May the kindness of God be reflected in your words,
and the knowledge of God flow from your heart,
that all might see his grandeur all around you
and in seeing, believe.

Believe. Believe in the face of desperation, devastation, and a hundred types of death. Believe when you're riddled with disease. Believe when your home has been destroyed, when bombs are falling, when the world around you is rubble.

Regardless, her father prayed. His wards repeated his words. And decades later his prayer is still stuck in Anneke's mind. It comes to her in dreams and reveals itself in the rattle of the car over rough roads and the roar of a muddy river. She hears it in the stop-start traffic on the freeway and the crash of the surf in Malibu—the words commanding the impossible. Believe.

The priest in Rosedale begins his own benediction. A conventional one from Romans. Armando and Hector lead Alva around to where the priest is standing. Anneke watches her swat their hands away as she steps forward to stand unaided. She takes a small scoop from the priest's hands and bends down to fill it with dirt from the mound on the side of the grave. She takes off her sunglasses so the crowd can see her eyes. Her mouth opens and closes several times.

What could she possibly say? What needs to be said?

Hector rubs her back. Alva takes a deep breath. Then her eyes find Anneke's, fixing on the one person standing apart from the proceedings. As if somehow that gives her strength.

"We will never know why," she begins. She stands up straighter and tries again, her gaze never leaving Anneke. "We will never know why," she says once more. She clears her throat. "We will never know why the Lord decided to take Julianna from us."

The space between the two women narrows. There's no open grave. No congregation of mourners. There are no tacky wreaths or muddy earth. It's just Alva and Anneke alone.

"We will never know why the Lord decided to take Julianna from us," Alva repeats as if Anneke might provide an answer. "We will never know—"

Anneke shakes her head. "If that's what you want to believe," she says, her voice clear and proud. "The Lord had nothing to do with it. Nothing at all."

The congregation turns. A few of Julianna's friends don't bother to conceal their laughter. One calls Anneke a *fucking cunt* and heads in her direction, claws out, before two friends restrain her.

Anneke's eye has stopped twitching. She relaxes her mouth and heads for the paved path out of the cemetery.

She feels calmed. She has spoken and she has been heard. Her feet strike the ground with precision and purpose. She doesn't turn when she hears someone behind her.

At the gates a hand grasps her arm. Anneke slows, pulled to a halt by Dorian. She looks down at the fingers on her sleeve.

"That was unnecessary."

"Was it? You don't believe that nonsense about the Lord?"

"I don't," Dorian says.

"Then there's one thing we can agree on," Anneke says.

"Today isn't about what I or you believe."

Anneke slides her arm from Dorian's grasp. "Isn't it?"

"It's about Julianna's family and their grief. You should respect that."

"I don't need you to scold me," Anneke says. "I've got nothing but respect. I have more respect for their daughter's life than they did."

Dorian's eyes widen. "You're blaming them."

"I'm just saying things should have been done differently."

2.

―――――

THERE ARE RULES IN ANNEKE'S HOUSE. THEY KEEP THE WORLD on its axis. Sit down to all meals. Breakfast is just juice, coffee, bread, butter, maybe cheese and a piece of fruit or possibly a boiled egg. Lunch is usually cold, sandwiches and salad. Once in a while soup. Dinner is a simple ceremony. The table is always set, water glasses, wineglasses, linen napkins. One glass of wine at the meal. A glass of sherry or brandy after.

There is always a pause before the start of dinner—a brief moment in which Anneke can check that everything is in order. A secular grace for what she has achieved through control.

Anneke has her own benediction:

Preserve your house.
Preserve your family.
Preserve your boundaries.
Preserve order and order will be reflected in you.
Preserve privacy.
Preserve appearances and everything will be preserved
    for you.

Upstairs, beds are made. Laundry folded, never left in the hamper to wrinkle.

Windows remain closed. No sense in letting the inside out or vice versa.

These are the minor things. There are others—things you don't discuss. You have to be rigid, set boundaries.

It's not a lot to ask but imperative. If you let one thing slide, then what? Well, Anneke knows. She's seen firsthand what happens when you live without rules, without structure or self-respect. There's a way to carry yourself with dignity in a tent, on the street, in a slum.

It never ceases to amaze her how here in Los Angeles, a cosmopolitan and metropolitan city, people fail to elevate themselves. They don't alter or improve their surroundings, their circumstances.

Preserve appearances.

Preserve order.

Then you have done enough.

Roger is home. Tomorrow he will leave early for the charter school where he teaches ESL—a brutalist building wedged beneath a freeway on-ramp. A chaotic tumult of kids caught between cultures. It suits him. The regimented lessons. The practicality. A goal—to speak better, clearly, intelligently, as opposed to the more abstract lessons of literature or history. With language there is no interpretation, no improvisation. The same class year after year. The same workbooks, the same tests.

At least his black mood lifted the day before when he'd turned off his ponderous war history, taken off his headphones, and headed out in the rain to see Marella's art show. She'd worried when he'd gone out.

Anneke worries. That's her crutch. That is the crack through which the chaos seeps in. The disorder of her worried mind.

But Roger turned up where he was supposed to.

Anneke can hear him now in the backyard pruning the hedge, the slashing of the metal blades amplifying the tension in her head.

She puts on water for tea. When it boils, she lets it steep for twice as long as she should.

She assumes there will be a wake next door. It will start quiet and respectful and then explode into one of those parties that keeps the block up into the night with people shouting over loud music. As if death should be celebrated.

The noise of the shears in the backyard is grating—a slice-slice sound. She discovers that someone has opened the kitchen window.

Tomorrow he will return to teaching. It's too much for the two of them to be home all day together. The house seems to shrink. Anneke often finds herself making excuses to run errands, do her citizen patrols on the women working Western.

Through the gauzy kitchen curtain she watches her husband— his dull gray hair, the steady movement of his hands bringing the handles of the shears together as the vines rain down on his feet. Like the cemetery, the garden is a mess of muddy grass and soggy plants. But Roger is meticulous and won't track a drop into the house.

Roger was her first boyfriend, long after her mother had given up on her meeting anyone. At twenty-six, Anneke was working as a women's health coordinator in a flimsy NGO in the Philippines. Roger was teaching English at a small international school in Lipa. He was boring, unadventurous. That was the attraction. He wasn't a danger seeker or an evangelist like her father or like a lot of the men she met. He didn't want to save people or change the world.

Anneke goes to the living room, her cup of tea cradled in her hands.

Even here the sound of Roger's pruning grates on her.

She closes her eyes as if the darkness might relieve the tension. Three deep breaths, blowing out the pain as the holistic therapist in San Salvador instructed her when her migraines intensified during her pregnancy. It never works, but Anneke keeps trying. As if pain is something she or anyone can control.

Marella didn't come home again last night. Anneke had driven to the gallery on Western to retrieve Roger in the storm. She'd waited for her daughter. But there had been a wild look in Marella's eyes, one of fear and recognition but also of defiance.

I'm not coming with you. I'm never coming with you.

All this because Anneke had not attended the opening? All this anger for that.

Marella hasn't picked up her calls. She hasn't appeared. But she will. Anneke's certain. Through all the tough love, the bitter lessons, the insistence that Marella hold herself to a higher standard, Anneke has carved out a safe space for her daughter in the house on Twenty-Ninth, a nest to which she can and will return.

I'll see you at home, then, Anneke had said.

There's a knock at the door. Anneke spills her tea and brushes off the liquid. She goes to the door and looks through the heavy leaded glass. At first it seems as if no one is there. A prank. Or someone who thought better of appearing. Or perhaps a delivery. She looks down to check for a package.

There's a child or a young person standing in front of the door. Her head barely reaches the window.

"Yes?"

"Mrs. Colwin? Do you mind opening up?"

This voice isn't a child's.

"What is this about?"

Anneke watches as the visitor steps back. She is not a child at all or even a teenager, but a woman. She reaches into her suit pocket and holds something up to the window. "LAPD," she says. "Detective Perry. Can I come in?"

Anneke opens the door.

Detective Perry comes up to her chin. She looks around, taking in the dark stained wood, the tasteful period furniture and décor.

"So," Detective Perry says. She unwraps a piece of gum and pops it in her mouth. The smacking noise is distasteful. Then she looks at Anneke as if seeing her for the first time. "You are Anneke Colwin?"

"Yes."

The detective's manner is off-putting, like she's not entirely sure why she's here, like she'd come without a true purpose. "Do you mind if we sit down?"

"I've already asked you what this is about," Anneke says.

Less than a minute inside her house and this detective has already done the thing that Anneke dislikes most about the police—she has ignored her. She has not answered Anneke's question.

That is another house rule: If you want to know something, ask. If you are afraid of the answer, don't.

"I'd rather sit, if that's okay." She pulls out her cell phone and starts tapping away at the screen, the click-clicking alternating with the slice-slice of Roger's shears.

"So?" Detective Perry makes a sweeping gesture with a hand toward the couch as if she is inviting Anneke to sit in her own home.

Anneke makes no move toward the living room. It's a height thing, most likely, this aggressive need to sit. It levels the playing field. Anneke feels no need to give in to someone else's insecurity.

"I don't think this should take long," Anneke says. "You're here about the birds, correct?"

Keep your house neat.
Keep the world in order and your world will be orderly.

Detective Perry is back looking at her phone, snapping her gum in time with her tapping. "Excuse me?"

"Aren't you here about those silly hummingbirds?"

From time to time Anneke had been brazen enough to return to check her work, satisfied to see the tiny creatures lying in the dirt behind Dorian's restaurant. Yet Dorian didn't take the hint. She kept feeding the women. The women kept coming.

Keep your surroundings safe.

Keep your surroundings neat.

Take measures to preserve order.

Preserve order so that order might be reflected through you.

The detective glances from her phone. "Hummingbirds," she says as if she's never heard the word before. "No." She resumes clicking.

The sound of Detective Perry's nail on the glass is infuriating. Anneke's hand goes to her eye to try to stop the tremor before it starts.

The detective keeps tapping. "Dorian saves them, you know. In shoeboxes. To do that I think she bakes them in an oven at a low temperature. Why do you think she would do something like that?"

"I don't know."

"I think you do." Detective Perry drops her phone in her pocket. "Now can we sit?" Without waiting for Anneke's reply, she settles herself in the wing chair facing the couch.

"I poisoned them."

There are things you have to do to keep the chaos out. Small sacrifices. Risks.

"I don't care about the birds." The detective stops chewing her gum. She's not scrolling on her phone. The only noise now is the slice-slice of Roger's shears.

Anneke puts her hand to her temple.

"Are you all right?" Detective Perry asks.

"My husband is gardening. The noise is intolerable."

"I don't hear anything," the detective says. Then she looks toward the backyard. "He's home?"

"I just told you he's gardening."

"Right," Detective Perry says. "You did." She pulls out a notepad and flips it open.

"I had no other choice," Anneke says.

"About?"

"Dorian had to stop feeding those women. The birds were a sacrifice. Like Isaac."

The sound in the yard is louder now. The shears are shrieking. Anneke half stands to check for an open window again but everything is shut.

Suddenly the detective's focus is razor sharp. She's not tapping or chewing or scrolling. She's crossed her legs, leaned forward, joining the conversation for the first time. "I'm not here about the birds, I'm here about something else you did. On July sixteenth of 1998, you made a phone call."

Anneke laughs. "A phone call?"

The detective slides a piece of paper from her pad and unfolds it. "I pored through hundreds of pages for this." She holds it out.

Anneke takes the page. She sees her name scrawled in the margin alongside her phone number.

Bring order into the world and order will follow you
    home.

"They didn't call back, did they?"

Anneke laughs again. "You're following up on a fifteen-year-old phone call?"

"You tried once more, didn't you, in early 1999?"

"I gave you the benefit of the doubt. I imagined you were going to do your job."

"That time you didn't leave your name. But this is you, isn't it?"

The detective passes over a copy of a small typescripted memo. "Woman caller, says she's called before but no one returned her call. Has information about her husband. Will give it if her previous call is returned."

"As I said, I was waiting for you to do your job and when you didn't call back, I figured my information wasn't important. I assumed I was wrong."

It's what she tells her family, don't ask a question if you don't want to hear the answer. Don't open yourself up to disappointment. She'd answered a question no one had asked, and in return no one had paid attention. That was the confirmation she needed.

Detective Perry clicks her pen twice. "And what was it you were going to say?"

Anneke inclines her head toward the garden. "You really don't hear that?"

"I don't."

"What I had to say didn't seem to matter then, so it doesn't now."

"You were calling about the murders around Western."

"Yes," Anneke says.

She wants to stand up and scream at Roger. He knows better than to make so much noise and to disturb the sanctuary of their house.

Keep your doors closed.
Keep your family to yourself.
Keep your problems inside.
Keep your world in order.

"It was about your husband."

Anneke blinks twice.

"It was about your husband, Roger," Detective Perry says.

Anneke glances around the room. The organization of things is startling. The precision with which the Rookwood vases are displayed on the mantel. The spacing between the Mission-style picture frames. She examines how the seams on the Morris wallpaper are actually seamless, no line between the sheets.

"Mrs. Colwin, were you or were you not calling the station about your husband?"

Anneke closes her eyes.

Sometimes you wait so long for something you forget all about it. The waiting devours you, then it becomes part of you, and then you cease to notice it. It's absorbed into the everyday, accommodated and then overlooked. And eventually you aren't waiting anymore. And you almost forget about the thing you expected for so long.

Then it happens.

Then it releases you.

The hollow feeling is gone. The sound of the shears stops. Anneke almost feels as if she's floating above the couch. It feels almost possible, to levitate, to lie back and fly. "Yes."

"Lecia Williams was babysitting next door. Julianna Vargas lived next door."

Anneke keeps her eyes closed. It's peaceful in the dark. She wishes the detective would stop talking.

"Mrs. Colwin? Mrs. Colwin? Did he know you called?"

Anneke opens her eyes. "I told him. He asked me so I told him."

"And he stopped because you called?"

Anneke glances around the room, looking for something out of place that she can hang this mess on.

"Or did he stop because of Orphelia Jefferies?"

"I don't know who that is."

"I imagine that you do. She's the one who survived."

That was Roger's mistake. That was how disorder might have got in.

"That's why you called," Detective Perry says.

"I keep my world in order and order is reflected through me."

Detective Perry clicks her pen rapidly as her eyes scan the room. "Is that what sets him off, disorder?"

"You haven't seen the world, Detective. You haven't seen the chaos and desperation. You haven't seen the squalor and the deprivation, the things people—women—do to survive. It's repulsive. But still you try to help."

"That's what Roger was doing? Helping? He was purifying the world?"

Anneke laughs. "You are looking for something rational. Something noble. Roger was attracted to the chaos, the depravity. And he hated himself for it. So he did what he had to do."

"He killed these women because he couldn't help his attraction to them?"

"Roger is weak. He has a weakness. But he understands it. He knows which parts of the world are worth preserving and which only lead to corruption. He knows how to maintain order. He knows he needs to maintain order for our daughter."

"Your daughter," the detective says. "Marella."

As if Anneke needs reminding.

"You sent her away right after you called the station. Now she's back."

Why is this woman telling her all the things she already knows?

Now the detective looks Anneke in the eye. The full force of her attention is unsettling. "I've been asking myself the wrong question," she says. "Actually, I've missed part of the question. I have been so busy wondering why someone stops killing that I never considered why he might start."

"I wouldn't know."

"You do," Detective Perry says. "Marella. He hates himself more for what he desires in those women when his daughter is around."

Anneke's eye is pulsing. Her head pounds. "I said I don't know. I'm not a psychiatrist."

"You tried to stop him. You called the station to tell them this."

"And no one listened."

Detective Perry whips out her phone and clicks through, looking for something. "You know they arrested Morgan Tillett?"

"Who?"

"The woman who staged the protest on the top of the arch on the Brooklyn Bridge. They got her for trespassing." The detective is clicking away at her phone. "She also made a phone call. She was telling us without telling us. No one heard what she was saying."

"I don't know who Morgan Tillett is," Anneke says.

Detective Perry spits her gum into a piece of foil and unwraps a fresh stick. "My partner is outside. We have a warrant to search the place. You should go talk to your husband."

3.

_____

THERE'S A FINGERPRINT ON THE EDGE OF THE DINING ROOM table. There's a thread loose on the back of one of the upholstered dining room chairs. The sponge in the sink hasn't been wrung out.

Anneke puts her tea mug on the counter next to the stove. She opens the back door and steps into the yard. There's a large patch of concrete surrounded by a granite path with grassy areas on either side. One wall is grapevines, the other rosebushes.

In the far right corner is a fountain that no longer works and a weathered bench no one sits on except during the dice game. The dice game—the one time Anneke allows the outside in. A gathering of men is how she justifies it. A safe place. But there's more to it than that.

If your house is in order, people will come to you.
People will respect you.
Only darkness keeps them away.
If they come, there is no darkness.
If they come, your house is in order.
They will see the order reflected in you and it will be
    reflected in them.
If they come, you have kept the world right.

It was more of a logical proof than a benediction, but one Anneke repeated every Saturday from her window overlooking the
men in the garden.

Roger is pruning the pink cabbage roses between their house
and Julianna's. He's using the same shears, but they aren't making as much noise. Anneke watches him change the shears for a
smaller set of clippers.

"Roger."

Snip-snip. His movements are deliberate and careful. He's
working without gloves, but avoiding the thorns.

"Roger."

Anneke swallows her exasperation.

"Ro—"

He turns. She watches him bring her into focus.

"I'm clipping the roses."

What should she say? What is there to say?

"Did you want something?" He hates distraction. Anneke
learned that the hard way. His meticulousness, his dull compul-
sions, came with a price.

"Have you had lunch?"

Roger looks at the clippers in one hand, a rose stem in the other.

"I'm making sandwiches," Anneke says. "I can bring you one."

"Is someone here?" Roger says. "Were you talking to someone?"

"I'll explain in a moment."

There's comfort in the small tasks. Anneke pulls out a loaf of
seeded bread. Sliced cheese. Some cucumbers and ham.

She can hear footsteps, a man's heavy tread and a woman's
lighter one.

She makes two sandwiches, slices them on the diagonal. She
finds two lunch plates, puts a paper napkin on each, lays the sandwiches on top, and carries them outside.

Roger takes a plate.

"Are these the last of the year?" Anneke asks, looking at the roses he's clipped and placed in a basket.

"Yes," Roger says. "We had a long season. The repeat bloomers will come back soon."

"Remember how hard it was to grow roses in El Salvador?"

"Not the *Rosa rugosa*. Those were easy. They like an ocean climate."

"It was too dirty for beautiful things to grow," Anneke says.

"The rugosa roses grew."

Anneke watches Roger eat his sandwich. She has no appetite.

What are they looking for upstairs? What have they found? There's nothing upstairs that she doesn't know about.

"Remember the woman in the water?" Anneke asks.

Roger finishes his sandwich and picks up his napkin, brushing crumbs from his beard. "No."

"The woman in the sea behind our house in El Salvador," Anneke says. "She had drowned."

"Oh, yes. Her."

"Marella thought she was a whale or a dolphin. She ran from the house to go see."

"I'd forgotten about that," Roger says.

"I found her screaming by the rocks. She screamed until her voice was hoarse."

"I'd forgotten that, too."

"She hasn't," Anneke says.

"Who knows," Roger says. "Who knows what children remember."

Anneke reaches for Roger's plate. She holds one side, him the other. "You should never have let her see a thing like that."

"You were the one who let her run to the beach."

Anneke fixes him with her firmest stare. There is no hint of the tremor in her eye. "I said, you should never have let her see a thing like that. She was a child." They continue to hold the plate. "Trust me, she has not forgotten."

"I didn't—" Roger says. Then he lets go of the plate.

"You did," Anneke says. "You did."

Roger takes up the small clippers and climbs the ladder, returning for the last of the cabbage roses.

"I know I don't need to tell you to do a good job," Anneke says. "But please do. The police are here. They are searching the upstairs. When you go, I expect you to go quietly without a scene. And leave the roses in perfect condition."

There's a momentary break in Roger's snip-snipping, a hair's breadth of resignation. "They won't find anything," he says.

"I know," Anneke says.

"Did you call them?"

"No."

Roger doesn't turn around. "At least not this time."

"Exactly, not this time."

He cuts the last rose. Anneke takes the plates inside. She glances down the hall and sees Detective Perry and another detective at the foot of the stairs.

"Did you find anything?"

"Do you go to church, Mrs. Colwin?" Detective Perry asks.

"My father was a missionary."

"That's a yes, then."

"No," Anneke says. "I don't go to church."

She looks past the detective and sees that the street is swirling with red and blue lights.

"I did find something in your possessions." Detective Perry holds out a piece of paper. Anneke doesn't have to look closely to see that it's a program from a church in Inglewood. "This is the church where Feelia Jefferies works."

"Feelia?"

"Orphelia Jefferies," Detective Perry says. "If you waste my time by telling me you don't know her, I'll take you down to the station along with your husband and charge you with felony stalking. That plus poisoning Dorian's birds should be enough for jail time for aiding and abetting."

Anneke takes a deep breath and puts her hand to her eye, trying to stop the twitch before it starts. To her surprise, her eye is still. "I know Orphelia. Not personally."

"But you've been stalking her."

"I've been watching her."

"Why?"

"I keep my world in order, Detective Perry."

"You wanted to know if she remembered the person who tried to kill her."

"I keep my world in order. I keep my world in order. And order follows me."

Detective Perry raises her eyebrows. "Is that so?" She tucks the flyer into an evidence bag. "Your daughter has already given us what we needed—a water bottle with a fingerprint that matches both Julianna's cell phone and evidence from one of the women murdered decades ago. When the DNA comes back, I'm sure that it will match two samples taken from two separate victims. I'm going to send Detective Spera out to get Roger now." Detective Perry nods toward her partner, who heads for the backyard.

Anneke glances around the kitchen, down the hall, out the window on the front door that is washed in red spinning light. She hears the back door open and close, then open again as Roger is led in by Detective Spera.

Anneke stands aside for her husband. If it weren't for hands cuffed behind his back, no one would notice anything amiss.

"Don't worry, the wives always claim they didn't know," Detective Spera says as they pass. "The neighbors, too."

The front door opens. From the hall Anneke can see a half-dozen police cars crisscrossing Twenty-Ninth Place.

She's not going to hide. She's going to follow Roger out, watch him go. There will be no denying what he's done.

She steps out onto the porch. Her neighbors are out—all of them. Some stay behind their gates. Others have ventured onto the sidewalk. A news van rolls down St. Andrews. Detective Spera hands Roger to an older detective who holds open the back door of an unmarked car and ducks Roger inside. He shuts the door. The window is tinted. Anneke can't see Roger as he is driven off.

She looks up and down the street.

At the far end of the block she can see Detective Perry on a mountain bike riding behind the unmarked cruiser carrying Roger. Before the car turns onto Cimarron, the detective peels away, makes a tight U-turn, and heads back toward Anneke's. She stops in front of the house.

Two officers are taping off the squares of pavement in front of the house. Two more are setting up some sort of command station in the driveway.

Detective Perry leans her bike against the fence and pushes past her colleagues. She rushes up the steps, pinning Anneke against the wall. "You knew about all of them."

Anneke can smell her fruity gum.

Anneke towers over Detective Perry. "There's knowing and there's believing."

"And there's being believed," Detective Perry says.

"Exactly. Now you, Detective, tell me which of those is the most important in this world." She holds the detective's stare.

She kept her house neat. No one can claim otherwise.

4.

———

DETECTIVE PERRY IS NO LONGER RUNNING THE SHOW. SHE'S been replaced by a cookie-cutter set of detectives in descending sizes like nesting dolls. A bulky, ruddy-faced man named Bourke is in charge. He looms in the doorway, blocking the square of sunlight.

The detectives keep the curtains closed. They've turned on all the lights.

It's like being abused, violated—the cops crawling all over the house, picking up objects, sifting through drawers, plucking fibers from the couch, the carpet, the towels. Like her fabrics are guilty. They march up and down the stairs, their heavy tread shaking the window frames.

Anneke goes to the kitchen and looks at the schedule for her shifts at the nursing home on the small corkboard. She's on at six tomorrow.

She uses the landline and calls West Seas. She's certain no one's going to complain about her filling in for the overnight shift.

She fills a thermos with soup. She doesn't eat the food she serves the patients. She checks everything in her purse and takes her car keys.

Bourke is still standing in front of the door.

"Going somewhere?"

"I'm going to work," Anneke says.

Bourke checks his watch. "Now?"

"Should I stay here and supervise you instead?" Anneke asks.

The detective doesn't move. He looks as if he is thinking up a reason to prevent her from leaving.

"Unless you are planning on arresting me, I'm going to work. I will come down to the station to answer your questions tomorrow. Last I checked it's not against the law to do my job."

Bourke steps out of her way.

The neighbors are still out. The street is a traffic jam of cop cars and news vans. Camera crews are roving from house to house. Anneke's car is parked in the driveway, blocked by an unmarked cruiser. It takes several minutes to locate the detective who has the keys.

Anneke stands by her five-year-old Honda. She doesn't shield her face from her neighbors. They know what she looks like. She doesn't hide from the reporters. She takes out her cell phone and taps Marella's name. But before she dials, her daughter is there at the base of the driveway.

She looks like Roger. She has his brown hair, his darker skin, his sturdier build. He is in her. He always will be. Marella will have to carry that forever. The sins of the father.

It looks as if Marella hasn't slept or showered.

"You need to clean yourself up," Anneke says. "You need to take care of your appearance."

Her daughter's mouth opens and closes like an empty nutcracker. There are bags under her eyes.

"They've arrested your father," Anneke says.

"I know." Marella's voice is shaky.

"I hear you gave them a water bottle."

"He was scary, Mom. Last night in the gallery."

"He's always scary. Or hadn't you noticed?"

"Had you?"

Anneke puts her hand to her eye to stop the twitch.

"Mom," Marella says, her voice growing steady, impertinent almost, "had you?"

"Did I raise you to repeat yourself?"

"You knew there was something wrong with him, didn't you? You knew and you didn't do anything."

"Don't tell me what I did and didn't do. I kept you safe from this world."

Marella folds her hands over her chest. "You sent me away. That's what you did."

"For your own good."

Marella's eyes widen. "You were keeping me away from him."

"I did what I had to do."

"Did you think he would hurt me?"

"You can't take risks. You can't take a chance that something undesirable brushes off on you. I kept you at a distance."

There's a dark look in Marella's eyes reminiscent of Roger's.

"He's your father," Anneke says. "One day you will understand him. I'm working tonight, overnight. I'm sure the cops will be finished with the house by the time I get back tomorrow. I'll see you at home for lunch."

She opens the car door. She'd kept her daughter safe. She'd succeeded. Her work is through. She doesn't need Marella of all people correcting her.

She gets behind the wheel and shuts the car door, cocooning herself—the walkie-talkies, the whispers, the gossip, the loud-mouths who want to be heard on the news, who want to be the news.

MARELLA STANDS AT THE BASE of the driveway. She doesn't move until Anneke turns the ignition and creaks backward.

Anneke is about to straighten onto Twenty-Ninth when she sees Armando Vargas standing on his porch. Two camera crews rush him at once, both greedy for the exclusive. But Armando isn't looking at the reporters. He's staring straight through Anneke's windshield. Her foot goes to the brake, jolting her forward. She takes a deep breath. She sits up straighter and makes sure the car is still in reverse.

She returns Armando's stare, pulls out onto the street.

Traffic is light until she reaches the PCH into Malibu, where she discovers cars at a standstill. West Seas Adult Care is not on the beachfront but up in the mountains, where the residents look from the floor-to-ceiling windows in the common room to catch a glimmer of the Pacific—a small tease of the world they will not visit again.

Emergency units are forcing cars to turn around on the two-lane highway. When Anneke reaches the front of the jam, she can see the road in front of her is a river of mud strewn with rocks and debris. Several abandoned cars are trapped in the flow, tossed haphazardly from their lanes.

Two Los Angeles County firefighters are blocking the road. When Anneke doesn't immediately turn around, one of them blows his whistle and signals that she should move into the opposite lane and head back.

She waits. She hears the fireman's voice through her window. "Ma'am, the road's closed. Turn your car around."

Anneke rolls down her window. The air still smells of smoke from the fires mixed with the damp, mildew scent of rain. An odor of burning houses and bodies. "I'm going to work."

"Road's closed. The canyon's being evacuated."

"I'm going to work."

"Where do you work?"

Anneke points up toward the hills.

"The whole area's under evacuation, ma'am. Turn your car around."

Anneke does as instructed. But at Will Rogers State Beach, she cuts across and up into the hills. It takes her an extra forty minutes to arrive at West Seas. She has to circumvent several road closures, two road crews clearing debris, and a constant flow of cars heading in the other direction.

She parks and heads for the nurses' break room. She changes into her starched uniform. It's the start of dinner hour, the time for shift change. Many of the residents are already sitting in the common room, waiting to be led to the cafeteria. Anneke watches the row of rocking chairs and wheelchairs lined up in front of the glass wall. The sun is plunging into the ocean, dyeing the water pale pink and bright, cold blue.

"I heard the mud is flowing," one of the women says as Anneke wheels her chair to the cafeteria. "Mud always flows after fire."

At dinner the talk is of disaster. Earthquakes and wildfires and mudslides. At West Seas the apocalypse is always waiting in the wings. The residents are prophets and survivors. They are forecasters of doom. They know earthquake weather and can sense it when the nursing home is preparing to tumble into the ocean. They can smell fire a county away.

They are alert to epidemics and outbreaks.

They know someone who has survived every tragedy—the loss of an entire family, a plane crash, three types of cancer, heartbreak, amputation, divorce. They know people who have fled regimes and domestic abuse. They know people who have survived unreliable housekeepers and thieving babysitters.

They know better than anyone on the TV or the radio.

They have seen everything and fear nothing.

And they have retired, turned away from the world, let it

continue its messy, disordered, chaotic, violent existence outside the walls and windows of West Seas.

Anneke applauds them.

Dinner comes out on trays—neatly organized, easy to cut, to chew, to digest.

As she removes her tray, a woman pats Anneke's hand. "You look well, sweetheart. Porcelain beauty."

Her hand feels like tissue. Her veins pop like worms, as if she's already on her way to decomposing.

After dinner Anneke hands out medicine in paper cups. She looks at the pills. Trust is humanity's greatest mistake. It would be easy to switch the pills, to cross-medicate or overmedicate. She hands the cups to willing, careless hands.

The women return or are returned to the common room. The evening activity is animal bingo. It's meant to keep the women's brains active. Anneke imagines the game is actually boring them to death, lulling them into submission with the same repetitive call of: rooster, chicken, pig, hen.

Rooster. Chicken. Cow. Cow. Duck.

Bingo, someone croaks.

And they go again.

Many of the women can't play and others simply don't. They either cluster in front of the windows, gaping into the darkness, or they circle around the television absorbing the nightly digest of local news and cheap game shows.

Another nurse has the remote and has tuned in to KTLA. And there in the middle of the screen is Roger.

It's a photo from several years ago, taken when Anneke and Roger went to visit Marella in San Diego. It's possible to see the faux grandeur of the Hotel Coronado in the background.

The photo was on a table in her bedroom. Seeing Roger's face on the news doesn't infuriate Anneke. The photo does. Who gave it to the press? Who had the right? Did they take it from the house? Did they take it out of the frame? Did they leave her a receipt?

What else did they take? What else is missing, disturbed? How many fingerprints? Footprints? How long before her house feels like hers again? Before it is a home instead of a crime scene?

How had this happened?

How had the outside come in?

She had preserved order.

She had done her part.

But life will go on. It must go on. She knows that people think she will stop living, that Roger has brought an end to her life as well.

The photo on the news changes. There's a shot of her house, almost unrecognizable with the cop cars and strangers at the gate and clustered on the porch.

Then the screen flashes to a grid of photos—all women, mostly Latino and black. Four are highlighted with red marker, indicating they are Roger's more recent victims.

There are seventeen in all. Seventeen women. In the brief moment the image rests on the screen Anneke recognizes Lecia, Julianna, and a woman who might have been Julianna's friend many years ago. Close, but not quite a bingo.

Her stomach rises. She rushes for the bathroom. A woman in a wheelchair grabs her hand as she passes.

"I could feel this coming."

Anneke keeps her hand over her mouth.

"Evil comes in cycles. But it can't touch you in here," the woman says. "Here we are safe."

The TV is now showing the steps of Southwest Station a few blocks off Western. There's a press conference under way with officials in suits and in uniform. In the background Anneke can hear voices rising over that of the blond woman who's speaking into the microphone. The camera pans across MLK to a group of protesters holding candles and poster board signs—some with slogans, some with images of the murdered women.

The mothers. The mothers are chanting. The mothers are heckling the police. The mothers are calling for justice. The mothers are holding photos of their daughters.

One mother steps forward. Dorian.

A reporter jams a microphone in her face.

"This is not about solving crimes that have reached over decades. This is about correcting an injustice."

Her voice is loud, furious, and confident. It unsettles Anneke.

"This is about finding out why our daughters' killer was at large for so many years, about why the police did nothing about our daughters' deaths. About why they didn't care. About why they looked away. This is about why the police think our daughters don't matter." Dorian holds up a poster with Lecia's face on it. "This is why," she says, pointing at Lecia's cheek. "This is why," she shouts. "Her skin."

Behind her the other mothers have raised their voices. *Our daughters matter!*

Anneke feels a hand tighten around her wrist. She looks down to see the woman in the wheelchair still clutching her. "She sounds like the other one."

"Who?" Anneke asks.

"She sounds like the woman in New York. The one who climbed to the top of the Brooklyn Bridge."

"Imagine that at sixty," another woman says. "Imagine doing that."

"The Holloway mother," the woman holding Anneke's wrist says. "She reminds me of the Holloway mother. You can bet this one is going to make a lot of noise."

As if on cue, Dorian steps closer to the camera. "We are not going away. We are not going to be quiet." She points to the wall of the building behind her. "See that? That's where we are going to have our memorial. A mural to all our daughters right there. Something the police will have to look at every day. Every day they will be reminded of how they failed our daughters. Every day they will be reminded of how they failed us. We will never let them forget."

The mothers pick up this chant. "Never let them forget."

The broadcast cuts back to the newsroom.

Anneke breaks free of the woman's grip and rushes to the bathroom.

She keeps the light off. She presses her hands into the cold porcelain sink. She runs water, splashes it into her eyes to make the grid of women disappear. It was easier before she'd seen them all. Easier before she'd seen the mothers.

Seventeen women who'd stirred something passionate and violent in Roger. Seventeen women who made him feel something so extreme he couldn't contain it.

But really there are more. There must be. The one in El Salvador and others like her, surely.

Anneke presses her knuckles into her eyes.

You can hope and pretend. You can imagine that the world is violent and that it has nothing to do with you—that the women who die nearby are a symptom of an abstract evil, a distant one. Because to do otherwise would be overwhelming, it would undo you from the inside out, rip you apart just as badly as if you were one of the victims yourself. In fact, to do so would be unimaginable because being in the presence of that sort of violence, confronting it at the breakfast table, reaching over it to turn out the bedside light—that, well, that is impossible.

But now that she's seen those women's faces, Anneke feels something rending her apart. She wants to slap them off the TV, break the screen.

Instead she keeps washing her face, more cold water until her eyes sting.

She can't linger here. She can't leave the women to themselves for more than a few minutes.

Keep your house tidy, your person too.

When she returns to the common room, a fireman is standing in the doorway arguing with the other nurse on duty. "He wants us to evacuate," the nurse tells Anneke.

She looks at the women absorbed in their activities, stuck in their wheelchairs.

"We can take them down in fire trucks and ambulances."

"Take them where?" Anneke says.

The fireman's walkie-talkie crackles.

"We're not going."

Anneke turns. The woman who'd grabbed her hand on the way to the bathroom has wheeled up behind her.

"We're not going," the woman repeats.

Anneke puts a hand on her shoulder. "She's right. We're staying put."

There's another burst of noise from the fireman's walkie-talkie. "You understand you might be stranded or worse."

"You don't need to tell me about worse," Anneke says.

5.

———

"DAMN, YOU'RE A HARD WOMAN TO FIND."

Anneke opens her eyes. She'd dozed off in a recliner in the common room. The first glint of sun has lit up the scorched hillside, bringing up the burnt bracken and charred earth. The intercom is on the table next to her. It had been a quiet night—no pages, no emergencies. And she'd slept.

"I said, you're a hard woman to find. The fuck you doing up in these burned-ass hills?"

It's a voice that Anneke has only heard at a distance but one she knows perfectly.

Anneke glances at the clock. Six A.M. "Working," Anneke says, sitting up.

"Looks like you're sleeping is what."

Anneke pushes the recliner's footrest away. She spins around in the chair and sees Orphelia Jefferies standing in the entrance to the common room.

"What are you doing here?"

Orphelia throws back her head and laughs. Even from across the room and even in the low light Anneke can see the jagged scar. "What am I doing here? What the fuck am I doing here.

That's motherfucking good. Going on fifteen years you've been popping up wherever the fuck in my life and now you ask me why I'm here. I'm here because I want to be."

Anneke stands. She wants to close the distance between them, get Orphelia to lower her voice, turn down that raspy cackle before it wakes the entire house.

"And what's more," Orphelia says, "I'm here because I want to see you. I'm a woman with questions." She glances around. "You got coffee up here?"

"I do."

Anneke goes to the table in the common room and pops a pod in the machine. "How did you find me?"

"You're not the only detective in this game. Saw your house on the news. You know what's some funny shit? Two weeks ago, nobody would talk to me. It was all crazy black lady's back with her crazy shit. Now everyone is all loose lipped. Everybody wants part of this mess. *She works at some old folks place in the mountains in Malibu.* Didn't take a genius after that. A phone call. That's about it. Hard part was getting here. My daughter, Aurora, drives one of those internet car things overnight. Ride-sharers. Had her drop me off. You know those motherfucking roads are closed. It's like you're a bunch of, what-do-you-call-them, pioneers up on the hill. Last people on earth." She clears her throat. "So let that be a lesson in how bad I wanted to talk to you. Walked all that way uphill in the dark."

The coffee finishes sputtering into a cup. Anneke adds nondairy creamer and hands Orphelia the cup.

"The powdered shit?"

"So why'd you come all this way?" Anneke asks.

"Because if I were you I'd split town tomorrow. Never be seen again. That's what I'd do. So I wanted to talk to you first." Orphelia glances over Anneke's shoulder into the common room. "You going to invite me to sit?"

"No," Anneke says.

Orphelia cocks her head. "Have it your way." She sips her coffee and winces. "Tastes like shit," she says but drinks it anyway. "So funny you asking me how I found you when the real story is about how you found me."

"How I—" Anneke says.

"Let's see, about fifteen years ago, you started popping up outside my house. Just every so often. Then the liquor store, the grocery. Then at my motherfucking job. So let me ask you clearly one more time, how did you find me?"

"He had your wallet."

"Shit, no. I had my own damn wallet at the hospital."

Anneke has no interest in explaining things to this woman. "I returned your wallet to your house. Someone must have brought it to you."

"So how come you kept coming back? How come you've been loitering around my shit for years?"

Anneke takes a deep breath and puts her hand to her eye. The tremor's going to come. There's no stopping it. She clenches her jaw and speaks through pursed lips. "I thought he was having an affair."

"You what?"

"You heard me."

"You thought your husband was having an affair." Orphelia laughs so hard she spills her coffee. "So when you found out the truth, you what—you kept watching me in case I could ID your husband? That's some motherfucking commitment."

"You assume I knew the truth."

Orphelia's hand flies to her scar. "Or maybe it was more fucked up. Maybe you thought you could make reparations. Maybe you were thinking to watch over me like a too-late guardian angel. Maybe you were trying to protect me?"

"Protect you?" Anneke lets out a sharp laugh. "I had no interest in protecting you."

Orphelia brushes a droplet of coffee off her arm. "So?"

Anneke folds her arms over her chest and fixes the other woman with a disdainful stare. "I was jealous."

"Wha—?" Orphelia's eyebrows lift, her mouth forms a wide O.

"You heard me." Anneke feels as if someone has knocked the wind out of her. The admission nearly leaves her breathless, overwhelmed by shame and weakness.

"I've heard some fucked-up shit in my time, but this is the take-the-cake winner. Jealous? Motherfucking jealous." Orphelia cracks a dirty smile. "Let me take a look at you. Let me see. Are you green? Are you green like a bag of spinach? Green like the grass?"

"Excuse me?"

"I'm just wanting to know if you're so green with envy that you watched me for fifteen years? Because that's got to be the greenest green in history."

She has no idea, Orphelia Jefferies. None. What Anneke felt for her wasn't pity or sadness. It even stopped being jealousy—it transcended jealousy. "You don't understand," she says. "It's more than jealousy. It's hatred."

"I'm all motherfucking ears. Explain to me how you can be jealous of someone your husband tried to murder?"

"You think it's crazy to hate the woman who brought out a passion in him so intense he couldn't control himself? It's a betrayal you'll never understand."

"Lady, killing a whole bunch of people is worse than anything he did to you."

Anneke laughs. She doesn't care how many people hear, how many of the old ladies she shakes from their sleep. "Oh," she says, "there's your first mistake. You think Roger picked you up just to kill you?" She shakes her head at Orphelia's stupidity. "He was attracted to the depravity of you and others like you and he hated himself for it. And I hate you too."

"So you just let him do his thing—kill women because you
hated them."

I keep my house neat.
I keep my family close.
I keep my world in order.
I keep the chaos out so that order is reflected through me.

Somewhere someone is stirring in West Seas. Anneke needs
to clear Orphelia out before one of the women emerges from her
room or before she must attend the morning's first emergency.
"Listen," Anneke says, "I did what I could."
"And what did you do?"
She steps closer to Orphelia. "I called the police. I reported
him. But no one followed up and that was all the proof I needed."
"Proof of what?"
"Let me ask you something. Did you ever go to the police
about me?"
"I did. I sure as shit did."
"And what did they do?"
"Jack shit."
"And did you think you were crazy, that you were making the
whole thing up?"
"Time to time, but you kept showing back up," Orphelia says.
"It's easier not to imagine the unimaginable. It's what you have
to do to survive. Now if you're done, I have to work."
Orphelia puffs out her lips and shakes her head side to side.
"I'm not done. I'm not motherfucking done. I'll never be done
with you. You fucking knew. You can lie to yourself all you want.
You can lie to the goddamn news. But I know the truth. And I'm
going to remind you every fucking day as long as you live. You
knew and you killed them."
There's a sound from the hall that leads down to the bedrooms.

Both women turn and see that two of the residents have appeared, one on foot, the other in an electric wheelchair.

"Now where did you come from?" the one who is standing says, looking at Orphelia.

"Did you fly up the hill?" the one in the wheelchair asks.

Orphelia throws them a dismissive glance, filled with streetwise hate for their old-women curiosity. Then she gives Anneke a look once more. "I'm telling you and don't contradict me: you knew. That's what I came all this fucking way to tell you. You knew."

Before Anneke can say a word, Orphelia is gone.

"All this way through the mud for bad language," one of the women says.

"Knew what, dear?" the other asks.

6.

———

SHE HATED THEM, THAT'S THE TRUTH. SHE HATES THEM. A jealousy that has crystallized into hatred. Every woman Roger had killed, he'd also killed a piece of Anneke, too.

"Knew what, dear?" the woman in the wheelchair asks. She's tugging on Anneke's sleeve. "What did you know?"

These women—give them a bone and they'll gnaw all day. West Seas is a world of petty fixations: how many letters your roommate received, who was overlooked for her niece's baby shower, whose paperback was stolen, whose son visits the most.

Today will be all about the woman who visited Anneke—what she wanted, what Anneke knew.

They will whisper about it. They will gossip. They will transform the story to get them through the day.

But they won't understand. They never will. And when they find out who Anneke is, it will be worse. She knew? What did she know?

She needs to find Orphelia and get her back, explain to her and to everyone that she didn't know, she couldn't have known because knowing would have been the end of it for her. She couldn't have known because then she couldn't have continued to exist. And she couldn't have known, because if she did the police would have followed up on her phone call.

"I'll be right back," Anneke says. And without checking to see if either woman needs something from her, she heads for the door.

She crosses the drive and opens the gate.

West Seas is on a steep street near the top of a hill. Anneke can make out Orphelia beginning her descent to the south.

"Wait."

She doesn't have her car keys so she follows on foot. The street is filled with gravel and rock loosened by the recent rains. The air still smells of wet char.

"Wait," Anneke calls again.

Orphelia skids on the uneven terrain. "You chasing me? You following me?"

"I said *wait*."

"And I'm supposed to do what you say?" Orphelia calls, but she stays in place.

Anneke picks her way down the hill on the opposite side of the street.

"I figured you wouldn't have much reason to be following me anymore, now that all this shit's about to come out. Yet here you are."

"You need to listen to me," Anneke says.

"I can't imagine what-all you have to say. I came up here to do the speaking. And I'm done."

"Listen," Anneke says.

"You know what, forget it," Orphelia says. "I'm not listening to shit." She starts heading down the hill. "Explain yourself to someone else. I just wanted to see you face-to-face. I wanted to see your face and let you know that I know. Lie to yourself all you want. But I know."

Anneke's eye is fluttering so fast it's blinding her. She stumbles but keeps up her pursuit. She hates this woman. She hates how this woman and the rest of them endangered her daughter, stirred something in her husband that brought the danger close to home.

"You wait," she says.

"The fuck I'm waiting. I'm finally fucking free. Free of you and your husband and the shit he did to me," Orphelia says. "Fifteen years I've been living with this shit. You know what it's like to experience nearly two decades of crazy, two decades of feeling your mind wasn't your own?"

Anneke does. Fifteen years and more. The uncertainty. The suspicion. The horror that comes so close you have to swat it away. That's enough to tip the scales, unbalance you, sending you tilting toward insanity if you're not careful.

But Anneke was careful.

"But I'm free now. There will be a trial and I'm going to be in the motherfucking front row when I'm not on the stand. I'm going to be testifying about your husband. But just so as you know, it's you I blame."

Orphelia continues down the hill, Anneke in pursuit. Up ahead the road is eroded so she scrambles up the slight embankment and picks her way through the bracken and debris. Soon Anneke has to change her course. Instead of doing what Orphelia did, Anneke chooses to continue down the middle of the road.

She checks behind her. She's gone too far. She needs to get back to West Seas before the morning unravels.

"Will you please stop?"

"No I goddamn will not," Orphelia calls. She's on an incline, looking down at Anneke, who is several paces behind her. "I will not. I'm only getting going. You know, I ought to thank you. You've given me a new beginning. A new motherfucking beginning." She throws her hands up in the air. "I'm reborn!"

There's a sound in the distance Anneke can't quite place—a roar like a rushing river.

"I came all this way to set me free. And you," Orphelia adds, "your trial is just about to start."

Orphelia stops walking. She stops talking. Her face is frozen, her mouth an O, her eyes wide to the whites.

This is Anneke's chance to catch her. She picks up her pace, hurrying down the strip of asphalt that remains the most solid section of road.

Orphelia's still not moving. She's laughing.

Whatever is roaring in the distance is getting louder.

Anneke feels it before she sees it—a riptide of mud that grabs her ankles. She staggers forward. There's a moment when it seems as if she can sidestep the flow, jump to higher ground like Orphelia. But then that moment is gone.

The mud is at her calves.

The mud is at her knees.

The mud is bringing her down.

It pitches her forward, her mouth open to its muck and rubble. Her nose is filled with its thick, foul flow.

Anneke rolls over. Coughing. Gagging.

She wipes her eyes. She is now downhill of Orphelia, who is still standing on the slight embankment watching.

The mud carries Anneke. There's a moment when she feels as if she is flying. Then floating. She closes her eyes, lets herself be carried.

Is this what the woman in El Salvador felt bobbing in the waves? Was this how she bounced against rocks, weightless on the water?

When did she stop caring?

Was it before she was tossed into the sea?

Or was it when the darkness came across Roger's eyes, a floodtide of black that swallowed his irises?

Down the mud goes.

The hills of Malibu are receding above her. The mud is rushing, invading some houses and skipping others.

Is this how the world slips away, in slow motion?

Anneke is spinning, buffeted from one side of the stream to the other. It's almost peaceful.

These women. These women, beautiful and wild. Out of control. These women he loved with a ferocity he couldn't tame. A passion he didn't understand. These women who tortured and tormented him. These women who would taunt, screw, and die. These women he loved and hated and destroyed.

These women. All these women who haunted Western.

Anneke had tried to keep them safe. She tried. What more does the world want?

The mud blankets her face, as black as Roger's stare. One by one things are lost to her: sight, smell, and now sound. She can no longer hear the mud roar. It has filled her ears. She continues down in quiet.

May God preserve you in his light.
May God preserve your family in your heart.
May the beauty of God be reflected in your eyes.
May the kindness of God be reflected in your words,
and the knowledge of God flow from your heart,
that all might see his grandeur all around you
and in seeing, believe.

This is how you lose things.
One at a time.
Enough time to remember each thing as it disappears. Enough to hold it in a timeless expanse in your mind—to turn it over, to see from all sides before it flees.
Enough time to regret all the things you knew.
And then there is black.

FEELIA 2014

AURORA, GIRL. TOOK YOUR TIME. DON'T WORRY, BABY. I
know you're working. I know you've been pulling in cash. And
this time I don't mind waiting. Walked all the way down that damn
hill. But still. It's cool. It's okay. Because look at that—that water.
You motherfucking forget. Forget that there's a whole damn ocean
right here at the edge of town.

Let this be a lesson.

I saw the most amazing goddamn thing. I saw a lady float away
on a river of mud.

Nah. I didn't stop her. Not my business. Like she was going for
a ride on one of the lazy rivers they have in Vegas. Who am I to
disturb her peace?

But there she went.

I know mud can kill.

I kept myself safe, baby.

It's a whole new world out there for me. Gonna fling my window open and welcome the day. New start. A beautiful goddamn
start.

Don't look at me like that, baby. I see you in the rearview.

Looking at me like I can't change. Like I'm gonna be loud and paranoid forever, scared of shit on my street.

Listen to me for a second. Just 'cause I live hard and saw some fucked-up stuff doesn't mean I can't teach you a thing. Listen, baby.

There's this place in my head. Probably in your head too. A place that belongs to you alone. I know that everything inside you should be yours. But live long enough and it isn't. The world eats away at that shit. The world comes and takes little pieces like a rat eating bread on the sidewalk. Nip, nip, nip.

That's what your brain becomes. A place other people nip away at, leaving their poison behind.

Where you going, baby? You taking some canyon road?

This Mulholland?

That's some fancy-ass shit. I don't mind. Let it twist and turn. Twist and turn away. I got all day. I got all week. Hell, I got the rest of my life. Got it back today in fact. So take your time. Take the scenic motherfucker.

But wait up. Don't get me off my train of thought about this place in your head. Mine got nipped away. Think of it like a plant with all them leaves and even berries. And one by one a flock of birds comes and steals the berries, shreds the leaves, so all you're left with is a weed.

That's what my head was, a weed. One of them straggly mother-fuckers grows in the alleys around Western, more pollution than plant.

Last fifteen years the world was nothing but a flock of vultures come to eat this plant. And I let them. I let them strip me bare till I had nothing.

Now listen up. You got to tend that plant. Spray motherfuck-ing weed killer all around it—and don't listen to anyone who tells you that shit isn't healthy or safe. You do what you need to do.

Don't let anyone convince you otherwise. Else we all wind up a bunch of weeds, plucked and tossed.

Me, I'm growing my plant back. Growing it back to all its glory. It's one tough motherfucker—that's for sure.

But listen up. It's easy to let that plant die. Let yourself go dead inside. Let people take even your own thinking away.

You remember how this all began, right? You coming to see me in the hospital. I was so mad because it took you so long to bring me my smokes. You didn't stick around too much. Had your own shit to do.

I don't blame you, baby. We're good now. We're all good.

The world messed me up hard. Or it tried.

I'm ironing that motherfucker out.

I'm gonna open the window. Stick my face in the wind.

Look at those houses, big-ass motherfuckers. Wonder if folks are happy behind those gates. Wonder if they think they're safe.

Still smells like smoke. What's that—a week now. Smoke and that shit that happens to fire with water. Smolder. Smells like a dragon breathed all over this shit.

But it's gonna come back. This city endures. It motherfucking endures.

Hold up. Turn back.

I said turn back. I want you to pull over. Back at that what-do-you-call-it, outlook.

I'm gonna get out. You come with me.

Check it, baby. Check this view. Sun coming up all over every-thing. Just perfect.

Check all that shit below us. That's a whole fucking city just rolling along.

You forget. You forget how big it is. Down these hills, cross that pass, into what's that, West Hollywood, Beverly Hills. Past that. Cross Pico, farther south. Down to our woods.

I want you to look at that. Take a look.

Motherfucking vast is what.

Bigger than big. Hard to imagine it at all. Hard to hold it in your mind. You feel me?

But I want you to. I want you to try. It's important, baby. I want you to see it. See the city. I want you to know it. Not to be in it, be played by it. I want you to understand it. To feel it.

And I want you to remember one thing.

We're a part of that place.

We're a part of it.

We own it.

It's ours, baby.

Don't let anyone tell you different.

ACKNOWLEDGMENTS

This book exists because of the expert guidance and critical support of my editor, Zack Wagman, who has championed it since it was a nebulous idea in my head. As always, thanks to everyone at Ecco: Dan Halpern, Miriam Parker, Megan Deans, Dominique Lear, and Caitlin Mulrooney-Lyski, as well as to my tremendous agent Kim Witherspoon at InkWell Management and Jessica Mileo.

For their support and inspiration, accidental and intentional, thanks to Alafair Burke, Megan Abbott, Louisa Hall, and Lee Clay Johnson. For help in too many ways to list here, an immense debt of gratitude to Jennifer Pooley.

I will always remain grateful to Susan Kamil who I believe watches over my literary career even now.

It remains a joy to share this book (and all my books) with my first and best readers, Elizabeth and Philip Pochoda, who remain two sources of inspiration and admiration.

And of course, to Justin Nowell and our wild and wonderful daughter, Loretta Pochoda—may she always be believed.